CONSPIRACY

Larry Jeram-Croft

Copyright © 2017 Larry Jeram-Croft
All rights reserved.

Cover image: Ian Andrews @ Crown Copyright 2002

Also by Larry Jeram-Croft:

Fiction:

The 'Jon Hunt' series about the modern Royal Navy:

Sea Skimmer
The Caspian Monster
Cocaine
Arapaho
Bog Hammer
Glasnost
Retribution
Formidable
Conspiracy
Swan Song

The 'John Hunt' books about the Royal Navy's Fleet Air Arm in the Second World War:

Better Lucky and Good
and the Pilot can't swim

The Winchester Chronicles:

Book one: The St Cross Mirror

The Caribbean: historical fiction and the 'Jacaranda' Trilogy.

Diamant

Jacaranda
The Guadeloupe Guillotine
Nautilus

Science Fiction:

Siren

Non Fiction:

The Royal Navy Lynx an Operational History
The Royal Navy Wasp an Operational and Retirement History
The Accidental Aviator

Prologue

September 11 2001

It was the culmination of some extraordinary planning that had taken years. The complex plan had to be fool proof and watertight but although complex, it also had to involve as few people as possible. The more people directly involved, the greater the chance of failure. However, the master stroke had been to convince the really bad guys to do it without them realising that they were being manipulated. Even those who thought they were in on the ground floor were, in reality, only party to certain aspects of the whole programme. Motivation had been the key and funnily enough, once people's ideology had been sparked into life it was amazing how dedicated they had become. This was not just the jihadists but sensible Americans as well. Feelings were running high on both sides and would only grow vastly stronger now.

The two men really shouldn't have been where they were as it had all been their idea in the first place. They were the puppet masters, not the soldiers but they had both agreed that they needed to see the culmination of their work for themselves.

When the two aircraft had smashed into the World Trade Centre buildings that afternoon, they had watched it first hand from a neighbouring skyscraper that one of the men actually owned. It had made a perfect vantage point and of course, they knew they were safe. Initially, everything had gone to plan. The timing was never going to be exact but both of them were surprised at how punctual their first two pre-programmed suicide pilots had been. The collapse of the towers had been a possibility and now it had actually and spectacularly come about. It seemed that things were going even better than they had hoped. Both men felt dreadfully sorry for the poor trapped people in the upper floors as well as the innocents in the two aircraft. But they both reminded themselves that in war there would always be casualties. It wasn't that they hadn't done their best to minimise things, having picked a day when the buildings would be mostly empty.

Conspiracy

However, now something had clearly gone wrong. Where was the third aircraft? It should have arrived and done its job by now.

The men turned to the large television set behind them that was reporting events as they happened. The news anchor was just finishing a report that another large commercial aircraft was seen crashing somewhere to the west. Details were sketchy but both men knew what it meant.

The first man sighed, 'I suppose it was just too much to ask for the whole plan to work. I think we'll have to invoke the contingency back up.'

The second man agreed. 'The towers were a bonus but that building has to go. There is just too much incriminating evidence in there. The investigation into this will probably take years and we know how to muddy the waters and drag it out but we can't risk it. Our primary aim will probably be met either way but I'd rather not spend my later years in a federal penitentiary. Shall I make the call?'

The other man nodded so he picked up his mobile phone and dialled a special number. He held out the phone but the other man simply nodded. 'You do it,' was all he said.

He pressed the send button and they both looked out to the north of where the dust from the two twin towers collapse had now just about settled. Another building was on fire but not badly. Suddenly, it simply collapsed as the hidden detonation of secret demolition charges did their work.

Building Seven, as it was known, was a large office block containing several government departments as well as commercial organisations. It also contained nearly all the records that the two men needed to keep secret. In the blink of an eye and a massive cloud of debris, it all simply vanished.

Chapter 1

Captain Jonathon Hunt didn't know whether to be happy or sad. However, he was having to force emotion out of his thinking. Taking a twenty thousand ton aircraft carrier in through the narrows of Portsmouth harbour was never an easy task. Although he didn't want to admit it even to himself, doing it with a thick head from too little sleep and too much booze the night before was never a good idea. Still, 'it was all in the best traditions of the Fleet Air Arm,' he thought wryly to himself. Anyway, he had a really good navigating officer, his Commander stood next to him and he knew that they would be looking out for him.

It was his last day in HMS Formidable as Captain. He had loved every minute of it. He knew it didn't get any better than this. The first few months working up had been hard. Then there was the excitement of a real operation off the coast of Africa which had been a hard act to follow but they seemed to have managed it. A world tour, taking in Australia and the Far East had been the icing on the cake. But now everyone in the ship was looking forward to getting home and seeing loved ones and families. It was with that thought that a pang of loss shot through him once again. He wondered whether he was the only person in the ship who would much rather turn around and keep sailing forever.

His last night on board had been a classic naval 'up channel' night. As the ship steamed slowly into the English Channel around Ushant, he had started off by subsuming his Commander's role and conducting mess deck rounds himself. It gave him a final chance to meet and say farewell to all his sailors in person. He had been touched by their attitude. They all seemed genuinely sad to see him leaving. He then had an invitation to have a drink with his senior rates which he knew he couldn't refuse, not that he would want to. It was just that there was a tradition in the navy that any officer leaving their mess should not do so in any state of sobriety whatsoever. Luckily, he had the excuse that he would be required in the wardroom for a final dinner so had to limit his time with them. That didn't stop them at least partially completing their task. Then it was off to the wardroom as the guest of the Commander for a farewell

Conspiracy

dinner. The Air Group were still on board as well as the ship's staff and the evening had developed much as Jon had expected. He was really touched by the leaving present they had given him. Someone on board was a really gifted craftsman as witnessed by the amazing model of the ship, complete with miniature aircraft on her deck, made completely out of some sort of metal. The Commander explained that it was, in fact, the remains of the missile that had hit them off the coast of Africa. When they were clearing up the mess they had found a large section of the casing and it had been put aside for just this eventuality.

The English Channel is a very busy piece of water and Jon knew he should really be alert for their overnight trip to Portsmouth but he also trusted his senior bridge watchkeepers and the Commander had made it quite clear that he would be off the booze and quite capable of managing the passage. The consequence was that Jon had invited the rest of his Heads of Department for a final nightcap in his cabin after Wings had insisted that all the aircrew required for flying the next day had gone to bed. He had finally crashed out himself well after two in the morning.

So now here he was on the bridge of the last warship he would ever command taking her into harbour for the last time.

The passage through the narrows past Southsea and Old Portsmouth turned out to be relatively simple as there was very little wind. They didn't even need any assistance from the two tugs that had been fussing around them as soon as they entered the main channel. Once inside the large harbour, they came alongside the main naval base jetty. The masts of HMS Victory could clearly be seen over the roofs of the brick buildings lining the jetty which itself was completely full of cheering people. Many were waving 'welcome home' banners. It was an occasion often repeated in the navy but one that never failed to bring a lump to Jon's throat.

As the First Lieutenant reported that all shore lines were secure Jon ordered, 'Ring off Main Engines' and that was that. The end of his command. He, like many of the ship's company, would be going on leave now but the next time he came on board he would be handing her over to her new Captain.

Commander (Air) came up to him before he could leave the bridge to go down to his cabin. 'All the Harriers and helicopters have arrived safely at Yeovilton Sir.'

Conspiracy

'Good, thank you Wings' said Jon. 'Always welcome news.'

'Yes Sir and can I confirm that's where you are heading for your leave?'

'Correct Wings, you know that. Why are you asking?'

'Sir, we have one more air movement to make. We thought you might like to leave in style.'

Jon looked at Wings and the Commander who were both grinning at him. 'Right, what have you two been plotting behind my back?'

'Well Sir,' Wings replied with a deadpan look on his face. 'We sent our Lynx off this morning as you know but he didn't actually go to Yeovilton. He stopped off at Lee-on-Solent. The airfield is still open and he's on his way back as we speak.'

Just then Jon heard the familiar growl of a Lynx in the distance. He went to the side of the bridge and looked aft to see the familiar shape flaring into the hover on the port side. 'I wondered why they wanted us to berth starboard side to. I assume you arranged this Commander?'

'Sorry Sir, we couldn't simply let you leave over the gangway. If you go down to the Line Shack I've arranged for all your luggage to be there as well as a full set of flying clothing.'

'Hang on,' Jon said. 'My girlfriend is meeting me here. We're going on holiday tomorrow.'

'Err, actually she's waiting for you at Yeovilton Sir,' Wings replied with a grin.

Jon knew when he had been stitched up and realised there was nothing he could do and what the hell? This sounded like fun.

Fifteen minutes later, he was strapped into the right hand seat of the 'burning and turning' Lynx. The machine had been fitted with dual controls so Mike Perry, the Lynx Flight Commander could still be classed as the aircraft Captain and fly the machine if needed. He had already made it clear that he had no intention of doing so and Jon was free to take control.

They completed the pre-take off checks together and then Jon made a hand rotating gesture to the marshaller and four aircraft handlers ran in and removed the four nylon lashings that were securing the machine to the flight deck. Jon then gave a thumbs up to the marshaller who looked over his shoulder and confirmed that the flight deck traffic light was green.

The radio came to life.'486, you are clear to launch, wind is red two zero at five knots. Goodbye Sir from the whole of Formidable. 'Jon recognised the voice of Commander (Air).

The marshaller started to wave his bats up and down. Jon pulled up on the collective lever and pushed in a little rudder pedal to anticipate the need to compensate for the torque as it rose. They lifted cleanly into the hover. The marshaller waved them off to the left and Jon cleared the flight deck.

'Not forgotten how to do it then Sir?' Mike asked grinning. 'I hope you're going to say goodbye in style?'

'Bet your life.' was all Jon said as he pushed the helicopter's nose down twenty five degrees and pulled one hundred per cent torque, accelerating level with the flight deck and off into the large harbour in front of them. He stayed at fifty feet until they reached one hundred and twenty knots before racking the Lynx around in a sixty degree, two G turn to head back towards the ship. He allowed their height to creep up to two hundred feet. Mike looked slightly surprised but said nothing although he had been expecting his Captain to do a tight wingover on top of the ship to say goodbye.

Jon had other ideas. As the ship started to slide past their left hand side he pulled the nose up a few degrees and then rapidly applied full left cyclic. The Lynx could roll faster than many jets and quickly started to rotate and invert. As they became fully inverted, Jon pushed the cyclic slightly forward to keep the nose up and then they were upright again.

'Nope, don't seem to have forgotten anything Mike,' Jon said with a grin, turning to his companion. 'I hope that was stylish enough?'

'Fuck me Sir, you get ten points for style. Where the hell did you learn how to do that?'

'Long story but last time I did it someone was trying to shoot me out of the sky. Right, which way is Yeovilton?'

Chapter 2

The sun was streaming through a gap in the curtains at the foot of Jon's bed. The shaft of sunlight was speckled with dust motes that sparkled gold in the early morning light. Outside, a dawn chorus of birds were making their normal racket as they greeted the new day. It was the noise that had woken him up, that and the need for the toilet.

He carefully slid sideways out of bed trying hard not to disturb the naked form of Ruth who was lying beside him. She was facing away and tucked up in the foetal position. Jon got an excellent view of her trim buttocks as he carefully swung his legs to the floor. He grinned to himself at the recollection of the previous night. Maybe coming home from a long deployment did have some benefits after all.

When he crept back into the room he saw that Ruth was awake. 'What time is it?' she asked, peeping at him over the bed covers.

Jon looked at the bedside clock on his side of the bed. 'Almost six, sorry did I wake you up?' He asked as he slid in beside her.

'No, those bloody overexcited birds managed that,' she said as she cuddled up against him.

'So, when do we need to get up?' Jon asked. All he knew was that Ruth had booked them on a holiday somewhere and despite repeated attempts last night to find out where, she had skilfully avoided answering all his questions.

'No, there's plenty of time yet,' she murmured as her hand crept down past his stomach. 'And something tells me that you can wait a bit longer.'

Sometime later, Jon padded down to the kitchen in his dressing gown and put the kettle on. While waiting for it to boil he looked out at his back garden. He had bought the house some time ago, it was in the same little Somerset village where he had had his first house. The garden was more of an orchard with several apple trees and a little summer house at the rear and quite beautiful. None of this helped his thought processes. He realised that this was a critical time in his life and despite agonising over the various options open to him, he still couldn't see a way ahead.

'Bugger it,' he muttered to himself. 'I've got two weeks holiday with Ruth and then I can worry about it.'

He returned to the bedroom and handed Ruth her coffee and sat on the edge of the bed. 'Right Little Miss secretive, it's time to cough up. Where are we going? I don't even know what to pack. So come on what's the plan?'

Ruth took a sip of her coffee and looked at Jon over the rim of her cup. She had enjoyed teasing him but decided it was time to come clean. 'We fly from Bristol this afternoon to Nice. I've rented a villa just down the coast. Its got a pool and we have the use of a car. There's even some diving and sailing if you want it.' She decided to keep the rest of her plan a surprise.

'Oh, that sounds fantastic,' Jon responded with enthusiasm. It sounded just the sort of break he needed.

That evening, their taxi drew up to the villa. It was up a long twisty track and they saw it as the came round the last bend. It was perched on the edge of a small cliff with steps leading to what was clearly a private beach at its foot. The walls were white and the roof had red tiles. Climbing plants covered most of the outside. Jon could see a veranda which overlooked the large pool. He could also see that it was far too big for just the two of them. Not only that but there were two cars already parked up on one side of the drive.

He turned to Ruth. 'Something you forgot to tell me?' He asked.

'Oops, didn't I mention that we wouldn't be on our own, silly me,' she laughed. 'Come on, let's go in.'

They paid the taxi driver and grabbed their bags. A short flight of steps led up to the pool area. As Jon breasted the rise he could see a large table under the veranda next to the pool and there were several people sat around it. They all turned when they saw him appear and got to their feet.

'About bloody time, you're late as usual,' Brian Pearce boomed out.

'Ignore him,' said Kathy, his wife. 'You're right on time.' and she gave Jon a great big hug. Brian reached past her and shook his hand.

Jon saw the other couple behind them. 'Rupert, why am I not surprised? And Gina too, haven't seen you both for a while. How are you?'

'We're both good,' Rupert responded with a grin. 'And I don't suppose my darling sister has told you everything about this little holiday she has been planning, or should I say plotting for months now?'

Jon turned to Ruth. 'There's more?' he asked with an eyebrow raised.

'Maybe you should tell him Rupert.' Ruth replied. 'Or should I say ask.'

Jon was getting confused. 'Will someone tell what's going on?'

'Sorry Jon,' Rupert replied. 'As you've found out, my sister likes a good conspiracy. It's actually quite simple. Gina and I have been engaged for a while now and we've decided to tie the knot. We want to do it while we are here. Would you be my best man?'

Jon was momentarily taken aback. Ruth had certainly caught him on the hop. He and Rupert went back a long way. Back to nineteen eighty two in fact when they had first met at Ascension Island at the start of the Falklands War. They had been firm friends ever since and he was absolutely delighted that he was being asked to take on the role and said so immediately.

He looked over at Gina who he knew had been Rupert's secretary. 'Are you sure Gina? I've known this man for a long time. I might have to divulge a few stories that could embarrass him.'

'Oh no you don't,' Rupert got in before she could respond. 'Most of those are highly classified.'

'Ah but as Gina worked for you Rupert,' Jon responded with a grin. 'Then she must have the same security clearances as you.'

'Ah, you've got me there. Oh well, do your best to keep it clean.'

'And then there will be the stag night and I'm sure Kathy and Ruth can manage a good Hen do for Gina as well.'

'You know, I'm beginning to wonder if this was such a good idea after all.' Rupert said ruefully.

'Nonsense old chap, now where's the booze? I'm now officially on holiday.'

The fortnight passed in a happy blur for Jon. The weather was idyllic and despite Rupert's concerns, the wedding ceremony went without a hitch. Several family members came out for the event which was conducted by the local priest. Gina was Catholic and although Rupert was of no particular persuasion, he was more than content to bow to her wishes. The event was held at the villa on a special stage set up near the cliffs, looking out on the blue Mediterranean and was an enormously happy affair. It even got Jon thinking on similar lines again but he and Ruth had already discussed the idea and agreed that neither really wanted the commitment. However, despite all the happy times and great company, there was the persistent dark cloud at the back of Jon's mind. He had hoped he would have been able to shrug it off while on holiday but in some ways, the relaxed atmosphere only made it worse.

It came to a head on their second to last day. All six had gone into the local town for lunch and when they returned, they decided to sit around the pool and chat in the sunshine

Brian started, 'Jon, you haven't really told us what's next for you.'

Jon didn't answer straight away so Ruth decided to interject. 'Yes and I know you well enough to know that something has been on your mind ever since you got back from sea.'

Jon looked at Ruth with a half smile. 'Bugger, is it that obvious? Look, it's a personal thing.'

'Bollocks Jon,' Brian said with feeling. 'Come on spill it.'

'Thanks Brian, you never were one to beat around the bush.'

'So?'

'Alright, you all know the expression 'it doesn't get better than this'? Well for me, that moment was when I took command of Formidable. Without doubt, it was the most fantastic time of my life. When I was taking her into Portsmouth for the last time it really hit me that I'll never get the chance to command at sea again or fly again for that matter. I'm too senior now. So what does that leave me to look forward to? Some bloody staff job or the senior staff course and a bloody staff job afterwards. You all know me. Me and a sodding desk are more than incompatible. Of course, I've already talked to the Naval Secretary and he's given me some options to consider but none of them excites me at all. So I have to make a decision now. Do I stay in the navy or should I consider bailing out and find something more interesting to do?'

His remark was met with a stunned silence. Rupert was the first to break it and surprised them all by agreeing with Jon. 'Goodness Jon, you and me both. In fact, Gina and I have been having very similar thoughts. I can stay in intelligence. I've been offered some pretty good prospects but like you, it will mean even more administration and paper pushing. They don't want old buggers like us to get the excitement it seems.'

'Now hang on both of you,' Brian said firmly. 'For God's sake Jon, you were a first shot Commander and Captain. You've achieved more than just about any other serving officer in recent times. Everyone knows you're destined for higher things, CinC Fleet even the First Sea Lord, you can't throw that away. And Rupert, I don't know much about your world but I'm bloody sure you've got a long way to go yet.'

The two of them turned to look at Brian. Jon spoke first. 'You, of anyone should know Brian that I don't work that way. I love the navy and will always do my best but I've never been ambitious like some people. I know there are plenty of other things I could do and now is the right time to consider them.'

Rupert nodded in agreement. 'Sort of sums up my attitude as well I'm afraid.'

'Come on guys,' Brian remonstrated. 'Yeah, you've both given your respective organisations good service but they've also supported you and given you those opportunities. Don't you feel any obligation to them?'

Rupert laughed. 'What like the spectacular pay and conditions of service? I don't know much about the RN but we just get civil service rates even when we're in the field. Sorry Brian, I know what you mean but life isn't a rehearsal and it would be crazy not to consider this now while there's still time left to make a career break.'

Brian's wife Kathy then spoke up. 'Jon, I can understand exactly how you feel. In fact, I'm surprised you didn't consider it when Helen died. But surely your prospects can't be that bad?'

'No, they're not Kathy,' Jon responded. 'And yes, I did consider bailing out when that happened and on at least one other occasion but there was always the lure of a flying or command job ahead of me. I'm sorry but I just like playing with the toys. It's that simple.'

'So what options have you been looking at Jon?' Ruth asked in a slightly hurt tone. She had to wonder why this was the first time she had heard about this. Surely he could have confided in her first before blurting it all out in public?

Jon caught the note in her voice. 'Sorry, all of you, it's been building up slowly for a long time. And although I've got itchy feet if you want to call it that, I haven't really thought about what I could do otherwise. I suppose I could go into commercial flying or become a professional yacht skipper. I really should think this through a bit more,' he finished lamely.

Brian snorted in derision. 'You swallowed the anchor when you were two years old sunshine, you just haven't realised it yet.'

Jon was about to respond when Marie, the villas cleaning lady came rushing up to them exclaiming loudly in rapid French.

Jon was the only fluent French speaker and managed to get her to calm down enough so he could understand what she was saying. 'She says there's something we must see on the television. I can't make much sense of what she's saying so let's go and look.'

They all got up and went into the large lounge where the television was showing a city from a camera clearly mounted on a building. Marie started to explain again when they all stopped and stared.

'Oh Jesus fucking Christ,' Jon muttered, as they all clearly saw what was obviously a large commercial airliner slam into the side of a skyscraper and a ball of fire erupt from the other side.

'You know, Jon,' Brian said. 'Maybe you might just find life in the services gets interesting again.'

Chapter 3

Jon sat back in his chair and gazed up at the amazing ceiling of the painted hall in the old Naval College at Greenwich. The Trafalgar Night mess dinner was coming to an end and he was feeling the effect of some extremely good wines and the last two glasses of port.

His neighbour, Paul Roberts an army Colonel, caught his gaze. 'Forty five and half pairs of tits so I've been reliably informed Jon,' he remarked as they both admired the mural depicting the triumph of King George and his wife Mary over the dastardly French. The two royals were surrounded by cherubs and bare breasted angels. 'Mind you every time I've tried to count them I get a different number.'

Jon was almost tempted to try himself but realised that it was never going to happen. Just craning his neck back for a few moments was enough to make him feel slightly dizzy. 'It's an amazing place,' he responded looking around at the massive room. 'Who would have thought that the walls are actually flat, it's just the stunning paintwork that makes it so special. And of course, there is this.' He pointed down to the floor. Underneath his chair was a small brass plaque. He read the inscription. 'In this spot, the body of Admiral Horatio Nelson was laid in state before his burial in Westminster Abbey. What a shame they gave the bloody place away. You know they said there wasn't room for a Joint Service staff college here but that was bollocks so they gave it up and all moved to Shrivenham. I know where I'd rather have been based.'

Paul Roberts nodded. 'I did the old Joint Services course here some years back while it still belonged to the navy. That was a fantastic course. It always made us laugh that when you enter the town there's a sign that says 'welcome to Greenwich, a nuclear free town' and all the time the college had a small nuclear reactor inside to teach your submariners how not to blow themselves up.'

'Yes,' Jon agreed. 'It was called JASON I seem to remember and as usual when they did the numbers as to why to close the place down they forgot to include the cost of decommissioning the reactor. Had they done so it would probably now be the joint staff college.

Silly buggers. Now we have to pay just to have the place for one dinner a year.'

Jon was feeling mellow and not just because of the booze. It was the last day of the Senior Command staff course that he had been part of for the last year. And what a year it had been. Within a month of the attacks on New York, the Americans, with help from other countries including Britain had invaded Afghanistan and effectively neutralised the Taliban and Al Qaeda. In some ways, it had seemed almost too easy. Jon found it quite unusual to be a spectator to a major military action. He normally seemed to manage to get caught up in them. However, because of the seniority of those on the course they had been privy to a great deal of inside information and what now seemed to be brewing on both sides of the Atlantic.

With what he now knew, his future job was going to be very interesting. He reflected back to his interview with the Admiral at Fleet Headquarters after he had relinquished command of Formidable. Having ones 'horoscope' read was a naval tradition for all officers when their confidential report was written. In days gone by one was only given a small précis called a 'flimsy' which told you virtually nothing. However, these days a policy of open reporting was in place and his whole report was read out to him.

When the Admiral had finished reading the formal words he continued in a more forthright manner. 'So Jon, that was a bloody good job, your whole commission not just the little African operation at the start. Now, I'm going to be absolutely frank. As far as the navy is concerned you are our major rising star. Your career so far has been without reproach and the results you've achieved are outstanding. And I include those I'm not cleared to know about even now but of which I have been given an assessment from very high up. So although you've only been a Captain three years we want you to take over as Commodore Amphibious Warfare. You've got the practical experience as well as the necessary talents. What do you say to that?'

Jon was taken aback. He had been expecting some form of MOD job or at best a desk in Command Headquarters which were now based in Portsmouth at Whale Island and where he was now. Another operational command was completely unexpected and then something struck him.

Conspiracy

'But Sir, now that we've made Commodore a substantive rank to align with the other two services I'm not senior enough.'

'Good point,' the Admiral responded. 'And anyway, the current incumbent has at least another eighteen months to serve. So what we are proposing is that you take a year to do the senior staff course and then there are several options for a study for another nine months to a year. That will also give you some MOD experience which you strongly need.'

'A study Sir? I don't understand.'

'It's quite common these days. Some higher up, quite often a Minister gets a bug up his backside about something and a small independent team is set up to consider the idea and report on it. There are several in the pipeline and we'll have a better idea once your course is finished. Then you are in the prime position to be appointed as COMAW.'

Jon realised he had been cleverly trapped and he had to admit to himself that he did actually need more experience of the inner workings of the MOD. However, the carrot of the operational job was there dangling in the not too distant future. As to all the talk about going further, as he had told his friends when they were on holiday, as far as he was concerned, the jury was still out.

So now the course was finishing and he had an appointment the next day back at Whale Island to be told what this short term job was all about. From hints he had been given already it sounded interesting but he would keep his powder dry until he knew more and more importantly that the promise of the operational command to follow was still on the cards.

The senior staff member, an RAF Air Vice Marshall, tapped his glass with a knife to get everyone's attention and then proposed the loyal toast. They all rose and drank to the Queen and then the atmosphere relaxed as the formal part of the dinner concluded.

'I just hope the bloody man keeps his speech short,' Paul said to Jon. 'He can be a right old windbag when he wants to be.'

Jon nodded, although he actually rather liked the man. 'What's going to be more interesting is hearing a Senior Crab talking about a major naval action and its hero. It took the RAF another hundred years to come into existence. Oh and before I forget we are still on for Silverstone this weekend I take it?'

Conspiracy

Paul nodded. 'Yup the car's ready so I'll see you there for Saturday practice?'

'You couldn't keep me away old chap.'

Chapter 4

Jon had a new love in his life even though she didn't belong to him. He gazed at the beautiful silver car, thrilled that in a short time he would be driving her flat out around one of the most famous racing circuits in the world.

It had all started some months ago at the beginning of the staff course. One of the first things all the participants had been asked to do was to introduce themselves to their compatriots and say something about both their military and private lives. Jon had casually mentioned that he was the proud owner of an ex naval Wasp helicopter, which had caused not a little surprise. That evening in the bar, Colonel Paul Roberts sat next to Jon for dinner and quizzed him about the machine. Jon told him a little about its history and how he had acquired it but carefully failed to mention how he had used it a couple of years ago to track down and subdue a certain senior RAF officer. The story had never made it into the public domain and even now the memory was too raw.

'Paul, you seem inordinately interested in my little toy,' Jon observed. 'Would you like to have a go in her sometime? But surely you've had your share of buzzing around in helicopters in your time in the army?'

'Surprisingly, not that much and it was all mainly sitting in the back being taken to some God forsaken spot for people to shoot at me,' Paul responded. 'When I was young I wanted to join the Army Air Corps but as I wore glasses that was never going to happen. For the Royal Engineers it wasn't an issue. In fact, my eyesight is no worse than many pilots I know but if it deteriorates after you're qualified they don't want to waste all that money they've spent training you.'

'Yes I know several pilots who fly with glasses,' Jon said. 'It's always seemed a silly rule to me but what do I know, I'm not a medic. Anyway, if you want a trip then I tend to use her at weekends in the summer. The RN Historic Flight look after her and it's mainly one of her pilots that does the public displays but I usually use her on non-display weekends. You're welcome to come along.'

'Thanks, I'll take you up on that offer. And maybe I can offer you something in return. I know flying is exciting but I have something that will get your adrenaline going, believe me.'

'Go on. Sounds intriguing.'

'Well you have Wanda but I have Ella. That's Ella the E-type Jaguar. She's one of the original lightweights that they built for racing some years ago and that's what I do with her. There are several two driver races coming up this summer and I need a co-driver. What do you say? I'll swap you a ride in mine if I can ride in yours.'

'Wow that sounds interesting but I can't just jump in and race can I? There must be all sorts of rules.'

'Yes but actually its surprisingly easy. You have to do a one day course at a circuit to get a race licence which tells you all about procedures and the flags and that sort of stuff. Then you will need some basic safety kit, helmet and overalls but I can probably lend you some. I would suggest we book a track day to go testing and teach you a little about the car but then off we go. So that's the deal, you give me some hours in your machine and you can come and play with mine.'

Jon sat back and thought about the idea. It was something he had never even contemplated doing but it sounded like great fun, then a thought occurred to him. 'And what happens when I crash the bloody thing?' he asked. 'Oh and surely if you've been racing a while you already have a co-driver?'

A shadow passed across Paul's face. 'No, not any more, he didn't make it back from Afghanistan. And if you bend it, you mend it, that's the normal deal. However, you have to remember that there is no such things as a written off racing car only one waiting its next rebuild. On top of that, she is insured so I would have to ask for a contribution towards the costs but nothing excessive.'

Suddenly Jon was quite excited at the prospect and said so. 'Deal.'

In the end, it hadn't quite worked out as they planned. Not the least because the course had them travelling far and wide on several occasions and the number of spare weekends available to them were far less than they would have wanted. Even so, Paul managed to get several hours behind the controls of the helicopter and Jon even managed to teach him how to hold a hover.

Jon managed to do his course at the nearest circuit which was Thruxton near Andover and was introduced to Ella a few weeks later when they had a test day at Silverstone. This was particularly suitable as the first race they would manage would be there just as the staff course was ending so at least he would know the track. He immediately took to the car and by the end of the day was lapping her within a second of her owner. However, it had been a great deal harder than he had imagined.

They had fitted a second seat in the car and Paul came with him for the first few sessions. Jon remembered his opening remarks. 'You are not Nigel Bloody Mansell Jon, although it seems that everyone who starts racing thinks they are. So take it easy. I expect at least twenty laps in this first session and they are to learn where the bends go. After that, we can think about speeding things up. We've got all day so there's no rush.'

Paul had been right. Despite promising to be careful and build things up slowly, as soon as they were on the circuit Jon had to fight the urge to simply floor the throttle and go mad. However, the presence of the car's owner sitting beside him and knowing exactly how much it was worth tempered his enthusiasm more than a little. As the day progressed, with Pauls' expert tutelage, he was able to start pushing. He did manage one quite spectacular spin at Copse but as Paul said afterwards, 'if you don't occasionally exceed the car's limits you'll never really know where they are.'

'Not an approach I would recommend with flying Paul,' Jon replied. 'But I know what you mean.'

'So next time you get to do it Jon there will also be twenty four other nutters trying to occupy the same piece of tarmac. Don't worry it'll be great fun.'

So here they were at last. Jon hadn't had butterflies in his stomach like this for years. The car had successfully passed its scrutineering checks and both he and Paul had presented their competition licences and signed on. All that was left now was to qualify and then the race that afternoon. Both drivers would have to put up a time but the fastest one would be used to allocate the grid position for the race. They would have twenty minutes each and Paul had decided that Jon should go first. When Paul took over it would be well warmed up and he was best placed to put in a good time.

The cars were all lined up in the holding area waiting to go on track. Jon was strapped in and waiting nervously with his helmet on. Paul leant in for some final words. 'It's only qualifying Jon so don't try to race anyone and if anyone is giving you hassle just let them past, all you need is a time. When you see the pit board saying to come in, just complete the lap and come into the pits. We'll practice a race handover even though we'll be doing it the other way around in the race itself, just to give us some more experience alright? Bring me back a nice well warmed up car and I'll do the rest.'

Jon nodded, he knew this already but also knew that Paul was just trying to calm him down. Suddenly, the marshall at the end of the holding area waved his hand in a circle. Jon turned on the battery master switch and pressed the engine start. The three point eight litre, straight six engine started first time and settled into an angry rumble. The marshall then started beckoning the cars onto the track and with a final pat on his helmet from Paul, Jon dropped the clutch and headed on to the circuit.

The next twenty minutes were some of the most hectic and exciting of Jon's life. It was an all Jaguar race but there were a number of different types on track in various classes and the speed differential was quite marked. On top of that, Jon needed to get a clear piece of track to allow him to put in a time unimpeded. Every time he thought he was clear someone blasted past him or balked him at the entrance to a corner. All too soon, he saw the pit board with his number on it and the word 'IN' in large letters. Cursing that he hadn't put up a decent show, he completed the lap and drove into the pits. As he approached their pit he had already released his harness. As soon as the car was stopped, their mechanic wrenched the door open and grabbed him by the shoulders pulling him clear so that Paul could jump in. Jon spun around and helped him with his straps. He was just able to manage a shout of, 'all's good, the car's fine,' before Paul had dropped the clutch and was away. Jon stood back and realised his hands were trembling slightly. Bloody hell he hadn't been this fired up for years. 'Bugger me if that was practice, what's the race going to be like?' he muttered to himself.'

Derek the mechanic must have overheard him. 'Don't worry Jon, you did fine. I timed you and although the official time might be

Conspiracy

slightly different that was good enough for at least the fourth row of the grid if not better, not bad for a first attempt.'

Jon was pleasantly surprised by that and said so but then also pointed out that his highest priority now was a visit to the heads and a coffee and definitely in that order.

Twenty minutes later, Paul brought the car back in one piece and although he employed Derek to look after it they all set to checking her over and getting her ready for the race. Paul knew that many people would just walk away and leave it to the mechanic but his view was that it was his car and he wanted to know all about how she was performing.

Just as they had the car up on jacks with the wheels removed to check the brakes and suspension another of the competitors came over and gave Paul a sheet of typed paper. Paul took it gratefully and then grinned when he read the numbers.

'Front row of the grid Jon. We were second to the other E-type but by only point two of a second. Look, your time was even good enough for the third row. Boy, it's going to be an interesting race.'

The rest of the morning passed in a blur. Once the car was checked over and made ready for the race there was little else to do. They had been the first practice session and would be the first to race after lunch. Unlike qualifying, the race would last an hour and half and each driver had to do at least forty minutes behind the wheel. They had already agreed that they would share the time equally unless something unforeseen happened. Paul had decided that he would do the start as it was probably the most critical part of the race when accidents were likely to occur.

It's simple Jon,' he said. 'Everyone says that you can't win a race at the first corner, you can only lose it. It's amazing how many people forgot that once the red mist has descended when the start light comes on.'

Jon was more than happy to concur, he was getting worried enough about the race itself without the added pressure of having to get off the line with a load of other speed freaks around him, especially as the car was on the front row.

To pass the time they went and had a giant full English cholesterol special in the race cafeteria and then went and watched some of the other races qualify but Jon's mind was finding it hard to concentrate. At one point he turned to Paul and asked. 'Is it just me?

Or do other drivers get the butterflies before a race? Frankly, I'm getting quite wound up.'

Paul laughed. 'Not just you my friend. I'm the same, it's just that I've been doing it long enough to get used to it. Some racing drivers go off and throw up before a race, apparently James Hunt did it all the time.'

Somewhat reassured, Jon decided to go back to the pit and sit quietly for a while.

All too soon it was time. Paul took the car out onto the grid and they all pulled away for the 'green flag' lap before forming up for the start itself. Jon watched everything from the pit wall. The start was amazing. A wall of sound and fury and then suddenly it all went quiet as the cars disappeared around Copse the first corner. Just over a minute later the first ones reappeared on the start finish straight. Paul was in second and not far behind the other E-type. It was clear that they were much faster than the others and as the race progressed slowly pulled well clear.

And then suddenly Derek tapped him on the shoulder. 'Get suited up Jon, I'm signalling him to come in this lap.'

With Jon ready, the car slid into the pits and within moments Paul was leaning over doing up his straps. 'Go for it Jon. The second driver of the other car is not as good as the first but watch out for traffic. The car's good. Off you go.'

Jon dropped the clutch and headed onto the circuit. It seemed surprisingly empty but that gave him time to settle down. He knew the other E-type was still out so well ahead but that would soon change and it did. Two laps later as he had just passed a rather slow, black XJS, he saw the other car pull out in front of him but well ahead.

Thoroughly fired up he set off in pursuit. It seemed to take forever to catch up but, lap by lap, he got closer. However, catching up and passing were another thing. When he saw that he was on the last lap from his pit board he knew he would have to do something brave, he just prayed it wouldn't be something stupid. The last bend before the finish is Luffield and it's a never ending open right hand hairpin. He had noticed that his antagonist tended to enter on a tight line and drift out as the corner progressed, presumably to stop Jon out braking him into the corner. Jon decided to do the opposite. He held off his entry and then cut in hard, holding the car in a progressive four wheel drift. Sure enough, the other car had gone so wide there was room for him inside and he had the speed to exploit it. The two cars exited the corner absolutely side by side and sprinted for the line. Jon could see the chequered flag being waved and looked to his left to see who was in front. In the split second as they crossed the line he couldn't work out who it was. As soon as he lifted off and started a gentle warming down lap, the adrenalin surge kicked in and he gave a whoop of pleasure. The car was in one piece, he was in one piece and he hadn't had so much fun for years. It got even better when he stopped in parc ferme area where they would be held for a few minutes before being released. Paul and Derek ran over with massive grins on their faces.

'Point zero one of a second Jon, you won and in your first bloody race. Fantastic.'

Jon was stunned and sat back for a second before pulling off his helmet. He realised he was drenched in sweat. 'Only one question Paul?'

'Yes?'

'When can I do it again?'

Chapter 5

Monday morning started as an anti-climax and the matter of a small hangover didn't help. Jon had an appointment with the Second Sea Lord at ten in the MOD Main Building in Whitehall and had travelled back to London late afternoon after the race. He met Ruth at her house in St John's Wood and took her out for a celebratory dinner, which had ended up rather later than planned for all sorts of reasons.

Ruth's comment after they had made rather spectacular love that evening was, 'well you'd better become a full time racing driver if that's what it does to your libido.'

Jon could only agree.

But now he was plodding down Whitehall towards the large grey building and wondering what the navy had in store for him now. He just prayed it wasn't something boring even though he knew it would only be a temporary assignment.

He gave his name to the MOD guard in the lobby and immediately a sandy haired young man introduced himself. 'Captain Hunt Sir, I'm Commander Peter Hardcastle. The Second Sea Lord's Military Assistant. If you'll come with me Sir?'

He handed Jon a temporary building pass and led him through the security air locks and up into the building.

'The Admiral apologises for dragging you to London Sir. As you know, he normally works from the naval base at Portsmouth but he had some other people with him he wants you to meet. I'm sure you'll understand.'

Jon wasn't sure he understood at all but kept his council. Things were starting to look more interesting by the minute. They went up in a lift to the top floor and it was clear they were in senior officer country by the fact that there was now a plush carpet underfoot and a series of oil paintings, mainly of old warships, lined the walls of the corridor. Unlike other parts of the building which were often hectic and noisy with people coming and going, this was a haven of peace and quiet. They reached a set of mahogany doors and the Commander pushed them open and ushered Jon in.

Conspiracy

They went in to what was clearly the Admiral's outer office and slightly to Jon's surprise Vice Admiral Bob Tucket was there ready to greet him. The Admiral was a small wiry man with receding sandy hair and a rather large nose. Jon knew it had given him his nickname of 'nosey' rather like the Duke of Wellington of the previous century. However, there the likeness ended. For a start, the Admiral had spent most of his career underwater in submarines and had almost certainly never sat on a horse.

'Jon, good to see you,' he said and extend his hand for a surprisingly firm handshake. 'Come into my office. Coffee?'

'If you wouldn't mind Sir,' Jon replied and immediately a cup was offered to him by the MA. Together they entered the inner sanctum and the doors were closed behind them. Instead of going behind his large desk, the Admiral took Jon to two leather arm chairs around a low coffee table and indicate that he take a seat.

'Now that your staff course is over Jon, I believe CinC Fleet indicated that there might be some temporary work for you before taking over as COMAW. Is that correct?'

Jon immediately wondered whether something was wrong and the promised job would not be forthcoming.

The Admiral saw the look of consternation on his face. 'Don't worry Jon, the Commodore job is still yours in due course.'

'Sorry Sir, but yes that was what was suggested.'

'Good, it's that temporary job I want to talk to you about. However, before we go any further I want to know what you think about what is going on in the Gulf at the moment.' He looked keenly at Jon as he asked the question.

'Err, well Sir, I know what's been in the press of course and we had several in depth briefings during the staff course. So I guess I'm fairly up to speed,' Jon replied not sure at all where this was going.

'No, that's not what I asked Jon,' the Admiral replied with a slight note of asperity in his tone. 'I want to know what you think about what is going on. What are your views?'

Jon sat back and took a sip of coffee in an attempt to buy some time while he thought. He did actually have some fairly strong personal views on the situation but why was he being asked? Clearly it had something to do with this temporary job he was being offered. He made a decision. 'Chatham house rules Sir?' Meaning that whatever he said it would be contained within the four walls of the office.

'Absolutely Jon, everything you say will be treated in strictest confidence.'

'Very well Sir, the whole thing stinks. This latest 'dossier' the government have just put out for example is a travesty. Did you hear that some journalist tracked down the author of some of it and it's an American student who wrote it as a university thesis? And this claim that we are under a threat that could be enacted in forty five minutes is just complete rubbish. For a start, the only British property that Saddam has the range to reach is our British Overseas Territory at Akrotiri on Cyprus and I know how fast we could act if we had to and it wouldn't be that fast so I'm damned if can see how he could do it. I have to say it does worry me enormously.'

'So, what do you think is really going on? How did we get into this position? You were involved just before the Gulf War weren't you?'

'Sir, the Americans have made it clear for years that they want to get rid of Saddam. Clinton and now Bush have said so openly many times, it's been official US policy. I have to say I find that particularly two faced bearing in mind that they supported him during the Iran Iraq war. They even supplied him with the chemicals and biological weapons that he used on the Iranians. So maybe there is some truth that he has these so called Weapons of Mass Destruction. After all, we gave them to him in the first place. I guess that after that war finished and he invaded Kuwait, the Americans had a change of heart and have wanted him out ever since. And then of course, there is the attack on the twin towers. Despite what the Americans claim there doesn't appear to be any credible link between Al Qaeda and Iraq but that hasn't stopped them claiming there is so I suppose that's just another way of ramping up the pressure. However, I think Afghanistan may be the key. The Taliban simply ran away and the American military, in particular, were left feeling triumphant but needing to keep on a roll. Everything I see so far looks like preparation for a pre-emptive strike. It's just a matter of having the justification. The UN Weapons Inspectors won't find anything. Even if Saddam has anything, which personally I don't think he has, they'll never find it. It's a very, very big country.'

'So you think it's all about forcing regime change then? That's not what our Prime Minister is saying as you well know.'

'Yes Sir of course it is. I'm sorry but the Prime Minister is blatantly distorting the truth. If he admitted it's because he wants a brutal dictator who oppresses his people out of power then people would be asking why we aren't doing the same about Robert Mugabe in Zimbabwe or Gadhafi in Libya.' Jon stopped and looked at the Admiral wondering whether he had gone too far.

'Very well Jon and if we are ordered to support the Americans in an attack on Iraq as military officers what would be your view?'

Jon didn't have to think too long. 'As long as it's adjudged a legal war then I would have no choice Sir.'

'No choice? That sounds like you would be reluctant then.'

'I'm reluctant to go into any war Sir and I've seen my share. More than most in fact. People die, all too often the innocents. If we invade a massive sovereign country how many people will we kill? I joined the service to protect my country I fail to see how attacking another country thousands of miles away does that. But if I am ordered to do so and it's demonstrably legal then of course, I would obey.'

The Admiral looked hard at Jon. 'Good, that's exactly what I hoped you would say.'

Jon realised he had just passed some sort of test. Quite what it was he wasn't sure yet but this could get interesting.

'So, what would you say if I asked you to become involved in seeing whether it is, in fact, legal or not. What would you say if I asked you to do some investigating into just that?'

The penny started to drop. 'As long as I am working within a legal framework then frankly I don't see a problem Sir.'

'Excellent, so if I asked you to head up a team and conduct a covert investigation of the situation, would you be prepared to do it?'

'Yes Sir, assuming of course, that I am not asked to operate outside the law.'

'No Jon, there is no question of that. In addition, you ought to know that this had the sanction of the Ramon Society. Any findings you make will be passed through them alright?'

Jon nodded, he had been recruited as a member of the society some years previously. He hadn't realised that the Admiral was also a member, he must be a fairly new recruit Jon realised. He wasn't at the last meeting that Jon had attended. Jon's friend Rupert in MI6 actually knew about them and called them the 'Old Farts Club.' However, that belied the purpose of the organisation which was to take a view on affairs that might threaten the sovereignty of the country and advise the government. It was all strictly unofficial but as it comprised some of the most important people in the country it had ways of being listened to.

Jon grimaced. 'Do you really think this Prime Minister will listen to anyone Sir? He seems to be pretty set on this course. Maybe we should be talking to the American President instead. He seems to be the only person the PM pays any attention to.'

'You may have a point there but we have to try Jon,' the Admiral responded. 'And look, you can't do this on your own. So on the basis that you will be doing a study, you will have three other officers, one from each service working under you. Your naval colleague will be your old observer Brian Pearce, as I'm sure you know he's just been selected for Captain on leaving his ship so he will be putting up his fourth stripe early. You already know the army officer, he was on the staff course with you, Paul Roberts. As a REME engineer he's perfect.'

Jon laughed and told the Admiral what he had actually been doing at the weekend.

'Good, then I know you two already get along pretty well. The third is Wing Commander Tony Deverell. The Air Force couldn't stump up a Group Captain at short notice. He's a Tornado pilot but recently had to eject and has sustained some minor back damage. He's fit for this sort of duty. The medics say it will be nine months before he's fit enough to fly again.'

As you need to be the senior team member we are going to promote you to Commodore early. We can do this on the basis that the rank can still be used in the old way even though you are still slightly too junior so it's temporary I'm afraid. But with the likely timescales, we can make it substantive when this is over and you take up your new job. The stated aim of the study is to look at how different countries, particularly the US and Israel support their aircraft at the front line to see if we can learn any lessons from them. This will give you access to operational units but more importantly, you will be able to talk to their staff people at various levels. In particular, you can find out how well this potential war is supported by the grass roots military in the States and the Middle East as well as listen out for any intelligence about what the American government is actually intending. We can talk about it in more detail later.'

'And my team members Sir, will they be in on it?' Jon asked.

'No, at least not to begin with. They won't know about your real mission but they will give you the credibility you need. That said, if in your judgement they need to know at some time, I'll leave that up to you. They've all been vetted and are completely trustworthy. However, it may not surprise you to know that there are people in MI6 who aren't all that happy either. The dossier that they produced was heavily amended by the PM's people and that's really ruffled some feathers. They've agreed to go along with us on this one and will also be providing a team member, although as far as the world is concerned, that person will just be a civil service assistant. However, they will be aware of the real mission.'

Just then the phone rang and the Admiral picked up the receiver and listened for a second. 'Show them in,' was all he said.

The door opened and Jon looked around. The first face that appeared was his old friend Rupert. However, the second face took him completely aback.

The two people came in. Rupert shook Jon's hand. 'You don't appear surprised to see me Jon.'

'Now, I wonder why that is,' Jon responded with a grin. 'We've worked together well enough over the years.'

'Not this time I'm afraid Jon, I'm too far up the tree.' Rupert turned to his companion. 'Jon, may I introduce Jenny Brooker.'

Jon looked at the girl. She was one of the most stunning women he had set eyes on. She had short blonde hair cut in a page boy style and two of the biggest brown eyes he had ever seen, set in an oval face with flawless skin. Slightly shorter than himself, she had a slim but generous figure that even the standard civil service jacket and knee length skirt failed to disguise. She was also quite young, he put her age at no more than mid-twenties. This was definitely not what he was expecting.

She put out her hand and smiled at him. Her fingers were cool but her grip surprisingly firm. 'Actually that's Doctor Brooker,' she said looking him in the eye. 'I have two first class degrees from Oxford and a PhD in modern languages. I'm to be your personal assistant.'

Chapter 6

The two men met in St James Park near Whitehall. It was a cold damp day. All the last leaves had blown off the trees in a gale two days ago. There was a smell of rain in the air again, complemented by the odour of rotting leaves.

The American had been early. He rather liked these grey autumn days although he was not a fan of the English rain that normally went hand in hand with them. Back in his home state of Virginia the 'fall' was a visually stunning time normally followed by snow. Not here and even if it did snow it was usually wet insipid stuff. Not that any of that was in the forefront of his mind. The task he had been set seemed to be pretty trivial and he soon wished he had decided to cut his timing finer.

Dead on time, a man in a grey overcoat with a briefcase sat next to him. He looked around at the almost empty park. 'Good place to meet. No one can overhear us on a bloody awful day like this.'

To the American, the man's English accent seemed almost a parody of what an American actor would attempt. Of course, it wasn't, some of them really spoke like that over here.

'Yes Sir, but we shouldn't stay long. We may not be overheard but we sure can be seen. Is it happening?'

The Englishman nodded. 'As I anticipated. There is a large cadre of people over here who are dead set against this policy. I'm not saying they will do anything overt to interfere but you had better be on your mettle to counter any attempts to railroad the process.'

The American chuckled. 'And your government should do the same. Your Prime Minister seems dead set on making everyone suspicious. That dossier idea was just plain crazy and now he's peddling this forty five minute claim. That was all his idea and from what I can see it's just making people very suspicious.'

The Englishman sighed. 'I couldn't agree more. I didn't vote for the bloody man but a great deal of the population did and he seems to think he has a mandate to do as he bloody well likes. I just hope that the real intelligence that you lot say you have is kosha, otherwise it's all going to hit the fan very quickly once it's over.'

'Don't you worry about that. We know exactly what Saddam has and what he's up to.'

'Alright then. Anyway, that's not my problem. Now the news I wanted to pass on is that some of the military are doing some digging. They've formed a team of reasonably high ranking officers to look into things. Ostensibly they are studying aircraft support methods in other countries. In fact, their remit is to travel around and try to find out what the real situation is.'

'Jesus, you mean spying?'

'No, no nothing like that. Simply put, they will be travelling around asking questions and trying to gauge the situation, nothing more than that. But as you and I both know there are some things we really don't want them finding out. A certain incident a few years ago for example.'

The American grimaced at the thought. 'Can't you stop them?'

'Absolutely not, frankly any attempt to do so would probably be counter-productive. All you need to do is to ensure that they don't get to meet and talk to the wrong people. Here are their details. Oh, and only the senior naval chap and the girl are actually involved. The others are just there as a smokescreen.' He handed over a small buff envelope. 'Now, I'd better be going. Don't take this the wrong way but I'd rather not meet again.'

The man stood and casually walked back towards Horse Guards Parade. The American sat a little longer and had a quick look in the envelope. It was one sheet of paper with five names and their ranks. With a sigh, he knew the afternoon would be spent setting the wheels in motion to get the dossiers on the names and then sit down with his boss and decide whether they actually needed to do anything about this.

Half a mile away, Jon was getting ready to meet the new team for the first time. He had been given office space on the second floor of the MOD Main Building and he and his new assistant had spent the morning sorting out the basics. It had also given him time to talk to her. He was intrigued and not a little concerned that she was the right person for the job.

The previous day, when the meeting with Second Sea Lord had broken up he had managed to grab a few moments with Rupert before he left.

Conspiracy

'Hey old chum, what's with this girl? She's clearly very bright but what's the deal?' he asked.

Rupert chuckled. 'Not only that, she's new and no one knows her. MI6 really can't be seen to be getting its fingers mucky in this and she's not on anyone's radar. She's got some other assets you might find come in handy but I'll let you talk to her about it.'

Despite Jon probing further, he got no more information out of his friend. But now was as good a time as any. The others wouldn't be arriving for at least another hour.

'Right Jenny, that's enough stationary and laptops, the coffee's brewed. Let's grab one each. We need to talk.'

She nodded and poured them both a cup and Jon indicated that they should sit around the little conference table in the main office. Jon looked at her. Despite her sensible clothing she still looked like Miss World. He couldn't for the life of him understand what Rupert had been thinking. He was just about to ask her to tell him something about herself when she got in first.

'You're wondering why MI6 would put me on your team. You know I've got brains but look like a bimbo and that's clouding your thinking.'

'Bloody hell girl,' Jon responded, completely taken aback by her candour but acknowledging to himself that she had hit the nail on the head. 'Alright, I think I get where you're coming from. So why don't you tell me yourself?'

She nodded and took a sip of her coffee before starting. 'Ever since I can remember people have told me I'm beautiful and men have looked at me in the same way that you did when we first met.' She saw Jon was about to say something. 'No, that wasn't a criticism. It's always been that way for me and I actually quite like it. Let's face it who wouldn't. But I have always had the problem that I'm also bloody intelligent and that's not hubris, simply a fact. I was always top of my class and was actually moved up a year to get my A levels early. It also made me incredibly unpopular with my female classmates although the boys didn't seem to mind. When I was at university things got much better. It's a place where brains actually matter. Even there though, my looks got in the way. Two of my tutors tried to get me into bed but strangely my male colleagues seemed intimidated by me and I was actually quite lonely. A female friend once told me that girls as pretty as me put men off because they can't imagine I don't have a boyfriend. It seemed a weird theory at the time but I slowly came to realise it was right.'

Jon didn't know quite what to say about this so just nodded for her to continue.

'So, I got my first degree in history and then was so fascinated by languages went on and got another in Middle Eastern languages. I then did a thesis on that for my PhD. But I realised I couldn't spend the rest of my life stuck in a university so eventually decided to look for something challenging. My father was a Chief Petty Officer in the Royal Navy. He actually served under you in HMS Prometheus so I know quite a lot about you.'

'Brooker,' Jon mused. 'I had a Petty Officer called that in my Operations room. Was that him?'

'That's right, he sends his regards by the way. Anyway, just as I was wondering what I was going to do with the rest of my life I spoke to dad and he suggested joining the navy. It wasn't a bad idea but I get sea sick crossing Westminster Bridge. However, it got me thinking. I actually believe in this country even though it seems fashionable not to these days. I knew MI6 were recruiting as, much to my surprise, they advertised in the Times so I applied and here I am.'

Jon looked at her shrewdly. 'There's more isn't there?'

Jenny looked down for a second and Jon knew he was right when he saw a faint blush appear on her cheeks. 'I'm also a bit of a cheat. When I heard that this job was coming up and you were going to be running it, I made every effort to get on the team. Being a cute blonde can be used to advantage you know.' She looked Jon straight in the eye.

'Why on earth would you want to meet me?' Jon asked, surprised.

'Dad told me all about you and what you did in the Gulf and I've looked you up. You've had an amazing career. I know about what happened to your wife and how you caught the man responsible in the end. There are also several parts of your dossier that very few people are allowed to see and I can guess that's not because you did badly at whatever it was. So I calculated that working with you was going to be interesting to say the least.'

Jon snorted a laugh. 'Not this time young lady. Our remit is pretty limited we're just going out there to listen and gauge the mood, nothing more.'

She shrugged. 'Maybe and of course, I can be of more value than you might think.'

'Oh, what do you mean?'

Jenny shrugged and suddenly her expression changed subtly. The look of sharp intelligence in her eyes was replaced by a slightly vacant expression and she smiled in an apparently innocent way. Reaching up, she undid the top two buttons of her blouse, exposing a spectacular cleavage. She leant towards him, looked him in the eye with her big brown eyes and said breathlessly. 'Tell me all your secrets Commodore,' she purred. 'I promise I won't tell anyone else.'

Jon rocked back on his heels. He was almost old enough to be this girl's father but it hadn't stopped the knee jerk reaction he had felt at the blatant sexuality she was suddenly able to conjure up out of nowhere. It was like looking at a different person.

'Bloody hell Jenny. Ok, I get the idea. But are you really happy to do that? It seems rather demeaning to me.'

Her normal expression returned and she did her blouse back up. She laughed. 'Yes, that was a bit over the top but don't worry. I've found that various degrees of 'blondishness' can be an amazing way of getting information as long as you don't mind of course.'

'I guess not, as long as you're comfortable with it.'

'Good, then I can be your secret weapon.' She smiled her normal smile back at him. Just for a second, Jon felt a pang of disappointment.

A few hours later the whole team were assembled. Jon did the introductions. Obviously, he already knew Brian and Paul and it seemed clear that they would get on well. Tony Deverell was an unknown but Jon's initial impressions were good. He was the last to arrive and apologised as he had been kept waiting by the medical centre who wanted to give him a final check over before signing him off as fit for the task. He was a tall and slim man with a shock of red hair. Jon could see that he was still in some pain purely by the way he walked but he was clearly determined not to let it get in the way.

Jon was quietly amused by the way they all reacted to Jenny when he introduced her as their admin assistant. To a man they looked surprised and then all grinned for a few second like schoolboys. He wondered if he had looked like that when he had first met her and mentally concluded that he probably had. It was clear within a few minutes that she was going to have them all eating out of her hand.

He called the meeting to order. 'Right everyone, the first rule for this team is that we are all in it together and we'll be wearing civvies for most of the time. So unless we're in uniform, in public, its Christian names please. Tony, I know you're the junior service member but as far as I'm concerned that's irrelevant. We have a job to do and that's that. So let's introduce each other and summarise our history and qualifications. We'll then go on to look at our terms of reference and start to put a plan of action together.'

The meeting carried on for several hours and with Jenny taking notes they soon had an idea of what they wanted to achieve. Jon called a halt at six and suggested they all go to a local hostelry.

As they walked up Whitehall to the pub, Brian pulled Jon to one side and spoke softly. 'Good meeting Jon and you almost had me fooled for a while but your priorities seem a little odd. When are you going to tell us all what this is really about?'

Chapter 7

Jon took his window seat in the Virgin Atlantic 747 with Jenny and Brian. The other two team members had seats in the centre aisle. They had been together now for several weeks and having done enough preliminary work travelling around various facilities in the country, were now embarking on their first and possibly most important overseas trip to the States. They had managed to cobble together a good itinerary and would be visiting at least three air bases operated by the US Marines, Air Force and Navy. Hopefully, this would give them a good oversight into the mind set of the front line forces that appeared to be slowly mobilising despite the fact that the UN Weapons Inspectors were reporting no results. They would then visit a couple of aircraft manufacturers. Although this was part of the cover story, Jon was quite interested to see how industry viewed the developing situation. Finally, they had appointments in Washington at the Pentagon and several other government departments.

Jon was relieved that the burden of the task was now falling on everyone's shoulders. After Brian's perceptive comment on day one, it was clear to Jon that trying to keep the real task confined to just himself and Jenny would never work. He had called on Admiral Tucket and told him of his intentions and obtained his blessing. The Admiral hadn't actually been that surprised.

That morning, after meeting with the Admiral, Jon called all the team together. Before he went ahead with full disclosure, he had individual meetings with all the team to sound out their attitudes just as the Admiral had previously done to him. He was not surprised to find that they all held similar views. He then called them all together and explained the real mission. Paul and Brian took it in their stride once they had been assured that it was just a general assessment exercise. It was Tony who surprised them all. He explained that his brother had been in Afghanistan with his army regiment and lost both legs to a roadside bomb when working with the Americans. It seemed he blamed several people for the tragedy. Firstly, the local American Commander who had been so keen to get into Kabul first he neglected to recce the route properly, the result being that the

Land Rover his brother had been driving had been blown to bits by a mine. The second being the morons in the MOD and army who had sent soldiers to a hostile country renowned for the use of mines and road side bombs in totally inadequate transport.

As Tony opened up Jon, realised he would have to keep a closer eye than he had expected on the young pilot. He clearly had an axe to grind. Privately, Jon agreed with everything he said but he definitely didn't want it ruining the objectivity needed to conduct their investigation. Jon had a quiet word with Brian and Paul about the subject later that day.

When the aircraft landed at Dulles they were met by a smart naval Lieutenant Commander who introduced himself as Eugene Porter who would be their liaison officer while they were travelling around their various locations. He would ensure that their security clearances were managed and make sure the planned visits took place on time. He took them to their first location which was actually the British Embassy where Jon made a courtesy call on the Ambassador. Jon had already been briefed that the Ambassador was not party to the real purpose of the visit and the meeting had been a quick formality. After that, they had proceeded to the Embassy Suites hotel in downtown Washington which had been booked for them for the whole of their visit. There was nothing else planned for that day and as it was still early afternoon American time Tony, Brian and Paul decided to go on a quick sightseeing trip around the capital. Jon had been to Washington many times and decided that an afternoon nap was more in order. They all agreed to meet in the bar for the hotel's notorious 'happy hour' that actually started at four and ended at nine in the evening. He was surprised when Jenny declined to go with the other men as she had already admitted that she had never been to the States before but she said she had a dreadful headache and wanted to sleep it off.

Jon entered his quite palatial hotel room on the fourth floor and did a quick inventory. Two massive double beds dominated the room but there was also a large desk with a television mounted on the wall above it which could easily be seen from the beds. Next to the desk was a fridge and a quick look inside confirmed that it was well stocked. He was not a fan of American beer but decided that one can would aid his sleep so he pulled the tab and looked at the sign on the desk. As advertised, there was a connection for the internet. It was something he was only just getting to grips with but they had all been issued with laptop computers and being able to get on line would be very useful. A quick check of the bathroom confirmed the standard American setup with no bath just a massive shower. That was fine, he preferred a bath but could no doubt manage for a few weeks. He next went in search of the air conditioning and turned it off. It was quite cold in the room but American hotel rooms always seemed to be too cold.

He had just unpacked and jumped on the bed with his beer to try out the television while preparing for a nap when there was a knock at the door. He went over and when he opened it he saw Jenny looking at him strangely with her finger to her lips. He ushered her past him and she walked in carrying a small device in her hand. It looked like a small table tennis bat connected to a small box with a wire. Without saying a word she waved the bat at several of the light fittings and frowned when a red light on the box came on. Jon realised what she was doing and stayed mute.

'Well darling, we are alone for a couple of hours now what shall we do?' Jenny asked in her seductress voice. As she spoke, she was frantically writing on the hotel notepad on the desk.

Jon leant over and read what she was writing. 'At least three bugs in my room too. We need to take a shower.'

As he read she continued talking. 'I don't know about you but why don't we get naked and have a shower together? Then we can spend the afternoon in bed like we did in London.'

Jon was startled to say the least but realised what she was up to and simply said 'Talked me into it, you raving nympho.'

Jenny took off her jersey and kicked off her shoes and Jon deliberately undid his belt noisily before noisily kicking off his shoes as well. Together, they went into the bathroom and Jenny checked it out with her little detector. She then turned the shower on full. As soon as the noise of the water started, she sat on the toilet seat and indicated for Jon to come closer. It was a weird situation for Jon. If what was going wasn't so serious it could have actually been quite arousing especially as Jenny only had a very sheer blouse on now and her full curves could be appreciated properly. Pulling himself together, he whispered at her. 'How did you know?'

Conspiracy

'I would have checked anyway as a standard precaution but the so called liaison officer was the giveaway so I was doubly careful and glad of it because these bugs are very cleverly hidden.' she whispered back.

'Oh, he seems quite genuine to me.'

'He probably is, in one way but my guess is that he knows who I am because he was completely unmoved when I was introduced. You know what effect I have on males but he barely registered my presence. That was enough to get me thinking. It's exactly what he would have done if he had been briefed on who I represent.'

'Or he could be gay,' Jon responded with a grin. 'But no, that does seem right. And anyway your little bug detector has proved the point. Shit, it means we are going to be under surveillance just about all the time we're here. Damn, how the hell did they, whoever they are, find out?'

'Could just be a standard precaution, it's a tense time after all but I suspect there has been a leak at home. It's going to make our mission bloody hard though.' Jenny responded.

'Ok, we'll need to warn the other three. You can write them a note. We can still ask our questions but I've a feeling that we are not going to be allowed to meet the people we want to now. Dammit, we're blown before we've even started.'

'We've still got a list of names that we would reasonably be expected to ask to be available. We should be able to get to at least some of them. The trick will be getting to talk to them in private. There are a few tricks I've been taught about how to do that but we'll need the other person's cooperation for them to work. But we'll have to assume that everything we say and do is being overheard from now on, especially when indoors.'

A thought suddenly struck Jon. 'You didn't think through your little charade earlier properly did you?'

She looked blank for a moment and then the penny dropped. 'Oh dear, that was a blonde moment wasn't it?' She looked Jon in the eye and grinned. 'Well, we can fake it I suppose but don't you think we should make things sound as authentic as possible? Purely for the sake of the mission of course.'

'Come on girl, I'm old enough to be your father.' Jon responded without conviction.

'Bollocks, I'm thirty two and that would mean you fathered me when you were a teenager. Come on let's have some fun.' She gave him her sultry look as she said it.

God, he found it hard to resist. She was absolutely adorable and every fibre of his body was screaming for him to give in. But he also knew that it would be a step too far. He had to maintain a professional reputation and dammit, despite what she had said, he did feel old enough to be her parent.

'No,' he said firmly. 'That's not going to happen. I already have a partner and I'll not screw up this mission with totally inappropriate behaviour.' He saw the look on her face. 'Let's see how good we can be at faking it.'

To his surprise, her sultry look disappeared and was replaced by something he couldn't quite analyse. 'Well, I hope you're a good actor then,' she said with a mischievous grin.

The ears of the two men who had been monitoring the bugs in the Brits bedrooms had pricked up when the naval Commodore's secretary had suggested a shower together. They listened even more intently when the two of them came back into the bedroom.

'Jesus,' one of them said after many long minutes. 'Have you seen the girl? That's one lucky bastard.'

'Judging from the noise she's making, she's pretty lucky too,' the other man responded.

Chapter 8

Jon's concerns that his secretive mission was compromised, soon seemed to become baseless. When visiting the various air stations, irrespective of the service running them the same atmosphere was clearly prevalent. The same could be said for the two aircraft manufacturers they visited. Far from having to be careful about asking questions about the political situation, they were given opinion from all sides and it was always the same.

After ten days of travelling around the country, they found themselves back in Washington in their hotel. They had managed to get their liaison officer to leave them for the evening and had gone out for a meal. Jenny had been careful in picking the restaurant and made sure they were in a secluded area at the rear of a rather pleasant Italian Bistro. They could not be seen from the road and no one could overhear them without being seen. Even so they kept their conversation guarded.

'Well,' Terry said. 'I think we can safely say that this whole trip has been a busted flush. The whole bloody country is paranoid. No one seems to care about the truth even if their own government has said that Iraq had nothing to do with Nine Eleven only months ago. I think we can report back that one hundred percent of the US military want nothing more than to find another Middle East country to invade and as soon as possible. Mind you I am surprised that everyone is focused on Iraq I thought that Iran was their big bad bogey man. Didn't they support Saddam at one time?'

'Yes they did,' Jon replied. 'And I think you've summed it up rather well Terry. A cynic might say that after years of watching other countries being subjected to continual terrorist attacks, it's been a shock to their egos to find that they are actually in the same world as the rest of us.'

'Good point,' Paul said. 'You know they had about as many casualties on Nine Eleven as we suffered in the thirty years of the troubles with the IRA. The only difference being that they got it all at once.'

'And don't forget that most of the money those murdering Irish bastards got came from this country in the first place.' Brian replied.

'Maybe it's a wake up call with some good coming from it despite the tragedy that happened. But Terry's right, not one person I've spoken to and that's not just on our formal visits, I even include the receptionist in the hotel, thinks that the matter is over. If anything could unite a country this is it.'

Jon looked thoughtful. 'You guys may be right but don't forget we've got the Pentagon visit tomorrow. I have to say though, that I'm pretty sure our report from here will be of total solidarity even if the logic looks skewed to us. Maybe the attitude in Israel will be different, after all they are close neighbours and stand to lose a lot more if things go wrong.'

Just then their waiter arrived with their food and several bottles of wine. They busied themselves with the food for a few minutes then Jenny spoke. 'It's funny, all you men seem to have the same opinion of what the atmosphere is like over here. I've been talking to some of the women in the margins, especially the non-military ones. I had quite a long chat with one woman in a shop when we were in Norfolk the other day and she had some interesting things to say. Maybe it was because she had no idea who I was. Most of the people we've been speaking to, even in the hotels know we are a military team even if none of us are in uniform. She was quite upset over the whole thing saying that Nine Eleven was all an internal setup to convince the country to take out Al Qaeda.'

'Oh come on,' Terry scoffed. 'There's been these silly theories going around ever since the incident. Can you really imagine the American government doing that to their own people?'

'No I can't,' Jenny responded. 'But ask yourself this. If Nine Eleven hadn't happened where would we be now? There would have been no viable excuse to attack Afghanistan. And no viable excuse to ramp it up to have a go at Iraq. I'm not saying that it wasn't a terrorist attack just that it's causing all sorts of mayhem now.'

'And my brother would still have his legs,' Tony said bitterly.

'You're right Tony,' Brian said sympathetically. 'But mayhem is just what that moron Bin Laden wanted of course. So his plan worked.'

'Ah but did it?' Jon replied. 'I'm pretty sure Al Qaeda has nothing to do with Saddam Hussein. I expect they're as surprised as the rest of the world over this. Anyway, this is not our remit. Our job was to see what the attitude of people over here is and it's pretty clear to me. There may be many of us with doubts at home but apparently not here. Maybe a trip to the Middle East is still called for but frankly I think this whole thing is a bust. The UN will hopefully have the final say although, as you know, some are already arguing that there are already grounds for intervention. It's also clear that our government will go in with the Yanks whatever happens. Anyone disagree?'

There were shaken heads around the table.

'Fine, then here's what I plan to do. We all know Jenny and I have been under surveillance for the whole time we've been here. The other rooms weren't bugged so whoever tipped off the Americans don't seem to know that we're all in it now. So, on the night before we leave, Jenny and I will go back to my room for a night cap and have a similar conversation to this one. I'll leave the rude remarks about our allies out of it of course. When we get back to the UK I'm going to suggest we write up what we've discovered about aircraft support to give a credible account of our time here and then maybe we can all go our own ways. We've still got the Pentagon to visit tomorrow but does anyone here think they'll hear anything different?'

'If they're that gung ho on the airbases and in industry, I hate to think what the attitude there will be. They got hit on Nine Eleven as well of course.' Paul observed.

The next morning an official mini bus collected the team from the hotel and drove them to the Pentagon. As they climbed out of the car it was suddenly obvious how big the building actually was.

'Bloody hell it makes the MOD building in London look like a garden shed,' Paul remarked as they gazed at the main entrance.

'Yes but don't forget our MOD is split over a load of buildings just look at the size of Abbey Wood at Bristol,' Brian countered.

'Come on guys,' Jon encouraged. 'Didn't you know everything is bigger over here? Doesn't mean it's better though.'

Just then as if on cue, their almost ever present liaison officer appeared and ushered them in through the main entrance portal. Once in the lobby, their identities were checked and then they went inside. They were surprised to see an immaculately dressed US Marine in dress blues and spotless white gloves standing smartly to attention as they entered.

He snapped a smart salute, even though they were all in business suits. 'Commodore Hunt Sir. I am Marine Thompson and will be your escort for today. We are in meeting room Alpha Seven. If you would all follow me.' Without waiting for an answer, he spun around and started down the long corridor.

Within a few minutes, Jon was hopelessly lost. The place was a rabbit warren and he realised now why visitors were escorted. He turned to Brian who was walking alongside the wide corridor they were in.

'Thank goodness for our shiny Marine Brian. I thought he was here for security but it's more likely that he's here to make sure we don't get lost.'

Brian laughed. 'There's probably been people wandering around in here for years trying to find the exit.'

Just then the Marine stopped and stood smartly to attention outside two mahogany doors. He knocked and immediately opened one of them and indicated for Jon to enter. They all filed in to find a pleasant meeting room with a large conference table draped in the de rigeur green baize covering. Standing at the far end were several military officers, all in uniform.

An American Admiral stepped forward and greeted them. 'Lady and Gentlemen welcome to the Pentagon. Especially Commodore Hunt. Hello Jon, long time no meet.'

He held out his hand to Jon, who just for a second couldn't place the man. And then the penny dropped. They had only met face to face once but it was at a particularly exciting time.

'Sir. Admiral Morrison. Goodness, it was a long time ago.'

The Admiral turned to the room and addressed them all. 'Gentlemen, the good Commodore here was in command of a Royal Navy Frigate, HMS Prometheus in the Gulf at the same time that I was in command of the Sacagawea. If it hadn't been for him and some pretty crazy tactics I probably wouldn't be here today. In fact, when I was subsequently teaching at Annapolis, I used the action as an example of one of the finest military encounters of the decade.'

'You're making me blush Sir,' Jon responded with a grin. 'May I introduce Captain Brian Pearce? I don't think you ever met at the time but he was my operations officer and just as responsible for that action as I was.' Jon then introduced the others and was secretly amused to see that the Admiral's reaction to Jenny was as predictable as ever.

The other American officers were the particular specialists that Jon had requested to talk to. Having made the introductions, the Admiral took Jon to one side. 'Jon I would be grateful for a talk in private before you leave.'

Jon looked around the room. 'Actually Sir, I think my team could easily manage without me. How about now?' There had been something in the Admiral's tone that had alerted Jon that this may not be a routine chat about old times.

The Admiral nodded. Jon turned to Brian and quietly explained what was going on and asked him to take over. He then followed Admiral Morrison to his private office which was thankfully quite close by.

Once seated comfortably in two chairs in the plush office, Admiral Morrison turned to Jon. 'I think we can dispense with rank here Jon, call me Jim please.'

'Fine Jim, I've always wondered how you got on after the Iranian attack was beaten back. As I'm sure you know we went on and found the merchantman.'

'We had to be towed in I'm afraid but the ship was eventually put back into service. My God but we learned a few lessons from it though. And you took out the Iranian with a broken Surface to Air Missile and those Stingray torpedoes I understand?'

Jon laughed. 'That and just about every small arms weapon we had on board but you're right it was the torpedoes that put her down.'

Jon was getting the strong opinion that the Admiral knew all this and was saying it for the benefit of someone else who clearly wasn't in the room.

'And your study? It's just a short term fill in I understand? Then I assume you're going on to something bigger and better? After your performance with that little carrier of yours, you must have good prospects.'

'Yes, we're just about wrapped up.' Jon realised the Admiral was writing something as he spoke so he kept going. 'After this, I'm hoping to get an appointment back to sea. It might be good timing for what seems to be about to happen.'

Conspiracy

The Admiral frowned at the remark but didn't comment directly. 'Now Jon, I understand that you are heading home next week. Mary, my wife and I would be absolutely delighted if you could come and stay with us at the weekend. I have a small house up near Trenton at a place called Washington Crossing. We could catch up properly and Mary has been dying to meet you ever since I got back from the Gulf all those years back. We keep a small boat there on a lake next to the Delaware River and I could take you Bass fishing.' He held up the piece of paper so Jon could see what was written on it.

Jon read the few words and the penny dropped. He also realised the Admiral was taking a big risk but all he said was, 'I'd be absolutely delighted Jim. Oh, could I bring Captain Pearce as well? As I said, he was there too and could probably tell you more.'

The Admiral looked slightly surprised at the request but Jon nodded firmly at him.

'Hey, I'd be delighted Jon. We can make a great weekend of it.'

Chapter 9

Jon looked out of the car window at the classic American house they were pulling up outside. 'Goodness Jim you actually have a white picket fence around the front garden,' he remarked.

Jim laughed. 'It's practically a legal requirement around here Jon. How many houses do you see without one?'

'Good point,' Jon replied. 'I have to say it's a really pretty place. It's like a village in England only spread out over twice the real estate.'

'You should see it in the Fall when all the leaves are still in place.'

Jon had to do a quick mental translation of the American term. 'So I guess it will be snowing any time soon?'

'Sure will. We normally get a white Christmas and snow is forecast for next week. Mind you it's warm at the moment.' Jim stopped the car just as a woman opened the front door. Even from a distance, Jon could see she was quite pretty although the jeans and rather loose sweater hid her shape well.

She came up to the car as Jon and Brian clambered out. 'You must be Jon, I'm Mary, I recognise you from Jim's description and you must be Brian.' She gave them both a quick hug. 'How was the flight? Did the Admiral pull rank like he normally does on a Friday afternoon?'

'Now my dear, as you well know it's a regular communication flight. It's just that I get priority over seats.'

'It wasn't like that when I first married you,' she laughed. 'Come on everyone lets go inside. It's getting cold out here.'

They all trooped in. Jon looked at Brian. 'Jim may be a Three Star but I know who the boss is in this house.'

'I heard that Jon Hunt and actually you're completely right.' Jim laughed.

'I know the feeling,' Brian replied.

'Oh, aren't you married?' Mary asked Jon innocently. 'I am surprised, a good looking man like you.'

'Not any more Mary. I'll tell you the whole story some time.' Jon responded.

She caught the look on his face.' 'Oh sorry have I been tactless again? Jim is always nagging me not to say the first thing that comes into my head.'

'It's alright Mary,' Jon said. 'She died in a car accident some years ago. It's all history now.'

A look of recognition passed across her face. 'Yes, I remember now. You were the naval officer who took a swing at that journalist on television. They showed it over here you know. Well done, we all cheered you.'

Jon winced at the recollection but before he could reply, Jim grabbed Mary by the arm. 'Come on my dear let's get our guests settled. You can continue putting your foot in it later over dinner.'

In fact, dinner was a great success. Mary had invited several of their friends over to join them and the evening flew by. It was well after one in the morning before their host bade Jon and Brian good night with the admonishment not to lie in in the morning as the weather looked good for the promised fishing trip.

Indeed the next day dawned bright, crisp and clear. After being given an enormous American breakfast of pancakes with syrup and bacon, scrambled eggs and gallons of coffee, Jim led them out to his garage where they got into his old shooting brake. He drove them a couple of miles to the lake. Tied to an old jetty was a modern looking aluminium open boat with an outboard on the back. Jim directed the other two to get all the tackle from the rear of the car while he got the boat ready. Within minutes they were speeding across the mirror smooth lake.

He made for a spot near the centre and showed them how to set up the rods and cast the bait he had provided into the water.

When they had settled down, Jon turned to his host. 'Alright Jim, it must look like we're fishing to anyone watching from the shore but they certainly won't be able to hear what we're saying. I hope this rather extreme secrecy is worthwhile. Before this week, we've only met once before and that was in the middle of a very tense military situation. I've trusted you up to this point, so come on what the hell is this all about?'

'Before I answer that Jon, I need to establish a couple of things if you don't mind,' Jim replied. 'Firstly, let me explain that I have a pretty good idea why you are actually here. I sit on several intelligence committees but more importantly I have connections with some of your people in England. A certain society if you understand my meaning?'

Jon nodded. He wasn't at all surprised but he turned to Brian. 'Sorry old chap but before you ask, this is more than top secret, especially Jim's last remark.'

Brian simply nodded.

Jim continued. 'Now, our intelligence suggested that only you and that pretty little secretary of yours were in on the bottom line but it seems that Brian is also in the know?'

Jon was thinking furiously. He wasn't surprised by the turn of the conversation but that didn't mean he felt he could completely trust this man. There again, this could be the turning point of the whole trip and he realised he couldn't afford to ignore it. Which meant he had to be honest or at least as honest as he could until he knew the complete lie of the land.

'No Jim, the whole team is. It was never going to be practical to keep the purpose secret within a close knit team. But if you are concerned, don't be. We're all worried about what seems to be going on and I assume you are too? Otherwise, I can't see a reason for all this secrecy and all these precautions.'

'Correct. Now could you summarise your findings so far? Just in general terms.'

Jon nodded. Recounting the results they had achieved so far wouldn't exactly be difficult. 'It seems very simple. Just about everyone we've spoken to so far seems dead keen on following your President's line and gearing up for an attack on Iraq. Frankly, we can't really understand why as the line about Saddam having anything to do with the World Trade Centre attacks is bloody thin. And then this spin about Weapons of Mass Destruction looks like just an excuse. Mind you our Prime Minister is pedalling it for all he's worth as well. Why? Do you know something I should know about?'

'One word Jon. Oil.' Jim sounded grim as he spat out the word.

Jon nodded. It made sense in some ways. Taking over Iraq would give America and presumably its friend's direct access to and control of vast oil reserves.

'Why am I not surprised?' Brian said. 'And there was your President saying that God had told him that Saddam should be removed.'

'He did say that, didn't he?' Jim said. 'And I find that even more terrifying than just plain old greed.'

Jon wasn't so convinced. 'Sorry Jim, I'm not sure I'm buying that. There has to be more than just Iraqi oil. Yes, Iraq has massive reserves but there is plenty elsewhere and they're finding more every day.' He decided to take the bull by the horns. 'Jim, you've dragged us out here so we can't be overheard. You're a Three Star Admiral, yet you're clearly paranoid about security and someone else knowing what you're up to. We are just a small British team here on a fact finding mission, albeit a covert one. To me, that means you are worried about something in your organisation and it must be something that you are in a minority about. Yes, I can buy the oil explanation but there is something more isn't there? And it's far more than just a power grab by the American government.'

'There are no flies on you are there Jon. Fair enough but you're wrong about one thing, it's not the government I'm worried about. In fact, I don't actually really know who it is. What I do know is that things are running out of control or should I say running under someone's control to a very hidden agenda. Let me ask you a question. What happened on Nine Eleven?'

Jon thought for a moment. 'Four aircraft were hijacked by Al Qaeda operatives. Two were flown into the twin towers and one hit the Pentagon. One crashed when the passengers tried to retake control.'

'And the towers?'

'They burned for several hours and the heat must have damaged them internally so much that they collapsed.'

'And was that all?'

'Sorry Jim, what do you mean?' Brian interjected.

'Did you know that a third building collapsed some hours later?' Jim asked.

Both British men looked confused. Jon responded. 'But there were only two aircraft there how did a third one come down? And why hasn't it been reported?'

'Good questions my friend. It was reported briefly at the time but little has been said since. World Trade Centre, Building Seven, was to the north of the twin towers and hit by debris and set on fire when they collapsed. The damage to the area had cut all pressure to the fire mains and so the building's sprinklers didn't work. It had a steel core

Conspiracy

and so eventually it too went down. Or at least that's the official story.'

'You obviously think there is more to it,' Jon observed.

'Damned right I do. It was a forty seven story building and mainly occupied by a Wall Street trading company who had just taken it over. They had carried out extensive internal rebuilding to make an almost separate internal division. The main occupiers were commercial organisations but also in the building were elements of the CIA, Department of Defence, Secret Service and the Office of National Emergency Planning. There are already stories circulating that there is no way the building could have been brought down by fire, it was just too strong. And here's another thing almost immediately after the collapse when they were clearing the area, all the structural steel was taken away and smelted down.'

'Sorry, what does that mean?' Brian asked.

'How does a building like that collapse if fire wasn't the culprit?'

Jon looked at Brian and then back to Jim. 'Are you saying it was deliberately demolished, that's just crazy.'

'Then why remove the steel so fast so that there was none left to analyse for residual explosive traces? If you watch the film you will see that the whole structure collapses in free fall, the only way that could occur is if all the supporting structure was removed simultaneously. I managed to speak to a cousin of mine who is in the demolition business and he is in no doubt. Building Seven was deliberately destroyed and not by Al Qaeda.'

There was silence in the boat while Jon and Brian digested the idea. Jim took the opportunity to reel in one of the fishing lines and pretend to check the bait before recasting out into the lake.

Jon eventually spoke first. 'Alright Jim, I guess I have to take that at face value at the moment. You know I can check everything you've said?'

'Oh yes, go onto the internet and the conspiracy theories are flying around like mad. It doesn't mean that some of them aren't right though.'

'Fair enough but the key question is why? Why would anybody do anything like that?'

'Well, first of all, you have to understand that no one was killed. They all had plenty of time to evacuate. So, if it was deliberate, then terrorism wasn't the prime reason although blaming it on that is a great way of hiding in plain sight. No, there was something in that building that had to be destroyed once the twin towers came down.'

'Hang on, that infers that the main attack was also part of some sort of conspiracy,' Brian said.

'Not that I can discover Brian,' Jim said. 'The perpetrators were all that the media have said they were, despite the conspiracy theories to the contrary. Even in such a paranoid country as this, I can't believe that the government would do that to their own people.'

'You must have some idea about what was destroyed Jim or you wouldn't be talking to us.' Jon said.

'Remember I mentioned that occupants of the building and one was ONEP, the Office of National Emergency Planning. The CIA and Secret Service and others were just administration wings but ONEP is something different. They had an operational cell there with all the computer and communication infrastructure that implies. Every time I've tried to get close I hit a brick wall. So much so that I've been warned off in no uncertain terms. It's one of the reasons I decided to confide in you. What I do know about ONEP is that despite the word 'national' in their title they are something much more. Their public stated purpose is making sure there are contingency plans in place for national disasters. They actually had some that helped with the Nine Eleven response operation. However, what I do also know is that they also plan for international threats to the country and that includes operations abroad.

'So they had some dirty secret that needed to be destroyed once the main attack was successful. I don't get it.' Jon said thoughtfully as he gazed out over the water.

'Frankly, neither do I Jon,' Jim said. 'But you have friends in high places over the water. As I said, I can't dig any further but you can. Will you report this back?'

'Of course, Jim. I know several people back home who can be trusted to look into it. But there's something more isn't there?'

Jim sighed. 'Look at where we are now. Ninety nine percent of Americans are convinced we are under some sort of attack. We took out Afghanistan with ridiculous ease. Iraq has been a political thorn in the side of the Bush family ever since they stupidly stopped at the Iraqi border after we kicked Saddam out of Kuwait ten years ago. Let's suppose they do invade Iraq and find these weapons. What happens next?'

'They'll be on an even bigger roll,' Brian answered. 'They'll be looking out for yet another excuse to keep going.'

'And the country that really bugs the hell out of American isn't Iraq, its Iran.' Jon said as realisation dawned. 'Ever since the Ayatollahs took over, America had been trying to intervene. They even supported Saddam during his war with them. Jesus, if Iran is attacked the gloves will really be off. Russia won't stand for it for a start.'

'Yes but Russia is a spent force at the moment.' Jim said. 'Then there is Syria, the Lebanon even Jordan all ripe for the pacifying. Just imagine the Middle East completely controlled from Washington. Apart from Saudi and some of the smaller states who are already allies. The whole region will be dominated from here and on the ground they will have local control in the form of Israel. Imagine what a stranglehold there will be on oil production. Guys, I love my country but this is not what I signed up for. And frankly, I'm not sure that this is government policy, at least not overtly. We are being manipulated and I've no idea who is doing it. What's worse is that the manipulation is so subtle and so convincing that no one wants to know.'

'Shitty death Jim, that's a lot to think about.' Jon stated as he stared unseeingly out over the lake.

'I know Jon and I'm sorry to dump it on you but maybe you can unlock some doors over on your side of the pond.'

'I'll try Jim, no guarantees though. Of course, there is one thing that could pour very cold water on the whole thing.'

'Oh, what?'

'If we do invade and take over the country and despite all the certainty, find out that there were never any Weapons of Mass Destruction in the first place. That would stop things dead in their tracks.'

Chapter 10

Jon and Brian returned to Washington with much to think about. They had both agreed not to say anything to the others until they were back on British soil. If an American senior Admiral was so concerned about security, then who were they to argue? The routine trooping flight operated by Virgin Airlines only flew out on Tuesdays and Thursdays so they all had a day to kill before heading off to the airport.

In the end, they all agreed to stay together and do the sights. In particular, Jon wanted to visit the Smithsonian Aerospace museum. He had never had the time to go there in the past and for an aviator it was fascinating. The team spent a happy morning there and then after lunch went on a wander down the centre of the city taking in the Capitol, White House and then a long walk down to the Lincoln Memorial.

As they walked down towards the large Romanesque memorial Jenny turned to Jon. 'This city is just a bit over the top isn't it? All this pseudo classical architecture.' She said as she looked around at the white marble buildings surrounding them. 'None of it is particularly original.'

Jon laughed. 'No it's not but then when you start with a blank sheet like they did, why not copy the best from the past. I actually think it's quite impressive which, of course, is the point. Mind you, go just a few miles from here and there are streets you really don't want to even drive down. It's the contradiction of the palace that amazes me. All this power and wealth and ghettoes literally within walking distance.'

'All this open space does have one advantage though,' Jenny observed.

'Oh, what's that?'

'It makes it very hard for people to stay out of sight when they are trying to follow you.' She said looking straight ahead.

'Ah, you've seen them too then?' Jon replied. 'They've been with us since we left the hotel this morning.

'Actually, they or others like them have been with us nearly all the time when we've been away from military bases or large corporations.'

Jon nodded unsurprised. 'I'll tell you all about our weekend and some interesting revelations Jenny but only when we are back home. For the moment let's just let them get on with their job and we'll do ours.'

She turned and gave him an odd look but said nothing more.

It wasn't much later that they all agreed that they were footsore and it was time to find a bar. Jon turned to the group. 'It's our last night before we head home, let's have a good time and we'll regroup back in London. No talking shop until then.' He emphasised the last remark looking hard at all of them in turn. 'So, let's head back to the hotel, we can hit happy hour and then go out for a meal.'

Several hours later, Jon and the team were in a small Italian restaurant that Paul had discovered over the weekend. It was the quiet backstreet sort of place where the quality of the food was inversely proportional to the simplicity of the décor. The proprietor was a rather rotund and extrovert character who took great delight in explaining how all his dishes were cooked although he singled out Jenny for most of his attention which amused Jon and to his surprise seemed to annoy Tony a little bit. Of course, Tony wasn't married so maybe Jon shouldn't be that surprised that he seemed hopeful of getting to know Jenny a little better.

They were finally left to their main courses, which were outstanding and definitely worth the lengthy explanations. Jon took a swig of his red wine and suddenly felt that maybe he had had enough to drink. He realised that the fact that they were heading home tomorrow and would get away from the constant surveillance had made him drop his guard. That and the free booze at happy hour. He looked around at his team. As usual, Brian looked none the worse for wear. He was renowned for having 'hollow legs'. Paul just seemed merry and he had noticed that Jenny was very careful over how much she had consumed. However, Tony was definitely cooking on gas. He was smiling at everything and was even starting to slur the occasional word. Jon decided he would need to keep an eye on him although to be fair Jenny seemed to be doing the same thing.

In retrospect, Jon wondered whether he should have done something earlier but hindsight was never much help and with what he eventually knew it would probably not have made any difference anyway.

The door of the restaurant opened and two young men came in. No one took much notice even when the proprietor put them at the table next to Jon's party. The restaurant was getting quite crowded and it was the only table left. At first, everything seemed normal then Jon noticed that one of the men kept staring at Jenny and then turning to his companion and saying something that made them both laugh. Jon couldn't hear what was said but it was clear that Tony could.

Before anyone realised what was going on, Tony pushed his chair back and stood looking at the two men. 'Would you care to say that again you oaf?' He demanded in a voice loud enough for the whole room to hear. It didn't help that he was swaying slightly on his feet. Jenny reached up and tried to pull him back into his seat but he was having none of it.

The American who had made the remark also got to his feet and confronted Tony. In a clear voice that all could hear, he repeated his remark. 'I said, you deaf Limey, that you are one lucky bastard sitting next to one of the most beautiful women I have ever seen.'

'That's not what you said at all you lying bastard.' Tony said even more angrily if that was possible.

Jon looked at Brian who was already getting to his feet. Unfortunately, the table was between him and the ongoing confrontation.

'Break it up Brian.' Jon called over to his friend. This wasn't the first time Brian had helped defuse a situation like this. His size was normally more than was needed. Unfortunately, Jon realised that both Americans were pretty well built, although Brian had a few inches and several pounds on either of them. Jon started to get to his feet as well and noticed Paul doing the same.

The two Americans grinned at each other as they saw the other men starting to stand. 'You pussy's want to make something of it?' The first man said.

'Oh shit,' Jon muttered under his breath. There was only one way this was going to end but he had to try. 'Tony sit down that's a bloody order.' Jon said firmly, although he had no confidence his words would have any effect.

Sure enough, they didn't. Before anyone could react, Tony took a swing at the man in front of him. To give him credit, Jon was impressed. Tony may have been half cut and only two thirds the size of the man in front of him but his fist connected perfectly and the man's head snapped back, sending him staggering back into his comrade.

Before the men could react further Brian arrived. He took Tony by the shoulders and forcibly pushed him back into his seat. 'That's enough Tony.' Without waiting for a reply he turned to the two men who were now back facing them and looking very angry. The man Tony had hit was holding his jaw with a look of surprise on his face.

'Do you people know who I am?' he asked angrily.

'No idea son,' Brian answered. 'But if you come here and insult one of us you should expect to pay the consequences. Now why don't you and your friend just leave before there's more trouble? You haven't even placed an order yet and there are plenty more restaurants in this city.'

The two men looked at each other and then back at Brian who stared stonily back at them. For a few seconds it was a battle of wills then the two men just smiled. 'Be seeing you,' one said and they turned and walked out.

As the front door banged closed, conversation suddenly resumed and the proprietor came over.

Before he could say anything, Jon spoke first. 'We do apologise for that Sir. If we could have the bill we'll be leaving.'

'Yes of course,' he replied. 'But I suspect you don't know who that was?'

'No idea,' Jon replied. 'Does it matter? They insulted my lady companion and one of us stood up for her.'

'Well, we did not hear an insult but more importantly that was the son of Senator Arnold Kennedy. He is a senior member of the new Department of Homeland Security and I don't think he will take kindly to his son being assaulted in public, whatever the provocation.'

'I see, well thank you, we'll be leaving now.' Jon replied with a sinking feeling. As he said the words, flashing lights appeared through the restaurant window as several police cars pulled up. Jon turned to Brian. 'Shit, why do I think we've just been set up?'

Chapter 11

'Jesus wept Jon. How the hell could you let it happen?' Admiral Tucket was not a happy man. That was quite obvious.

Jon was exhausted. He and the rest of the team had only landed at Heathrow a few hours earlier. He was jet lagged, exhausted and thoroughly pissed off, both with the bastards who had set him up and at himself for letting it happen. Luckily, it seemed that the press hadn't realised that they were arriving and there were none to greet them. Jon had been dreading yet another confrontation with bloody journalists.

'Naivety, overconfidence, I don't know Sir. It was hardly the sort of thing I would have expected to occur. It was clearly entrapment but that wasn't obvious at the time. It was only the next day after the police had let us go that I realised the full extent of the damage. The press had clearly been well briefed.'

'You're not wrong there Jon. The headlines were bad in the US but over here they had a field day. 'Drunken Military Team Pick Fight in Washington Bar.' 'Naval hero Falls From Grace.' I could go on. Talk about a public relations disaster.'

'Yes Sir but you're asking me the wrong questions I'm afraid.'

'Eh? What do you mean?'

'You haven't asked me about the trip and what we discovered,' Jon replied wearily. 'And you haven't asked me why someone thought it necessary to try and discredit us. This goes far beyond me and my team.'

The Admiral sat back and thought for a moment. He had clearly caught the simmering anger in Jon's tone. Had he been caught out in the same way he would probably feel the same. He also realised that Jon had a point. 'Why don't you tell me then?'

'Firstly, we were under surveillance for the entire time we were there. My and Jenny's hotel rooms were bugged. That and the fact that the others rooms weren't, means someone was warned of our coming but they thought that Jenny and myself were the only people they had to worry about. So, firstly we have a leak and need to find out who it is. But no matter who we spoke to over there, they all support the Bush line of Saddam having these damned weapons.'

'Didn't that American Admiral invite you to his house for the weekend? What was that all about?'

'Nothing Sir. You may remember I helped a US ship during my time in the Gulf in Prometheus, He was in command. He never really got a chance to say thank you in person so that was his opportunity. I took Brian because he was my Ops officer at the time.'

'And was there anything else to it?' the Admiral asked.

'No Sir, nothing. That was all it was about.' As Jon said it he was nodding his head as hard as he could.

Admiral Tucket looked at him as if he had gone mad but Jon continued to nod and then pointed to the ceilings and walls.

'Oh come on, you can't be serious.' The Admiral said before realising that anyone listening might realise what had just happened. He thought quickly. 'Surely you must have found something out?' he asked hoping that the question would sound like a response to Jon's last statement.

'No Sir, the whole mission was a busted flush. I can't see it's even worth going ahead with any further work. There's nothing to find out. I suspect the surveillance was just precautionary.' As he spoke Jon held out a piece of paper he been writing on and handed it over to the Admiral. It only had two words on it 'MI6, noon'.

Admiral Tucket nodded but said nothing in direct response. 'Well, if you say so Jon. I'd like a written report to that effect as soon as you can.'

'And my team, what happens to them Sir?'

'Well, the girl can go back to her old employer and we'll have to look at new assignments for Pearce and Roberts but I'm afraid that the Wing Commander's career is at an end. His RAF Lords and Masters take a dim view of fighting in public but I'm pretty sure we can avoid a court martial as no charges were ever made, merely some incredibly damaging press reports. But Jon, it's also a problem for you I'm afraid.'

A feeling of dread stole over Jon. He could make a guess at what was coming next but guessing and being told were two completely different things.

'You're a very public person Jon. In the past, the press have liked you with the exception of one particular fracas we all remember but things like the Uganda incident and the rescue of the hostages in Africa have made you a bit of a media darling. But as you know

Conspiracy

there's nothing the press like more than a fallen star and I know it's desperately unfair but they've managed to make most of the mud stick to you over this one. The Minister himself spoke to me the other day and asked what you were meant to be doing next. When I told him that we were going to give you command of our amphibious capability he absolutely forbade it. I'm sorry Jon but COMAW is now out of the question.'

There it was. Right between the eyes, yet oddly Jon just felt numb. He had been expecting it of course, he was no fool and knew how the world worked. He realised he was now at the watershed he had talked about when they were on holiday what seemed like an age ago.

'Understood Sir,' was all he said. 'I'd like to go and talk to the team if you don't mind they're down in the office and then some sleep for all of us wouldn't go amiss.' As he said it, he pointed to the piece of paper he had written on.

'Fine Jon, get yourself sorted out then we'll talk some more. And I am really sorry. You are still the best man for that job in my opinion but we both know how politicians think I'm afraid.'

'Yes Sir, thank you.' He stood and left.

Just after midday, Jon, his team, Admiral Tucket and Rupert Thomas met in a secure room in the MI6 building on the south bank of the Thames.

Rupert assured them that the room was completely secure and they could all talk freely at last.

Jon took the lead and with the help of Brian, gave them all the complete story and included everything that Admiral Morrison had told them.

When he finished there was a stunned silence for a few seconds then Rupert spoke. 'We know about Building Seven of course, but not that rational people are really considering that it might have been brought down intentionally. We have a small team who keep an eye on the various conspiracy theories that are going about but that particular one hasn't been high on the list I have to say. I think we'd better have a closer look.'

Brian responded. 'I got the impression that although that was some sort of corroborating evidence to Admiral Morrison, the real issue he was worried about was that someone is manipulating the

American nation and very effectively at that. He also wasn't convinced it was the government. But that was far as he was able to go. He was rather hoping we might be able to come up with something.'

'Not much chance of that I'm afraid.' Rupert replied. 'No one is going to talk to you now.'

'Yes but it was the end game that Jim Morrison was really worried about,' Jon said. 'His concern wasn't just about Iraq. If they are successful there, then Iran and other countries will end up on the list. He seemed to think it could end up in nothing less than an American take over of just about the whole Middle East apart from the few countries that are already allied to them.'

Jenny had been silent throughout the discussion but now felt she needed to say something. 'As you know, I have a degree in Middle Eastern languages as well as a PhD in the subject. You can't go that deep into language without understanding the history of the countries concerned as well as the politics. I don't think America is behind this, they are being led by the nose. Who stands to gain most out of this in the local area?'

Tony Deverell was the first to answer. 'Well, Israel obviously. They are surrounded by enemies. Iran and to a lesser extent Iraq have said they wish to see an end to the country. They've managed to piss off all their neighbours in one way or another. If it wasn't for the military and financial support they get from the States they'd have gone under years ago.'

Jon was pleased that Tony was still contributing to the debate. After all, he had been through and with the knowledge that his career was just about dead, it was encouraging that he was still motivated enough to work at the problem. Mind you, he had to remind himself, keeping up his own motivation was going to be an issue now as well.

'I agree,' Rupert said. 'It makes more sense than the Americans crashing planes into their own buildings or blowing them up.'

Paul wasn't convinced. 'I think that might just be too simplistic. I lost a friend and Tony's bother was maimed in Afghanistan. When that happens it makes you look at things in a different light.'

'Go on Paul,' Jon said. 'What are we missing?'

'Ok, ask yourself why they went into Afghanistan in the first place.'

Conspiracy

'Hang on,' Brian interjected. 'Everyone knows why. It was being run by the Taliban who were hosting Al Qaeda. It was a direct reprisal for Nine Eleven.'

'Really?' Paul replied. 'AL Qaeda were as much hosted in Pakistan as Afghanistan and they weren't invaded. In fact, America calls them allies.'

'Maybe because they have nuclear weapons.' Jon pointed out.

'Good point but my original question still stands. If our suspicions are correct and some agency is manipulating public opinion for their own ends, why go into Afghanistan? There's no oil, bugger all minerals, just mainly rocks and sand.'

'And poppies, acres of poppies,' Jenny said. 'They were the biggest heroin producers in the world. They aren't now.'

Silence met her remark as they all thought it through. Rupert spoke. 'I haven't said much until now but I personally think that Jenny is right. But first some background. As you know we were commissioned to produce a report on the regime in Iraq. Once it left here, the spin doctors in Number Ten sexed it up. There were and still are a large number of very unhappy people here because of that. What's the point in having intelligence experts if all you do is take their findings and twist them to your own purpose and quite blatantly at that? I hear what you say about attitudes in the US. To a large extent they, whoever they are, are getting away with it over here as well, although there is a growing groundswell of opposition unlike on the other side of the Atlantic. One government Minister has already resigned and the government's legal advisors are far from happy. Just because we made our report doesn't mean we have stopped work, far from it. Jenny has a good point about heroin. Since the Yanks went in, they have made enormous efforts to stop the growing of poppies and output has already fallen by almost two thirds. We have a theory about all this and it's not far from the conclusions you have come to as well. Remember the President of the US has strong religious convictions and his country has a major drugs problem. The logic of going into Afghanistan starts to make a lot more sense if looked at that way. Frankly, far more than the logic of attacking Iraq but if your theory is correct and it's the start of an attempted pacification of the whole of the Middle East it all starts to fit together. Afghanistan was a test and clearly the test was passed with flying colours.'

'So my brother lost his legs because of an American drug problem?' Tony asked sourly. 'How many more are going to die because of this fucked up situation?'

'Look, we can't save the world,' Jon said. 'But maybe we can do something, however small. There are two things that come out of this. Firstly we know someone tipped off the Americans about our trip, if we can find out who it was, it could give us a lead. And on that point we need to sweep the Admiral's office for bugs.'

Jon looked at the Admiral who nodded assent. 'I can start making some discreet enquiries. Not many people knew the real purpose of your trip Jon. If the office wasn't secure can we trace the source of any eavesdropping?' He looked at Rupert as he said it.

'Maybe but let's see if there is anything to find first' Rupert replied. 'And your second point Jon?'

'The man in America who provoked Tony. We know who he is. He must have been put up to it by someone. Can we get to him and maybe find out who that was? It might take us further.'

Before anyone else could comment, there was a knock at the door, a man came in and passed a piece of paper to Rupert and left without saying anything.

Rupert studied the words for a brief moment and then looked up. 'Last night, US time, Admiral Morrison and his wife were travelling in a US Navy helicopter from their home in Maryland to a formal dinner in New York. The helicopter crashed and there were no survivors.'

Chapter 12

'Should have gone to the bloody Caribbean,' Jon muttered into his beer.

'Oh do shut up Jon,' Ruth replied in an exasperated tone. 'You know all the flights and hotels were booked. It's close to Christmas and the place just gets full up. This isn't bad and at least the diving's great.'

Jon looked around at the view. Ruth had a point. The sun was setting and illuminating the distant hills of Jordan across the blue isthmus that separated it from this northern tip of Egypt. The last rays of the sun behind them were turning the distant coast line a shining gold colour, which contrasted with the ever darkening deep blue of the sea.

Taba had been a last minute impulse. Encouraged by Ruth, who knew all about the events of the last few months and also his personal demons, he had acquiesced to her suggestion that they get the hell out of the country for a while. They had originally tried to book to Antigua or St Lucia but this late in the day there were absolutely no places left on any flight or hotel for that matter. Egypt had seemed a good alternative and the small resort of Taba just next to the Israeli border right at the top of the Red Sea had plenty of affordable accommodation and offered some excellent and uncrowded diving. As a break from reality it was working, as a method of getting him out of his depression, it was failing.

'Shame the water's so cold though. I expected it to be much warmer.' He wasn't ready to stop feeling miserable. Maybe it was the beer.

Ruth sighed to herself, she felt she knew what he was going through even though he had actually said very little. As a part time employee of MI6 herself she was cleared to know all the facts. However, most of the story she had got from Rupert her brother, rather than her suddenly taciturn boyfriend. Not only did she know about his visit to the States but also about the sudden loss of his career prospects. He may not have said anything directly about the situation to her but he knew that she knew. She had spent the last few days desperately trying to get him to open up, to no avail.

'It's a darn sight warmer than in the spring. I dived in Sharm in March a few years ago and that was really cold. At least the sea has only just started to cool down from the hot summer. And come on we saw a leopard shark today, how good was that?'

Her only answer was a non-committal grunt.

'Oh for God's sake, will you just stop being sorry for yourself and snap out of it.' Ruth had suddenly had enough. The softly, softly approach of the last few weeks had clearly failed and so at last had her temper.

Jon turned to look at her. He stood, saying nothing and walked off. 'Oh shit,' Ruth muttered under her breath but didn't follow. He was going to have to work this out for himself and anyway she knew where she would find him.

Sure enough, several hours later she went to the hotel casino and there he was. He had discovered the place on their first night and seemed to want to spend all his evenings there. It wasn't even that he was losing money, the damned man had been winning for the first two nights and it looked like he was in the process of doing so again. She took a seat next to him at the roulette table. The place was very quiet. Apparently, it only got really busy on Friday nights when the rich Israelis flooded over the border to spend their hard earned cash and all the minimum bets went up accordingly.

Jon turned and nodded to her but said nothing. Ignoring him, Ruth took a couple of his chips for herself.

'The travel rep says we can go across the border tomorrow and swim with the dolphins. So, I've booked us on the trip. We'll need passports and she says to ask them not to stamp them when we go through immigration. Apparently, they will but you have to ask them. Otherwise, there are some countries around here that won't let you in with an Israeli stamp in your passport.'

'Fine.'

Ruth saw the croupier scoop up the two chips that she had placed on red. 'Alright, I'm going to have an early night, that deep dive this morning has knackered me.'

'Fine.'

Realising that was all she was going to get, she gave him a perfunctory peck on the cheek which he ignored and she went off to their room.

Conspiracy

The next morning Jon seemed to have regained some of his normal outlook and they made their way along with several other tourists in a mini bus to the border. There they were ushered through immigration. It was a reasonably painless process although the Israeli woman who checked their passports gave them a sour glance when they requested she didn't stamp them. Then there was another mini bus waiting at the other side. In only a few minutes they were drawing up to the beach where a couple of wooden huts were the only things in sight. A local man greeted them, took their money and ushered them to the huts where they could change.

Very soon, armed with masks and snorkels, Jon and Ruth were gently drifting across the large lagoon off the beach. Suddenly, out of the gloom three grey shapes appeared. Two large adult dolphins and a baby appeared and started to swim around them. They could clearly hear the clicks they made as they talked to each other. The family seemed happy to stay with them for several minutes and they were both careful not to reach out and try to touch any of them as they had been briefed before entering the water. Then for no apparent reason, the dolphin family turned and swam off into the blue.

Half an hour later, without having seen them again Jon and Ruth swam to shore and towelled themselves off in the warm sun.

'Wow, that was fantastic. I've always wanted to do that,' Ruth declared happily. 'And the baby, that was a definite bonus.'

'I have to agree,' Jon answered. 'Although it's a shame they have to keep them captive in this lagoon even if it is quite large. Still, it's better than the local fishermen trying to kill them because they think they take all the fish. So what shall we do now? There's plenty of the day left.'

The rep said we could take a taxi into Eilat as our temporary visa is good for twenty four hours. Apparently, taxis regularly come to the car park. We just need to tell them we'll make our own way back this evening.'

'Let's do that then,' he replied.

They made their way into the dusty car park. There was only one couple ahead of them in the queue and they were soon picked up. Just as they were about to get into the taxi that had pulled up for them, a man pushed them aside and attempted to jump into the cab.

Conspiracy

The driver shouted at him and reluctantly he got back in the queue. Jon and Ruth jumped in wondering what that was all about.

The diver, a young man in his twenties with a mop of unruly blonde hair apologised. 'Bloody Israelis. Rudest race in the world.'

'Hang on,' Jon said smiling. 'Aren't you Israeli as well?'

'Yes but I'm the nice one,' the driver replied. 'Now where would you like to go?'

'Eilat please, we just fancy some lunch and a look around before heading back to Taba this afternoon.'

'Well my friend, you've got the right taxi. I can recommend an excellent restaurant and if you like I can pick you up and show you the sights before taking you back.'

'Let me guess,' Jon said. 'Your cousin owns the restaurant and you will give us the best price anyone could ask for.'

The driver laughed. 'My sister actually and yes I am pretty reasonable. Also, I grew up in Eilat and can show you things and places that aren't on any tourist map. What do you say?'

Jon looked at Ruth smiling. 'Why not? Getting a local to show us round should be fun.'

Ruth agreed and then showed her harder side by having a good haggle with the driver over the price. In the end they were all satisfied and they headed off towards the city which was only a few miles away. Just for once, Jon decided to put the real world on hold and just enjoy the day. He reached over and squeezed Ruth's hand.

Daniel their driver was true to his word and they stopped at a small café overlooking the old harbour. While they had a light lunch he disappeared inside and left them alone. Afterwards, they jumped into the taxi. Daniel explained the history of the area. It had become important in Egyptian and Roman times as an area where copper was mined. He took them to some outstanding Roman ruins and by the end of the afternoon they were getting not a little footsore and ready to head back. As the car headed back towards the border on an isolated stretch of road, Daniel suddenly pulled off and headed up a rough track. Within seconds they were hidden from sight and he stopped the car.

'What's up Daniel,' Jon asked. 'I thought we were heading back to the border?'

Daniel didn't answer. Instead, he turned around in his seat and Jon found himself looking down the barrel of a nasty looking black pistol.

'What do you want?' Jon immediately asked. 'We don't exactly have much cash on us.'

Daniel just laughed. 'I don't want your money. I want your attention. There is someone who wants to talk to you and the pistol is my insurance in case you don't want to talk to him. We haven't far to go, Commodore Hunt Royal Navy and Miss Brooker of MI6.'

Chapter 13

Jon didn't think. He had recognised the weapon, it was a nine millimetre Browning pistol that he knew well from his service time. It was the standard weapon of the British military. He also knew when the safety catch was still on. He simply reached over, grabbed the weapon by the barrel and pulled. The look on Daniel's face as the gun was simply snatched from him would have been funny if the situation wasn't so serious.

'Right, you silly sod,' Jon said as he pressed the button to release the magazine and pulled the slide back to clear the barrel only to realise there wasn't even a round in the chamber. 'What the fuck do you think you're doing pulling a gun on us? You clearly know who we are but equally clearly have no clue as to how to use a gun. But believe me sunshine, I do.'

The look on Daniel's face was a mixture of embarrassment and anger but he didn't apologise. 'Look, I really need you to meet someone and I thought you wouldn't be too keen, especially as we're in Israel. I know something about what you have been doing but my grandfather knows a great deal more. He wants to meet you. He's parked up about a mile from here in a secluded place where it's safe to talk. Please, I'm sorry about the gun, that was my idea and obviously not a good one but this is just so important.'

'Really? I'm not so sure about that. Why don't you just drive us back to the border now?' Jon was angry and the adrenalin was starting to stoke the flames.

'Shit, I knew the gun was a bad idea. Grandfather said I should say something to you that would encourage you but I didn't think it made any sense.'

'Go on.'

'He said to tell you, he knows why Building Seven came down,' Daniel answered not sounding convinced.

The words hit Jon like a physical blow. He turned to Ruth. 'Do we risk it?'

'Do we have any choice?' she answered calmly.

Jon looked in the pistol's magazine. It was fully loaded. He reinserted it into the weapon's grip and pulled the slide back chambering a round before flicking the safety on.

'Very well my friend, you can drive us there but I now have the pistol and unlike you, I know exactly how to use it. Do you understand?'

Daniel simply nodded, looking apprehensive. He started the taxi and they drove down the rutted, sandy track.

They didn't travel far. One thing that had caught Jon's attention was that Daniel had called Ruth 'Miss Brooker' so he obviously thought that Ruth was actually Jenny. This clearly had something to do with their States trip. Ruth was clearly thinking on the same lines. She leant towards him and whispered 'Who should I be Jon? He clearly thinks I am the girl who went to America with you.'

'We're going to have to play it by ear. But maybe at last we're going to learn something concrete.'

Before he could say anything more, the car swung round a tight bend and pulled up next to a small cliff. Built up against it was the remains of a Roman temple with the entrance to a small cave clearly visible at the rear. Parked to one side was a silver van.

They all got out and Daniel pointed towards the ruins. 'He's in the cave.' It was all he said and then he walked ahead leading the way.

They went through the ruins to the small cave. It was very dark but Jon could see the outline of something inside. At first, he couldn't make it out and then he realised he was looking at a man in a wheelchair. Not only that but there was a plastic tube which ran from the chair and went to his nose with a little clip. Jon realised he must be breathing oxygen. This was clearly a very unwell man and no threat at all to them.

The man seemed very calm and not at all surprised to see them, even with Jon holding the pistol. He spoke first. 'Commodore Hunt and Miss Brooker, welcome, call me Adam, it's as good a name as any. It's even one I've answered to in the past. I worked in the Israeli security services for many years and I know all about you Commodore. I have followed your career for many years, especially after that incident with the cruise ship Uganda. I also know about you Miss Brooker, how you work for MI6 and that the two of you were in the US only recently with a small team trying to work out what the fucking hell is going on in America and your own country for that matter. It also looks like I have to apologise for my grandson. I told him what to say to get your interest. Clearly, he didn't believe me and it looks like you've made him see the error of his ways.'

Jon simply nodded and looked hard at the old man. He looked very ill. How on earth had he even got here? He wondered. 'You're very well informed. But as the Americans knew all about us I'm not surprised you lot found out. But aren't you a little old to be involved in all this?'

'Maybe so and as you can see I've not got much time left on the planet. And in case you're wondering I came in that van outside. It's been specially modified for me. I have Multiple Sclerosis and the government in their compassion paid for it to be modified. Also, in case you are wondering, I chose this place for several reasons. Firstly, it's impossible for anyone to overhear or see us and secondly, this is the place where I proposed to my wife, God bless her, many years ago. This is the cave of an oracle and the temple was for her. You know what an oracle is?'

'Someone who claimed to be able to see the future I believe,' Jon replied drily.

'Correct, so quite an appropriate place for us to meet. Everyone thinks I'm on a last trip around the places of my life to say goodbye. They even think that Daniel there is just keeping an eye on me so if they see the cars outside it won't be suspicious. But we don't have too long as if I'm late they will send someone out to look for me even though Daniel is here.'

'So you'd better say what you've come here to say then.'

'I will but let's be absolutely sure about one thing. I am here to give you information to help you try to stop what is almost certainly going to happen once Iraq is invaded. I think we both know stopping the actual war itself will be next to impossible now. I will only do this if you tell me, on your word, that this is also your aim.' The old man looked hard at Jon and then at Ruth.

'Yes,' Jon answered. 'That's exactly what we want, you have my solemn word and that of Miss Brooker as well.'

Ruth nodded but said nothing.

'Very well. Let's start with a question. Why do you think the US President and your Prime Minister are so certain that these dreadful weapons will be found? After all, the UN Inspectors have discovered nothing. Don't answer that, I'll tell you. It's because they have been given irrefutable proof that they will be found and it gives them the excuse they need. But please note, I didn't say that they have proof that they are currently present, although that is what they think. Do you see the difference?'

Jon thought for a moment. 'You mean that they will be put in place to be found when necessary?'

'Exactly, whoever is orchestrating this whole charade has the resources to ensure that the missing evidence will appear. If you think that's rather extreme, remember they managed to get terrorists to attack New York and generate this incredible groundswell of hate.'

Ruth spoke. 'What has that got to do with Building Seven?'

Adam laughed and then broke into a coughing fit. When he finally finished, he looked at them both. 'Not just Building Seven but the Pentagon as well. The third aircraft was meant to take out Building Seven but there was never a fourth one. Look at the photographs of the damage to the Pentagon. It was claimed it flew into the side of the building. Alright, so where was the wreckage? The wings, twisted aluminium, internal fittings and engines you would normally see littered around a vast area. There is even a television clip of a journalist standing outside the place only hours afterwards asking just those questions. It was only aired once and was never seen again. On top of that, the building has the most CCTV coverage of any in the world yet only one video tape was ever released and that doesn't show an aircraft, merely an explosion. I have copies of both, along with some other evidence that you can take away with you in the brief case I have with me. And you are a pilot Commodore Hunt. Can you imagine how low you would have to fly to hit the side of a building like the Pentagon? It's no skyscraper. You would have had to get down low, well before you hit just to make sure you didn't fly right over the top. The official account has it that five street lights were clipped by the aircraft's wings. Can you imagine just how low you would have to fly to do that? Yet strangely, there are no eye witness accounts at all of a large jet flying low over the river and onwards as there would have had to be. No, the Pentagon was hit by something else possibly a missile of some sort or a bomb but the reason for it and Building Seven being demolished is exactly the same.'

'And that was?' Jon asked.

'To get rid of evidence. There's no way this conspiracy could have been successful without at least some of the military being involved even though most of them probably never knew the full story. I surmise that in the case of the Pentagon it was necessary to make sure certain people were eliminated. I have a list of all those killed, the real one, not the one given to the media. In the case of Building Seven, one of the resident organisations was the ONEP, the Office of National Emergency Planning. We can't be sure but we think the organisation was infiltrated and used as the core structure to manage and implement the whole plan. It certainly had the right connections in the US and abroad and ONEP personnel or those pretending to be members, would be able to go to many places without arising suspicion.'

Jon was thinking furiously. Everything this man said tied up with the suspicions of Admiral Morrison. But this was almost too simple. Where was the catch? There was always one.

'Alright, what you are telling me is interesting and fits in with what I already know. Now, why don't you tell me why you are confiding in me like this? It would seem to me that Israel is going to benefit from the situation so why do you appear to be so against it.'

'Young man, when I was a child I resided in a place called Belsen, maybe you've heard of it?' Adam said flatly. 'Don't ask me how I survived because I don't really know myself. I came here when we were given our country back, full of the shining ideal to create a paradise in the desert. In those days I would have done anything for my country and sometimes I did. However, I always clung to my strongest belief that we must never repeat the mistakes of the past. That we should never repeat the abominations perpetrated by the Nazis. Murdering innocent civilians in New York and using the whole situation to start wars is exactly what they would have done. I have been retired for some years now but there are many who think like me, although we tend to be of the older generation. Some of them still work in government and the intelligence services. I was asked to contact you. I'm expendable you see.' He said the last words without discernible emotion.

'Why me? Why us?' Jon asked looking at Ruth. 'What on earth do you think we can do?'

Adam looked at them both. 'Well firstly when we heard you were here, it seemed the perfect opportunity to make contact. We did have other plans but they became unnecessary. Correct me if I'm wrong but do you not represent a small faction in Great Britain that sees the enormous crime that is about to be perpetrated and are actually in a position to do something about it?'

Jon laughed without humour. 'See the crime yes. But being able to do something about it is a totally different matter. Look, this is all very well. All this talk of Building Seven and the Pentagon is useful but there is no way it can be used in time to stop things. Even if it was made public with full supporting evidence it would just be dismissed as a crank conspiracy theory. Maybe in the years to come it will all come to light but not in the next few months.'

'Agreed but you could use it to convince more of your people over the need to act.'

'And do what exactly?' Jon asked in frustration.

'As I said, if the weapons aren't there now but will be when the military arrive then they will have to be moved into position. Who do you think has the resources to produce them and make them look convincing? Who in the area has the resources to move them and pay others to look the other way?'

Jon sighed in frustration. 'You mean Israel. There's no need to pretend. Let's be absolutely honest with each other please.'

Adam grimaced. 'If I could give you names and places of course I would. But just as whoever is behind this, are using the American government, then they are doing the same over here. Most officials in Israel see this as a marvellous opportunity to make our lives more secure. The few of us here who have not got their heads stuck in the sand are doing what we can but it's precious little. If we get any more information we know how to contact you. In the briefcase are some one time code words to identify anyone contacting you. I'm afraid that's the best we can do.' Adam offered a small black attaché case to Jon who took it noting it was locked.

'The combination is your birthday. I suggest you change it as soon as you can.' Adam said.

Jon nodded. 'One more thing. Do you have any idea what form these weapons will take? I'm assuming that nuclear is out of the question.'

'Good question and I agree it's highly unlikely to be nuclear. The current rhetoric has it that they are deployable within forty five minutes which is of course, complete nonsense. That would mean they would have to be loaded into a weapon almost ready to fire. The obvious weapon being a Scud missile. In that case we are talking either a chemical or biological agent. Moving several Scuds into Iraq during the war, when satellite coverage and other surveillance will be almost total would be just about impossible. Our best guess is that as long as evidence of the presence of the weapons is found then the forty five minute claim will be conveniently forgotten. This also means that they could be infiltrated any time from now on, maybe to somewhere the UN Inspectors have already been. But the whole thing has to be credible so it will be more than a few boxes containing Anthrax or Sarin. There will have to be some sort of manufacturing facility as well, even if it's a small one. There are some notes to that effect in the briefcase. And now I really must be moving on. As I said, if I stay too long it could raise alarms. So good luck my friends. Daniel will take you back to the border now and I will leave a few minutes later.' He held out his hand. Jon only hesitated a second and then grasped it. The man's grip was weak but the look in his eyes was of steely determination.

Chapter 14

Once back at the hotel, Jon and Ruth decided to stay for the rest of the week in case anyone wondered why they had decided to leave prematurely. Despite the excitement of the meeting with the Israelis, they continued with their diving and tried to act as normally as possible. One thing Ruth was secretly grateful for was that the whole episode seemed to have jolted Jon out of his introverted misery. Mind you, it hadn't stopped him going to the casino and he still managed to win. By the end of the week, he had made enough to settle their bar bill and pay for the diving. They had decided to say as little as possible about the encounter whilst still in Egypt. Clearly, other people had discovered they were there and without Jenny's little box of tricks they had no way of finding out if their room was bugged. The best place to talk had been on the dive boat and even there they had been very circumspect.

It was on the last day that everything went horribly wrong. It started with a minor irritation. They were packing after breakfast as the transport to the airport was due to pick them up at eleven. There was a knock on the door and their holiday rep told them that the flight had been delayed and that the transport would be an hour late. Then Jon noticed that his dive computer was missing.

'Have you packed my computer with yours Ruth?' He asked, as he continued rummaging around with his equipment.

'Didn't you ask them to change the battery? If you haven't got it then it must still be there.' Ruth replied.

'Oh bugger, yes you're right I meant to pick it up last night and clear forgot. I'll nip down and get it now. There's no rush as the transport is going to be late anyway.'

'Fine,' Ruth said. 'I'm just about packed so I'll sit on the veranda and read my book.'

Jon nodded and made for the lifts as they were on the fifth floor. He walked around the side of the hotel past the pool to the dive centre. He just hoped there was someone there as they didn't have many staff and most went out on the boat. Luckily, one of the girls had stayed behind. Being changeover day there weren't that many out on the boat. She went to look for the offending device.

Five minutes later, she returned with the wrist watch sized computer and confirmed that the battery had been changed. Jon thanked her and left. As he went outside he took a last look around. Despite all the strange events of the last few days, he suddenly felt alive again. The view was fantastic and there was a warm wind blowing down from the hills. The visibility was crystal clear and the hills on the other side of the gulf looked almost pink in the bright sunlight. He realised he was looking forward to getting home again. The frustrations of previous months had gone. He didn't know how but somehow he was going to use the information they had been given and do something positive. One way or another, he would bloody well make a difference. Fortified with the thought, he started back towards the hotel.

He was just walking around the pool when the blast hit him. It was so unexpected and so incredibly violent that he had no time to think. Afterwards, he couldn't remember any sound, just an invisible hand that picked him up and flung him backwards with a savagery almost beyond belief. As he flew through the air, he briefly saw the whole side of the hotel burst outwards in a cloud of debris and then his head slammed into something and the world went black.

He was drowning. Somehow he had lost his regulator and they were thirty metres down. Where was Ruth? Where was his diving buddy? He needed to share her air. The reef looked odd, they must be quite shallow because the water was very light. But hadn't they gone on a deep dive? What the hell was going on? He took an involuntary breath and started to choke on the water he had inhaled. Panic completely set in and he started flailing his limbs uncontrollably. He knew he was going to die. This deep, he would never make the surface without air. Suddenly, pain flooded up his leg, his foot had hit something hard. What the hell? Still choking he forced himself to look around, this wasn't the reef. He looked up and the surface was a mere few inches above his head and above that, the sky. He spun around and suddenly everything came into a blurred focus. Reaching out he grabbed the silver bar in front of him now and pulled himself up. Up into the air.

He tried to breathe but had swallowed so much water it turned into a choking retch. He was trying to drag in air at the same time as his stomach was trying to void its contents. However, within a few seconds he was able to take in a few life saving gasps and then the pain at the back of his head really kicked in. Putting his hand up it came away sticky with blood.

Ruth! Ruth was in the hotel. He remembered the whole side of the building blowing out. The side their room was on. Ignoring the pain and the almost overwhelming desire to curl up and make the world go away, he managed to climb the little ladder out of the pool and turn to look at the hotel. The whole front was missing as well as the side nearest to him. He could see broken rooms with beds still in them. There was debris everywhere. Staggering forward he made his way towards the mess. He didn't get far, spots started to form in front of his eyes and the world slowly turned grey. As he fell to his knees, it all went black again.

Sometime later, light and consciousness returned. The first thing he felt was the headache although it wasn't as bad as before. Then recollection hit him and he tried to sit up. He didn't manage it. Instead, he decided to open his eyes and saw he was in some sort of hospital room. There were beds in a row to his right and they were all full. He tried to call out but only managed a croak. A harassed looking nurse must have heard him because she came over to look. She must have said something but all he could see were her lips moving. He realised he was deaf. She turned away and quickly came back with a glass of water. He tried to grab it but she resisted him and only let him take small sips. It tasted wonderful. She then turned to the chart at the bottom of the bed and took out a pen. When she finished writing she held it out for Jon to see.

'Explosion at hotel. You fine just concussion and head wound should get hearing back soon.'

Jon grabbed the paper and gestured for the pen. He wrote 'my partner in room 501, alright?'

The nurse read it and made a waiting gesture at Jon and went away somewhere. Jon waited in mounting frustration and after a few minutes, a man in some sort of uniform appeared. Jon thought he might be a policeman. He was obviously talking to the nurse and then turned to Jon moving his lips. Jon shook his head and immediately wished he hadn't as the pain was immediately intense.

The policeman looked at the nurse. She shrugged and gave him her pen and another piece of paper. The policeman wrote carefully and then with a strange expression handed the paper to Jon.

Conspiracy

'All floors on that side of hotel gone. No survivors. Very sorry.'

Jon realised he must be on some sort of drugs because he felt no emotion at all but an overwhelming weariness overcame him and he slipped into oblivion again.

When he next woke it was even more disorientating. His bed seemed to be bumping down a cobbled street and the ceiling was far too close. The face of what had to be another nurse swam into his vision.

'Can you hear me Captain?' She asked.

Jon wondered why she was asking and then realised that he could hear her although she sounded very far away. That was some relief. 'Yes, where the hell am I?' He croaked.

'It's alright,' she said. 'You're going home. This a medical repatriation flight. We'll be landing at RAF Northolt in a couple of hours. Try to rest. You've still got a nasty concussion but they X-rayed your head and there was no fracture. You were very lucky.'

Memory flooded back. Maybe there was still hope. 'What about my partner, Ruth Thomas? They said in the hospital that she was dead but surely it was too soon to know for certain?'

The nurse looked pained. 'I'm sorry but I don't know any more than you. We just flew in to collect you and straight out again.'

Jon had an idea. 'Is this a military flight?' he asked.

'Yes it's an RAF aircraft. I'm a military nurse. Does it matter?'

'Bloody right it does. Get the pilot to radio on ahead and get a message to a Mister Rupert Thomas at MI6. He's my partner's brother. If anyone can find out what's going on he can.'

The nurse nodded. 'Alright but you need to lie back and stay calm.'

Jon nodded in weary acceptance. In fact, he never got an answer from the pilot as he slept until the jolt of landing woke him up. However, when he was unloaded from the aircraft in his stretcher, Rupert was there in the ambulance waiting for him.

As soon as the ambulance set off, Jon was about to ask Rupert what was going on when he was pre-empted.

'A suicide bomb. A ton of explosive packed into a lorry and driven into the lobby. Ruth didn't stand a chance, I'm sorry. Current thinking is that it was Palestinians who wanted to bomb Israel but couldn't get over the border. Israelis use that hotel so it became a target.'

'Should have been me as well,' Jon replied. 'I had to go to the dive centre to collect something I'd forgotten. Shit, it should have been me.'

'Now, don't start going on a guilt trip,' Rupert replied firmly. 'It was nothing to do with you. You were not at fault, don't you dare even think that.'

Jon heard the words but wondered if he would ever truly accept them. Then another thought hit him. 'Oh Christ. Rupert we had a small black leather attaché case with us. I won't go into detail but it contained some really important information regarding the same thing we went to the States about. Shit, is there any way we can find out if it survived?'

Rupert looked startled for a second. 'Hang on, I thought you two were on a diving holiday. How the hell did you get something like that?'

'Long story,' Jon replied. 'I'll tell you all about it soon but getting that briefcase is really important.'

Rupert didn't look convinced but took out his mobile phone and spoke to the duty officer. 'There, I can't do any more. Do you know what was inside?'

'We glanced at it but I didn't want to talk about it with Ruth in case we were bugged. I was going to study it with you when we got back.'

'Bugged?' Rupert looked confused. 'Jon what the hell happened over there?'

Chapter 15

The pews in the little village church were completely full. Jon and Rupert sat together at the front next to the coffin. Ruth hadn't left a will but Rupert knew that she would have wanted a Christian burial. Jon went along with it although he knew that, like him, she had been leaning towards a humanist approach to life. Jon had seen too much death, injustice and pain to believe that any God, if he existed at all, gave a toss about him or anyone else for that matter. However, now wasn't the time. The vicar had finished whatever he was saying and made a gesture towards Jon. He had agreed with Rupert that he would say a few words.

Feeling heavy at heart, he made his way to the pulpit. He was still feeling the after effects of the blast. Bruises had appeared in all sorts of unlikely places but the previous day the doctors had declared him fit to be discharged from St Thomas's where he had been taken by the ambulance. So he stiffly climbed the stairs and when he arrived, he looked down at the full church. Ruth and Rupert's family were there along with another throng of friends and relatives. Brian and Kathy had also made it along with a surprising number of Jon's friends.

'Thank you all for coming. I just want to say a few words about my friend and my lover, Ruth Thomas. We met some years ago after I lost my wife. She was the first person since that happened who made me feel alive again. I owe her my life in some ways. We decided not to marry but we decided to stay friends, close friends.' He felt himself choking up and stopped for a second. When he had gathered himself he continued. 'Her death was completely unnecessary. The vicar tried to tell me everything is God's plan. As far as I'm concerned that's complete rubbish. She didn't need to die, nor did all the other poor people in that hotel. If that's part of a plan I want nothing to do with it. Sorry, I'm going off the point. I loved Ruth Thomas, she kept me sane kept me grounded. She was the rock I turned to when I needed support.' He stopped for a second and looked hard at the audience. 'But know this, if I find out why this happened. If I find out there was more behind it than some stupid random act of needless terror then whoever is responsible had better watch their backs.' He pulled himself together again, decided he had probably said enough, nodded and left the lectern.

As he sat next to Rupert, his friend leant over and talked quietly into Jon's ear. 'Thanks Jon. I know exactly how you feel and we're going to work on this as soon as we're back in London, alright?'

All too soon, they were standing by the open grave as the coffin was lowered into it. About the only thing Ruth had ever said about her funeral was that she absolutely did not want to be cremated and Jon and Rupert had made strenuous efforts to get a place in this local graveyard in the village where she was born. The vicar was muttering more Christian inanities which Jon was ignoring. He said his own personal goodbye and then it was time to leave.

'One thing we can be sure of Jon,' Rupert said. 'The one place she isn't, is here. I agree with what you said just now but wouldn't it be wonderful if life did go on somewhere?'

'It certainly would, I guess we'll all have to wait our turn to find out. I'm more concerned about the here and now. This isn't over by any stretch. I've been thinking about the whole affair. Had our flight not been delayed we would have been in the lobby checking out at exactly the time that lorry was driven into the hotel.'

'What? Do you really think it was an attempt to take you both out? That's getting a bit paranoid isn't it?'

'Is it? I've told you all that happened when we were there. The Israeli intelligence service must have been tracking us quite closely for this Adam character to know how to intercept us. His grandson had plenty of time, once he had managed to pick us up to contact his grandfather and for the two of them to arrange the meeting. If we were being watched closely, maybe their precautions weren't as good as they thought.'

'Fair point. We need to dig further.' Rupert said thoughtfully.

'And there's something else and we might be able to use it to our advantage.'

'Oh, what?'

'Both the Israelis seemed to think that Ruth was actually Jenny and we didn't disabuse them of the idea. Maybe there's some way we can use that to our advantage. But now's not the time let's discuss it when I see you tomorrow.'

The navy doctor had told Jon to take two weeks leave and take plenty of rest. He didn't disabuse him of the idea but time off was the last thing on his mind. He got together with Rupert and Jenny the next day back in the MI6 building. He had given Rupert the outline whilst in hospital. Now he could talk freely, he told them the full story in as much detail as he could recall and all the conclusions that he and Ruth had come to.

'As I said, this guy Adam thought that Ruth was Jenny. Now, Jenny and I did a little play acting while we were in the States and gave the eavesdroppers the impression that we were an item. So if the Israelis got intelligence from the Yanks then that would make sense.'

Rupert lifted an eyebrow and looked at the girl. 'I don't suppose I'd better ask how you did that.'

Jenny laughed. 'As Jon said, it was play acting but it was quite fun knowing that we were being listened to.'

'I'm not sure I want to know more.' Rupert replied sourly. 'But I agree, if that's the case then it would appear that there's been surveillance of you two ever since you got back and when you went to Taba the Israelis were tipped off. They must have assumed that taking a girlfriend meant that it was Jenny. It doesn't help really though as we know that Mossad and the CIA are pretty much in bed together these days. So, I'm going to summarise where we are. The Admiral's office was not bugged that we can discover and we've got nowhere in trying to discover who it was who tipped of the Americans in the first place. Oh and there's no sign of that briefcase you mentioned but as none of your luggage survived either I'm not really surprised.'

'But we must have a list of those who knew we were on the job,' Jon stated. 'Admiral Tucket told me that the Ramon Society was in the know so that includes the First Sea Lord but was anyone else involved?'

'No Jon, that's the complete list but as you know the society members are all pretty highly placed. We've got nowhere so far with them but we are continuing to dig. As for the young man who provoked the fight in Washington, we know exactly who he and his friends are but getting to them is another matter and proving almost impossible. Also, the accident to Admiral Morrison is being widely

Conspiracy

reported as pilot error. The weather was poor and the pilot apparently tried to stay low and flew into power lines.'

Jon barked out a laugh. 'That's got to be bollocks. The guys on those flights know the terrain. It's their back yard and they're all fully qualified to fly on instruments. They would never go low in those circumstances. That explanation stinks.'

'Be that as it may Jon, that's the official line and there's no way we can investigate it further.' Rupert responded. 'Now we have your trip to Egypt. We know who this Adam character was and it looks like he was kosher if you'll excuse the pun. But here's the thing, he died the day you got back, natural causes apparently. But his grandson crashed his taxi the same day and also went to meet his maker. There's a bit of a pattern emerging here don't you think?'

'Jesus,' Jon sat back in his chair. 'This is just getting crazy. So to me, it looks like our meeting was spotted somehow and then there was a massive clearing up operation. If our plane had been on time then Ruth and I would both have been blown to bits. These people are totally ruthless. With the hotel casualties that's another eighty four deaths to add to their list.'

'That's what I now believe too Jon. The question is what happens next.'

'Well, assuming that the idea of bombing the hotel was to remove me and Jenny from the equation as well as the information in the brief case then it failed, as I survived. If their surveillance is that good, they must know that I'm home so the need to take me out of the equation is a little irrelevant. By now they also must have realised that I wasn't with Jenny and that they took out the wrong person. So all those precautions, if that's what they were, have been wasted purely because I was lucky and survived. Mind you, they won't be sure whether I managed to hang on to the brief case. My guess is that they will be worried but there's not much they can do about it now unless they try to kill half of MI6 and the complete Ramon Society and that might just raise some suspicions.'

'Agreed,' Rupert replied. 'But I still think you need some protection or to get the hell away from here to somewhere safe. We actually had you under quite close surveillance while you were in hospital. We're going to keep Jenny in a safe house for the moment and I would like to suggest that you stay there as well until we know more.'

Jon thought about it for a moment. It seemed like a sensible idea for the short term at least.' I've got a meeting with Admiral Tucket at MOD Main Building tomorrow to discuss my future so, yes thanks for the offer.'

Rupert nodded and handed Jon a piece of paper with an address on it. 'One of our drivers will take you and Jenny there when we've finished.'

Jon nodded. 'I'd like to go via St John's Wood and pick up some personal effects if that's alright?'

'Fine, let me know how the meeting goes and we can work out a way ahead after that.'

Chapter 16

The totally innocuous Ford Mondeo was parked in St Johns Wood and Jenny was sitting in the back seat. She was starting to fret. 'What on earth could be taking Jon so long,' she wondered. He said he was going in to pack some personal effects and would only be a few minutes. He had explained that he been staying there with Ruth before they went on holiday and hadn't been back since. Rupert had collected his suit and few other items for him to attend the funeral.

Jenny could see how upset he was but she could also see a core of anger shimmering inside him. She was glad she was on his side because it was clear that if he ever found out who was responsible for Ruth's murder they wouldn't stand a chance.

She made a decision and leant over to the driver. 'He's taking a while. I'm going in to see what's keeping him.'

The driver was reluctant at first but Jenny knew the house had no rear exit so it wasn't as if Jon had done a runner and he eventually agreed. She made her way across the road to the door of the tall mews house. As she expected, it was open. The hallway ran the length of the house. The first floor had the kitchen and dining room which were both empty. Once on the first floor, she immediately saw that the large living room that took up all the space was also unoccupied. She went up to the next floor which presumably had some bedrooms. She was standing on the landing wondering which room to try first when she heard a noise from the door in front of her. She carefully opened the door and peered in. Jon was sitting on the bed with a half packed case in front of him. Tears were streaming down his face. In his hand, he was holding a small, scruffy, teddy bear.

He looked up at Jenny. 'This was hers. She had it as a child and it lived in her bedroom all her life. Stupid little thing but she loved it. He's called Bernard.'

Jenny didn't know what to say so simply gave a little smile.

'I must be some sort of Jonah Jenny. I'd stay away from me if I was you. All the women in my life who I've loved have died.' Another sob wracked him and he threw the bear back on the bed but didn't move.

Jenny went and sat by him. She put her arm around his shoulder. 'That's total bollocks Jon and you know it. Neither the death of your wife or that of Ruth were your fault. You can't blame yourself.'

Jon nodded, 'that may be true but it doesn't feel like it.'

'Jon, do you remember when we were in Washington and I came on to you when we knew the room was bugged?' She didn't give him time to answer. 'You turned me down. I think I can safely say that you are the only man I've met who would have done that. I don't really know why I did it. It's not something I make a habit of doing but you're not like other men. You're strong in many ways and you'll get over this. You need to because we need to nail the bastards who did it.'

Her last words made him sit upright. She could feel him stiffen at the words.

He turned to look at her. 'They say revenge is a futile exercise. But I got the man who killed Helen and that felt pretty good. You're right girl and I won't rest until I get these bastards too. And there's more to it because, if we're right, then the same bastards are trying to pull one of the most dangerous, stupid and immoral stunts the world has seen.'

He pulled himself together and started to put a few more clothes in the case. Jenny helped him. Soon they were back in the car and heading to a block of flats in an old part of dockland which had been renovated some years ago.

The apartment was modern and sterile but it had two bedrooms, a well stocked kitchen and a bar. Jenny had already been in residence a few days so while Jon unpacked she busied herself cooking a meal for them both.

When it was ready, she went into the lounge to find Jon sitting in front of the television. On the table next to him was a large bottle of scotch and he had a brimming glass in his hand.

'Jesus, listen to this will you?' he said pointing to the screen.

'What is it?' she asked.

'Just our fucking Prime Minister lying to the general public yet again. He just repeated this stupid forty five minute claim. Surely he must realise it's clearly rubbish. We couldn't react in that time so I'm damned sure Saddam bloody Hussein can't either.' He took a swig at his scotch. 'It's the bloody politicians telling the big lie of course. Repeat it often enough and people will start to believe anything. Still, this time he's having to drag it out again because one of his cabinet has just resigned in disgust. Who knows, maybe they'll all desert him. That would be something.'

'You may not have heard Jon but even the government's legal advisors are warning him we shouldn't move without a further mandate from the United Nations, that and at least something concrete from the weapons inspectors.'

'Hah, he'll just get another bloody lawyer to say the opposite, just you watch. But you know, the more I hear, the more convinced I am that he and the American President know something fundamental that they're not telling us. Why bang the drum this hard and stick to such a firm line if they don't? They wouldn't be that confident unless they know for sure that they will be vindicated in the end. Which all goes to confirm to me that that old Israeli was right.'

'What? That they will plant the weapons? I have to say I still find that hard to swallow.'

'No harder than deliberately blowing up your own building in New York?' Jon asked angrily.

Jenny decided the last thing Jon needed now was to get even more wound up. She reached over and hit the button on the remote control to turn off the television. 'That's enough,' she said firmly. 'Supper's on the table. Let's just forget the whole world for the evening.'

After supper, they watched a film. Well Jenny did. Jon seemed lost in a world of his own, that and a world of Scottish whisky. By half past nine, he had consumed three quarters of the bottle and Jenny could see he was falling asleep. Although he wasn't a big man, she knew she wasn't strong enough to get him to his bedroom on her own.

'Come on Jon, its time you went to bed,' she chided him as his eyelids drooped once more.

He looked at her. 'What's the time?' He didn't slur his words but she could clearly see the effect that so much scotch had achieved.

'Time you were in bed, that's what. Come on off you go.'

He nodded and tried to stand and almost made it. She rushed over and put an arm under his shoulder and managed to get him upright before he could collapse back on the sofa. They then staggered across the lounge to his bedroom. His eyes were already closed by the time his head hit the pillow. She managed to swing his legs onto the bed and carefully removed his shoes. She leant over him and gave him a kiss on his forehead. At the touch of her lips, his eyes opened briefly and then closed again.

She wasn't quite sure what he said then but it sounded like. 'Good night darling.' And then he was gently snoring.

The next morning, Jon woke with a pounding head and a desperate need for the toilet. The only problem was that he couldn't work out where the hell he was. The room was totally unfamiliar. He lay back and thought for a second and the events of the previous days rushed back. Now realising where he was, he carefully swung his legs over the edge of the bed and looked at his watch. It was nine o'clock. His meeting with the Admiral wasn't until after lunch so that was fine. Then he realised he had no clothes on. In fact, they were neatly folded up on a bedside chair. 'Oh God,' he said when he realised who must have done it because he never folded clothes. Hanging on the back of the door was his old dressing gown. He donned it and then went out looking for the toilet. What he discovered was Jenny in the kitchen and a marvellous smell of bacon.

'Good morning Jon,' she called cheerfully over the frying pan. 'The loo and bathroom is over there if you had forgotten and there's coffee on the go when you come out.'

Jon looked at where she pointed and then turned back to her. 'Err, I didn't do anything inappropriate last night, did I? I'm afraid my memory is a bit blurred.'

'What? Apart from getting totally pissed? Which frankly you needed.' she laughed. 'No, of course, not, although I did have to provide a little help getting you into bed.'

'And to remove my clothes,' he said.

'Ah, you worked that out did you? Well, it had to be done and anyway how did you know?'

'Oh that's simple, if it had been me then the gorilla would have been involved.'

She arched an eyebrow at him in query.

'Yes, well, it's an old naval tradition. When you go to bed after a few more drinks than is sensible, the gorilla comes in and throws all your clothes around the bedroom, steals your wallet and does something unmentionable in your mouth. What he doesn't do is fold up your clothes neatly. So I guessed it must have been you.'

Jenny laughed again. 'Anyway, don't worry, I didn't take advantage of you if that's what you're concerned about. Now, go and have a shower. Breakfast will be ready when you're ready.'

Precisely at two that afternoon Jon was once again ushered into the presence of Admiral Tucket.

The Admiral indicated a chair and the two of them sat down. 'Seems I never manage to get to my proper office in Portsmouth whenever you're around Jon.'

Jon smiled. 'Sorry about that Sir, trouble just seems to follow me around these days. Mind you, if I remember rightly it was all your idea in the first place.'

'Indeed and look, I'm terribly sorry about your partner. That was never part of the plan, nor for you to get blown up as well.'

'Understood Sir, but it does sort of show that we've overturned a bit of a hornet's nest. What can we do now?'

'We're working on it. Your chum in MI6 has set up a clandestine working group and I'm doing something similar with some trusted military people. But you have to realise we are going up against government policy here. Some would even call it treason so we have to be very, very careful.'

'So what can I do?' Jon asked.

'Hmm, well probably not a lot more at this stage. You are too well known now to be able to do anything effective and you may also be a target of some sort from what MI6 are saying so I think I need to get you out of the country soon.'

Jon's ears pricked up at the remark. 'Another ship Sir? I'd be pretty secure surrounded by steel.'

'Hah, you never stop trying do you. No, not a ship I'm afraid. Look, you should be aware that you have quite a lot of friends in the service and when the word got around that the Minister had succumbed to trial by journalism after the Washington incident, words were spoken. He's climbed down but I'm afraid that the COMAW appointment won't happen. We're too close to fully mobilising in the Gulf and we can't upset the chain of command at this late stage. What I have in mind is getting you into theatre in a role that could just put you in a position to do some practical good if the chance arises.'

Jon leant forward, this sounded hopeful.

'Jon you need to go to Wiltshire. To Wilton to be specific.'

Chapter 17

The two men sat in a hotel room overlooking a large green park. The trees were bare and a nasty wet, winter wind was whipping them into a frenzy. Grey scudding clouds obscured the sky. Neither man was taking the slightest notice.

'I said we were over reacting and look what a fuck up that became.' The first said sourly.

'No, we did the right thing. We had those Palestinian idiots all primed and ready. If we hadn't used them that way they would probably have done something even more stupid.'

'Yes but the naval officer survived and we're not even sure whether he had managed to keep the bloody dossier that the Israeli gave him.'

'Does it actually matter? I don't think so. Anyway, I've come up with an idea to ensure that the man doesn't get in our way again.' And he outlined the idea.

The first man laughed grimly when he had finished. 'At least that way we'll be able to keep him in plain sight and getting rid of him will be easily explainable. Machiavelli has nothing on you.'

'I'll take that as a compliment and anyway things are far too advanced to stop us now. They may have some ideas of what we are about to do but they can't prove it and they certainly will have absolutely no idea about how we intend to implement it.'

'So we killed all those people for no reason?'

'How many times must we have this discussion? We have to do everything to minimise risk and therefore must accept losses. We both know that the alternative will be far more catastrophic. The Middle East is a basket case. There are more factions and versions of the same bloody religion than anyone can count. They all espouse peace and love and are all out for the main chance using a medieval approach to everything from how to treat their women to how to deal with crime. It has to stop and we are the only ones who can see it. Successive western governments have interfered over the last hundred years and completely fucked the place up, from imposing national boundaries right through whole communities to encouraging despots for short term gain. It has to stop.'

The first man nodded but still looked pained. 'I just wish there was a way to do it without so much death and destruction, that's all.'

'We have to be strong. We know it's for the best for everyone. There will be far more death and misery if we don't act.'

'Hmm and it won't do our bank balances any harm either.'

'Agreed but that's just a peripheral bonus.'

The first man wished he felt that his partner really believed that. 'Anyway, what's the latest on the ground?'

'Almost there, the South African made a report yesterday. The infrastructure has just about all been repaired and he will be finished by today. Then he'll just be waiting for the final delivery.'

The South African in question had no idea that two men vastly removed in both distance and status were talking about him. He neither knew nor cared. He had a job to do and intended to make sure it was successful. It was nothing to do with patriotism or duty, merely money but in this case lots and lots of money. Ronnie Jansen or RJ as he was known to his parents and very few others was a mercenary and a bloody good one. More than that he was not the normal run of the mill paid killer. He had two degrees, one in engineering and one in modern languages of which he spoke four fluently. A member of the South African Special Forces until the political situation forced him out, he was one of an elite few in the world who could command enormous respect and massive remuneration. Just as importantly, he operated under the radar and very few people actually knew who he was and what he could do, unless he wanted them to of course.

Looking at him, one would not even be able to assess his origins. With remarkably plain features, he could fit into any situation given the right clothing. Today he was 'Musa' an Iraqi engineer leading a team of workers all of whom thought that was exactly what he was. Dressed in a slightly scruffy business suit, no one would have guessed at the finely toned and muscled body that was hidden underneath.

The dimly lit corridor was stifling hot, even this far underground. This was partly due to the savage desert sun above them but also because of the number of men working with no air conditioning.

Satellites couldn't see through solid rock but they could pick out anomalous temperature changes and it was imperative that the whole area continued to look as it always had been after the Israelis blasted the place to pieces some years back. All the major above ground buildings had been left as they were after the air raid but some of the smaller ones were being used as stores for 'yellow cake'. This mildly radioactive substance could be turned into Uranium suitable for reactors or bombs but was in itself inherently safe. The UN weapon inspectors had even been to see it a few months ago and declared it to be not part of a weapons programme. This was because the process to turn it into something lethal was so clearly beyond any capability left to Iraq after their nuclear facility had been bombed into the last century. RJ had to smile to himself when the inspectors finally left. If they had known what was going on, literally under their feet, they would have taken an entirely different line. And that of course, was the problem for them. Iraq was a massive country and hiding even large quantities of chemical and biological weapons was easy. Nuclear material was less simple because of the need for large processing plants and they could not be hidden. Also, tracking consignments of radioactive material was quite simple whereas the importation of various chemicals could always be explained by saying they were needed for quite innocuous reasons.

Just then Yussef, his deputy came around the corner. 'I think we're just about finished Musa. Would you like to come and see?'

'Yes, show me.'

They went further down the corridor. The first room they came to was clearly an office then what looked like a canteen and then finally they turned into a large room at the end. It looked like a cross between a factory and a clean room used to assemble delicate instruments or handle very dangerous substances. The latter was the case or would be soon.

'It's all fully functional?'

'Yes Musa, all you need is the finished product. The store is over here.' He led RJ to a large steel door with various chemical hazard warning signs on it. It was similar to the one that led into the corridor further back. Inside, there were racks for storage. All empty at the moment. There was also a large refrigeration and air conditioning plant that would have to be turned on before the delivery. It could easily alert a watcher to the change in status of the place but by then that would be what was wanted.

'Very well Yussef, you know what needs to happen now?'

Yussef didn't look happy but nodded assent. He went over to an intercom microphone on the wall and ordered all the remaining workers to get ready to leave.

'Don't worry, Yussef they will all be fine. None of them know what is really going on and they have been warned to keep quiet. They are at far more risk from the current regime but of course, think that that is who they have been working for. No one will risk saying anything.' As he said the words he wondered if they were really true. He knew his masters had a habit of scrupulously cleaning up after them. Still, it wasn't his business, he had other things to worry about now. He spent another few minutes looking around. The set up looked remarkably authentic. The old equipment had been repaired and even the new replacement stuff had clearly been used before. Once satisfied, he told Yussef he could leave as well and they would meet in Baghdad the next day at their usual place.

Now that he was completely alone, the whole place took on an almost menacing air. He hadn't realised how much the muted chatter of the workers made the place feel alive. However, there was one last job to do and it was one no one else could be involved in. Yes, they had managed to produce an authentic looking chemical weapons factory, after all that was what it had been in the past. There was one piece missing that was a crucial part of making the whole place authentic.

He climbed the ladder and out of the small personnel hatch. He left the much larger hatch used to bring goods in and out shut. It needed a block and tackle to lift it and it was best left well alone. He emerged from the building built over it into blinding sunlight. He blinked for a few seconds to get his bearings and then checked around to make sure the place was deserted. The tracks of the lorries that had picked up the workers could clearly be seen and Youssef's old Land Cruiser was kicking up a plume of dust in the distance on the way back to the capital. Satisfied, he went to the rear of his modern Range Rover and opened the large door. In the back were three large crates. One at a time, he lifted them out and staggering under the weight, made his way back to the entrance to the underground facility. One crate he left at the top, the other two he took inside. Then starting at the main door he removed the canisters of explosive. The receptacles were already there. Yussef had confirmed their whereabouts as he had been the facilities manager when the factory had been in full production. They were all well hidden above the suspended ceiling tiles. RJ had checked them as one of the first things he had done when he surveyed the site. It was a symptom of the paranoia of the regime, even when it had been a working facility during the Iran war that the authorities had rigged it to be demolished at the touch of a button. Anyone inspecting the site would expect something like this and everything had to be totally convincing to be credible.

   He took a small step ladder out of his car and over the next few hours, replaced all the demolition charges in their original positions. The wiring was a different matter. Most of it was still functional but he had to be sure so spent some time doing continuity checks on the wires. Where they were suspect, he rigged replacements but made sure he did it in a slightly shoddy fashion as a true Iraqi electrician would be expected to. And then there was the final touch. He knew that the main command wire ran well clear of the facility into the building above and at the far end. You would not want to be near when you pressed the button or you would be committing a rather silly form of suicide. He disconnected the wire and attached it instead to a large battery powered doorbell he had purchased the day before. It should be loud enough to hear. He climbed out again. The building space he was now in resembled a small warehouse, which is what it had been used for in the past. At the far end was a small room used by the security guards when there had been a need for them. He went in, the room was deserted except for a metal desk in the far corner which had been welded to the wall. Reaching underneath, he found the switch and flipped it over. In the distance, he could clearly hear the bell start to ring which meant the remote command system wiring still functioned. That was a relief because having to rig up a replacement system would have been a nightmare. His next task could be tricky as there was very little wire to play with. He looked under the table and saw the switch was right next to the wall and there was no sign of the wires, they must go straight into some sort of conduit. He decided he would have to work on the other end.

Having made his way back down into the underground corridor, he disconnected the bell and looked into the little box on the wall. The first thing he did was make sure the main arming circuit breaker for the individual firing lines was open, a mistake at this stage would be catastrophic not to mention bloody stupid. He had an idea and reconnect the main firing wires. However, he made sure it wasn't done correctly. He snipped the bare wires back to the insulation and inserted them into their sockets and tightened the clamp screws. They looked perfectly normal but with the insulation present no electrical contact would be made. The last thing he needed was the system to actually work. It was definitely not part of the plan for the explosives to actually do their intended job. His last task was to close the cover and lock it with the little key Yussef had given him.

Finally satisfied, he took one last look around and then knocked off the main electrical breakers and plunged the place into darkness. He then climbed the ladder and lowered the hatch. When the weapons inspectors had been present, both hatches had been covered with a variety of rubbish and old oil cans. These were piled up on one side now. At the time, the inspectors had been focused on nuclear threats and didn't even contemplate that there might also have been a chemical facility there as well. They hadn't looked hard and once they left RJ then had the opportunity to reactivate it giving the place a clean bill of health. There had been other options but because it had been declared safe it had proved to be the perfect solution.

He took half an hour rearranging the detritus to once again completely disguise the entrances to the facility. When he took delivery of the last part of the plan he would leave the entrances half exposed but for now it was worth maintaining the camouflage.

Finally satisfied that he had done all he could, he would now go back to Baghdad and await his next instructions. However, he was now sure that even without the final damming evidence, he had created a true facility capable of creating chemical agents right under the noses of the United Nations and Saddam Hussein.

Chapter 18

'What do you know of the Joint Helicopter Command Sir?' The young army Major asked Jon as he settled in on the first morning of his new appointment at HQ Land in Wilton.

'Oh, quite a lot. I'm an ex Jungly pilot so have always taken an interest.' Jon replied. They were in a modern office block within the grounds of the army's main headquarters in Wiltshire. 'That said, I was never quite sure how the army managed to win such a prize, presumably in the teeth of RAF involvement. Isn't it true that this command has more aircraft than the rest of the RAF put together?'

The Major laughed. 'Yes it is but as you know the actual head honcho job rotates between the services so it's all very 'joint service' even though we live under the army umbrella. But to answer your first question. The whole concept was floated during the 1996 Strategic Defence Review after a letter from the Assistant Chief of the Air Staff proposed the idea. However, it wasn't well received as no financial savings could be attributed to it, although, of course, the SDR was not meant to be about saving money.' The Major said with a cynical grin. 'Then the logistics guys took a look and reckoned that rationalising the fleets would mean that we wouldn't need so many airfields and that would save quite a lot. When the question was put to the army and RAF only the army was prepared to offer that sort of saving and so we won the prize. It was quite funny really because ACAS then tried to withdraw his letter but of course, by then it was too late.'

'And did the army close a base?'

The Major smiled. 'Not as of yet Sir.'

'Hmm, but the concept seems to be working quite well I understand?'

'Indeed Sir, we've been working bloody hard to make it work and to be honest most people drop their single service prejudices and just get on with the job. The only real issue that still catches us out are the different operational rules the individual services use. The light blue are quite strict about things like crew duty hours and the like. We, the army tend to just get on with it and although the naval Commando helicopters are not fully part of the command because of their amphibious role, we do use you once in theatre and naval rules are different again.'

'Tell me about it. My last appointment was in command of HMS Formidable and we operated navy and RAF Harriers so I've been there and got the T shirt.' Jon said with feeling.

'Well, our first real test is coming up as you well know Sir. Ark Royal and a naval Task Group are on their way. It's apparently the biggest naval fleet assembled since the Falklands. We are almost ready to deploy into theatre. Some aircraft are self-flying out and some are being loaded into transports. You've certainly joined at an interesting time.'

Just then a familiar face appeared around the door. 'Hello Jon,' said Paul Roberts cheerfully. 'I didn't think I'd be seeing you again quite so soon. Terribly sorry to hear about what happened in Egypt by the way.'

Jon stood and shook his friend's hand. 'Thanks Paul. What are you doing here?'

'Ah, well, you're about to find out all about it. Looks like we'll be working together again quite soon and of course, there's an E-type that will need some driving when the season starts. Mind you that's sort of on hold at the moment.'

'So what now Paul?'

Paul looked over at the Major. 'It's alright James. I'll take the good Captain to see the boss now, thanks for looking after him.'

The Major nodded and left, leaving the two men alone. Paul looked oddly at Jon. 'Did they tell you exactly why you're wanted?'

'Not really, simply that the staff of JHC needed augmenting for this upcoming stupid bloody war.'

'As you know I agree with that comment but it's going to happen whether we like or not. I see our duty as making damn sure it goes as effectively as possible and that we don't lose too many of our people in the process.' Paul stated grimly.

'Agreed but why do I think there's something more to all this?'

'Ahah, always the perceptive one. Come on I'll let the great man tell you all.'

Jon followed his friend down a carpeted corridor to a large office at the end that spanned the width of the top floor of the building. As usual, there was a small outer office, this one was manned by a middle aged lady in classic twin set and pearls.

'Commodore Hunt, Margaret.' Paul announced.

'He's waiting for you, just go in.' she replied. 'Coffee?'

'Yes please. Right, in we go Jon.'

Jon entered first. Sitting at the large desk overlooking the main entrance to the Headquarters was a tall, very thin, white haired, man in RAF uniform. He rose to his feet and held out his hand. 'Welcome Jon, it's been a couple of years I believe?'

Jon studied Air Vice Marshall, Mike Todd. The last time they had met had been at a meeting of the Ramon Society in a rather quaint estate in Scotland. He hadn't changed as far as Jon could see. He still had the striking, blue eyes and steady grip of a seasoned fast jet pilot. 'Yes Sir, that rather interesting shooting weekend in Scotland I seem to remember.'

'Hmm, I don't remember much shooting but I do remember the whisky tasting.'

Jon laughed. 'Oh yes, I seem to recall the hangover the next day as well.' He knew he had to choose his words a little carefully as Paul was not a member of the rather secretive bunch of people who got together on regular occasions in various parts of the country.

'Grab a seat guys,' Mike Todd said as he came around the desk to join them.

Just then, Margaret came in with a tray of coffee and silently placed it on the table before leaving as quietly as she had arrived.

'So first things first. No rank for this meeting please. This is private and informal.' Mike said. 'Now Jon just confirm to me that you are physically and mentally fit after that bloody awful ordeal you went through.'

'Yes Sir, sorry Mike. Yes I'm fine.' Jon replied firmly.

'Good, I was desperately sorry to hear about your partner but maybe, just maybe, what we're going to ask you to do might help.'

Jon's ears pricked up at the remark. This was starting to sound interesting.

Mike continued. 'I know all about what you, Paul and the others were up to in America. I've been fully briefed on that and the outcome of Egypt. Your friend in MI6 has been very useful and is keeping us up to date. But that's not directly why we asked for you. Your background is eminently suitable for what we have in mind. You've commanded a Commando helicopter squadron as well as a Capital ship but more than that you've proved to be remarkably adaptable when things don't go to plan. You also seem to have a number of friends over the pond in the US military who specifically supported your name.'

The last remark caught Jon by surprise and he said so.

'Yes, we were a little surprised too,' Mike responded. 'But it seems you impressed certain people during your recent trip. That said, at least one of them is now dead as I think you already know.'

Jon nodded. 'I'm guessing that Admiral Morrison wasn't working in isolation. Anyway, you've got me intrigued, what is the job?'

'As you know, COMAW will command the amphibious assault from Ark Royal but once the Marines and their aircraft are ashore they will come under army command for the land battle. However, the Americans and ourselves have agreed on the need to form a small separate force whose role will be to go ahead of the main attacks and conduct operations behind the lines. Their prime role is reconnaissance, sort of like the Long Range Desert Patrol Group in the Second World War in Egypt. They will have the direct support of some Special Forces aircraft and we want you to take command.'

'Hang on, I'm not a land commander. I do ships and sailors, not soldiers.' Jon protested. 'And anyway, surely special operations like these are standard part of military operations. This can't be a last minute thing surely?'

Mike laughed. 'You're going to love this. Someone in government came up with the idea that because we know that there really are WMDs in the country, the Iraqi's may try to sneak them out once they realise the battle is lost and believe me they will lose. So the prime task of this team is to go deep into the country and find them before they can either be destroyed or removed.'

Jon was completely taken aback. 'This makes no sense. Why would they choose me?'

'The decision was taken by the Minister believe it or not. The word on the street is that one of his advisors came up with the idea. There was pressure from several quarters for you to get the job. The Americans were already thinking on the same lines and when your name was put forward they liked your track record. They reckon your results over the Uganda incident and time in the Gulf were more than enough to recommend you. But don't worry you'll have a US Army Colonel as your deputy and Paul will be your engineering expert. The team will form up in Kuwait and embark in several ships until the assault begins. Assuming that it does of course.' Mike said with a cynical smile. 'Oh and one more thing, because your deputy will be a full Colonel it has been agreed that your temporary promotion to One Star will be substantive forthwith so congratulations Commodore.'

Jon was completely taken aback and having to try to think this all through. The news of his early full promotion was totally unexpected but before he could get his thoughts together the desk phone rang.

Mike answered, listened for a second and then replied. 'For goodness sake, yes of course, send her up.'

He turned to the other two men. 'Seems like we have some breaking news from our friends in MI6.'

A few moments later, the door opened and Jenny came in looking as vivacious as ever. She was dressed plainly in the female version of a business suit with black tights and still looked like a supermodel. She smiled at them all. 'Sorry to interrupt but Rupert wanted you to know this. However, he wanted to keep it as secure as possible so he sent me to brief you verbally.'

'This sounds good.' Paul observed.

'Maybe,' Jenny replied. 'It's a start anyway.' She looked at Mike Todd. 'I'm not sure how much of this background you have Sir, so I'll just backtrack a bit. We know someone tipped off the Americans almost as soon as Jon Hunt's team was formed up. However, we also know that the information was slightly premature. It seems that the fact that the whole team quickly became aware of the real purpose of the study, not just Jon and myself never reached the US. Because of this, when Jon was in Israel the man he met there thought that Ruth, his girlfriend, was in fact me. By backtracking on this we managed to produce a very short list of people who would have known about what Jon's team was really doing. One person in particular was party to the original briefs but then went abroad for business reasons and would not have known about the change.'

'Go on Jenny,' Jon urged. 'Don't keep us in suspense.'

She gave him an odd look. 'It's the same man who proposed your name for the job of leading this new team. He's one of the Minister's special advisors, probably one of the last people you would ever suspect. He actually went to school with the Minister and they've been close friends ever since. He's a banker but with impeccable credentials. His name is Sir Giles Merriot.'

Chapter 19

RJ had taken on a yet another new identity. Now he was a simple businessman trading agricultural chemicals. The expected message had come through two days after the facility had been finished. He had left Yussef in Baghdad to keep an eye on things and to be ready to open up when he got the word. It was now time to ensure that the delivery took place. A flight out of Baghdad to Paris had been followed by a trip to his apartment that he kept there under another name and a change of identity. Then as 'Marcel Tilbury' he had boarded another flight to America then to Tel Aviv. Anyone arriving in Israel from the States got an easier ride with immigration. In fact, the bored immigration officer barely glanced at his passport, not that it would have mattered as it was completely legal.

He had then headed for Jerusalem and booked into a good hotel, doing everything that would be expected of a man of his standing including engaging the services of a very attractive young lady for the night. She had proved extremely versatile and capable. He hadn't had a woman for several months and he kept her up most of the night while he made up for lost time. When she left, he gave her a note to deliver to an address in the city. Using prostitutes as unwitting couriers had proved effective in the past and once again the method worked. Later that morning, a piece of paper was pushed under his door with a time and the name of a taxi firm written on it.

As he got ready for the meeting, he looked out over the ancient city that was standing out starkly under the blazing sun. He mused on the fact that Jerusalem had been a focal point for so much intrigue and violence for literally thousands of years; from the Roman occupation, to the forces of Islam and Europe in the time of the Crusades, to modern times when the re-establishment of the country of Israel had caused its own conflict and grief. Now it was going to be the starting point for yet another round of Middle Eastern intrigue and violence. He often wondered why he continued with these jobs. It wasn't that he needed the money. He had two accounts in Switzerland and two more in the Turks and Caicos. Each one would keep him in comfort for the rest of his life. However, every time he thought about retiring something else would come up and the anticipation of excitement and violence would overwhelm him. He just couldn't ever see himself lying on some boring, bloody beach in the sun while his brain slowly rotted from too much booze. Maybe things would change when he got older but not now. Now he had a job to do and it was fun.

Donning his slightly scruffy suit and loosely knotting a tie, he picked up his packed bag, left his room and went down to the lobby. He informed the desk that he was checking out and paid his bill with cash. Outside, the cab he had booked earlier was waiting for him. He jumped in and studied the back of the driver's head. His hair was shaved almost to baldness and there at the base of the skull was the thing he was looking for. It was a tiny tattoo in the shape of the Christian symbol of a stylised fish. Even so he was still cautious.

'The Wailing Wall please,' he requested.

The driver nodded. 'I can't get too close, you will have to walk the last part, Victor.'

He sat back in the seat. All was well, 'Victor' was the word he had been waiting for. 'Alright, let's go to the rendezvous instead.'

The driver nodded but didn't speak. Half an hour later, after fighting through the downtown traffic, the taxi entered an industrial area and pulled up outside a rather scruffy looking warehouse. It was a large building which could have been an aircraft hangar had it not been surrounded by other buildings on all sides.

'I'll wait here,' was all the driver said as RJ got out.

'No need,' RJ replied. 'I'll call if I want you.' He knew he wouldn't. His brief tenure as Marcel Tilbury was over. A new identity would be waiting for him inside.

He went to a side door and knocked. It opened immediately. Inside it was dark and for a few moments he was almost blind after the glare from outside.

Suddenly, his hand was gripped hard and he was pulled into an almost crushing bear hug. 'RJ my friend, how are you? It's been too long.' A booming voice blasted his right ear.

He pushed himself clear and looked up at the smiling pock marked face of Pieter, his old colleague from days gone by. Both men had served together in South Africa for over ten years and had shared many actions and hardships. The bond between them would never be understood by anyone unless they had shared the same experiences. However, the physical comparison between the two men could not have been more stark. RJ, despite being superbly fit, was relatively small. In fact, he relished the role of the 'grey man'. He was always the man on the side lines, the one that was always overlooked. Right up until it was realised that overlooking him had been a serious error of judgement. Pieter could never take on that role. He was over six feet four and built like a professional wrestler. His face was complemented by a nose that had clearly been broken at some time in the past and a crew cut that emphasised the harsh angles of his face. However, he played this to his advantage. His size and build often made people assume his intelligence was in inverse proportion to the size of his muscles. In fact, he held a PhD in modern Philosophy. When he played RJ at chess, the matches could often take weeks. Like Special Forces soldiers the world over, size and power were no bad thing but it was intelligence and dogged application that were the defining characteristics.

'It has old friend,' RJ replied smiling. 'Four years now. How are you?'

'Good, I'm good,' Pieter replied. 'I'm glad you're here now because we always made a good team.'

RJ laughed. 'We certainly did and will do so again. So how are things?'

'We took delivery last week. The vehicles were fitted out ready by then. The only thing we had to do was to transfer the stuff. I tell you RJ that was the scariest thing I've ever done. It's all in special canisters. We had all the correct protective suits and took all the right precautions but handling that stuff was a nightmare. I don't mind admitting that it was the most terrifying thing I've ever done. But it's all secure now. Come and have a look and see.'

'Before I do. Have you paid off the hired help?'

'Yes, that's been taken care of. There were only five of them. They won't be talking to anyone. The drivers are a separate team and know nothing. They've been working for the company for some time now. They think this is all above board.' Pieter said the words with no trace of emotion.

Inside, RJ was glad he had not been involved. He was not squeamish in any sense but avoided violence as much as possible. He considered it as very much a last resort. Pieter, on the other hand, revelled in it. He knew the man was a borderline psychopath but there again how many soldiers of his type weren't? And the need for absolute secrecy now was paramount.

'Good, come on then, show me the beasts.'

Pieter led the way into the rear of the building. At the back, parked in line, were two massive, blue painted, bulk liquid tankers. Clearly painted in black on the front and sides of the cab was the name of the haulage company that owned them.

RJ went up and examined the first one carefully. He paid particular attention to the rear of the massive tank noting all the correct hazard warning symbols were in place. He then ducked down and looked at the trailer identification plate. Satisfied, he conducted the same examination on the other tanker. Pieter said nothing but his smile of satisfaction grew as RJ's examination continued. Finally, RJ wetted a finger and rubbed it on the rear of the tank of the second vehicle. As he rubbed, the white came off to reveal a dark green paint.

'This will all wash off quite easily?' he asked.

'Yes, they've been painted in this colour scheme since we bought the outfit but once we need to get rid of it, each truck carries enough water to do the job.'

'Good and the vehicle ident plates can be changed to Iraqi ones quite easily?'

'Yes, they are only riveted on and each truck has the tools to drill them out, replace the plates and then rivet the new ones in place.'

'Excellent. Well, I can't tell. Which one is it?'

'The front one. Let me show you.' Pieter said smiling broadly. He went to the rear of the truck and pointed up to the tank. 'The whole rear section is basically a large dish shaped piece of steel which is welded on to the main tube section. However, on this one we ground off the weld and pulled the whole thing off. Inside we put another smaller tube which runs the length of the tank. It's basically a smaller version of the main tank and the cargo is inside in sealed containers. When we put it back together we welded it back up but made sure the welds are much easier to grind off. Both tankers are now full of the liquid fertiliser and there's no way of seeing that the inside of this one is different. We also ballasted the cargo so if you put them on a weighbridge, they weigh the same. If someone wants to dip the tanks we've made sure that the inspection hatch opens clear of the internal storage so a dipstick will give a true reading.'

RJ was impressed and said so. 'Bloody good job Pieter and the paperwork?'

'Come with me,' he replied and they went over to a small office that took up one corner of the building. Inside there was a desk and a couple of scruffy chairs. 'This company has been in existence for several years now and has had the contract for some time. We bought it completely legitimately six months ago and we've already done four runs into Baghdad and Basra. For the coming trip, we are scheduled to go to an agricultural complex outside Baghdad. Of course, we won't get there but by that time we will effectively have disappeared. The border crossings are used to seeing us and we always provide a little financial lubrication when needed. We've got to the point where they want us to cross and even facilitate things by giving us priority.' He reached into the desk and pulled out a sheaf of papers. 'Here we are, export papers, cargo manifests and we've even got UN certificates. They are all one hundred per cent authentic. I've also got our Iraqi uniforms and identity papers. I get to be a Sergeant you're just a grunt I'm afraid. Did you bring your paperwork?'

'Yes, fully authorised military travel instructions and they are all genuine as well.' RJ said. 'My only concern is that we will be travelling in tankers that say we are carrying gasoline but which is actually fertiliser. However, I've made the orders clear that we are on a special mission and are not to be delayed. Hopefully, we will be less than a days driving away from our destination by then. We can't allow for every eventuality but that should be enough.'

'Good, we work well together as a team, we always have and there will be several critical points. On previous runs, once inside Iraq, they have given us a small armed escort. It's a nominal gesture, last time it was just one Land Cruiser and four troops. It may be that we don't even get them this time as they are all gearing up for what's coming. But if they do, we will need to get rid of them at some point and there are the drivers as well because this is a one way trip. I could manage the drivers myself but with you with me it will be a great deal easier if it comes to taking out the escort. I've stashed some weapons and protective gear in the trucks. It's all very well hidden. Although if they were found no one would be that surprised.'

RJ nodded in acceptance of the logic. 'And if all else fails there is always Plan B. I take it that you have allowed for that?'

'Everything is installed and wired up but I pray that we never have to use it.' RJ replied tight lipped.

'You and me both. And at the other end, I have my man Yussef but no others now so the three of us will have to do the unloading.'

Pieter grimaced. 'I'll not look forward to that. Two hundred litres of Sarin is enough to decimate half the bloody country.'

Chapter 20

At last, Jon felt free. Free from conspiracies, free from emotional entanglements, free from the land. As he gazed over the calm blue waters of the Gulf, he felt he was secure in the only home that mattered to him. In this case, the home was the grey painted, slightly rusty and definitely ageing warship HMS Intrepid. A veteran of the Falkland's War, until recently she had been relegated to the role of Dartmouth Training ship and was due to be de-commissioned but with the need for as many ships as possible in the Gulf, she had been reactivated to take part and meet the needs of Jon's new command. In other ways, she represented the end of an era as she was the last warship in the Royal Navy to be powered by steam turbines. If it hadn't been for the fact that her sister ship, HMS Fearless, which was already out of service, had been cannibalised for spares, Intrepid would probably not have made it this far.

Jon was remembering when he had been told that she would be the Command Ship for his enterprise. It had come as quite a shock. He hadn't even realised that she was still afloat let alone serviceable enough to actually travel the thousands of miles through the Mediterranean then through the Suez Canal, into the Red Sea and thence the Gulf. At one stage it looked like Cyprus would be as far as she would get when a major problem with the boilers manifested. It was only heroic work by her Marine Engineers that eventually got her going again. Not that Jon was aware at the time as he had spent the time she was in transit setting up his team and making plans. He and Paul plus a small team of subordinates had then flown out to Kuwait to join the ship.

He remembered his last night with mixed feelings. As he was due to fly out of Heathrow he had stayed in the MI6 safe house the previous night to his flight although by then he was beginning to feel that the precautions were completely over the top. He had said so to Jenny who was also in agreement but as it was giving her free accommodation in London she was making the most of it. Once Jon was out of the country she would be flat hunting as she hadn't found permanent accommodation in the city before she had had to move in. They had decided to ignore the rest of the rules and went out to dinner. Jon didn't want a late night as he had a long day ahead. He had excused himself quite early. He read for a while and then turned off the light. Just as sleep was overcoming him he heard the door open and soft footsteps approach. He opened his eyes just a slit and saw the beautiful sight of Jenny approaching. She was completely naked. Without a word she slid into bed and nuzzled up against him. Taken completely by surprise, he wasn't sure at all that this was what he wanted. He was lying on his side and he could feel her nipples pressing into his back. Although he was incredibly physically aroused, suddenly, he didn't know what to do.

He felt her lips kiss his ear as at the same time a smooth leg slid over his. 'I know you're awake Jon,' she whispered. 'I need this as much as you.'

When he didn't respond, her hand slid down and stroked his rock hard erection. It was enough, more than enough and for a while, all thought was suspended. However, even now, days later, he was worried that he had done the wrong thing and still guilty about betraying Ruth. He knew that was silly but the thought was still there, deep inside. The next morning, when they had parted Jenny had said very little except to smile at him and give him an almost sisterly peck on the cheek. He was still trying to examine his feelings and fathom hers when he heard footsteps behind him.

'Morning Sir.'

Jon immediately recognised the voice of Captain Tony Wright, the ship's Commanding Officer. Putting his personal reflections away he turned to greet the man. Tony was always smart and always very respectful but there was something about him that set Jon's teeth on edge. Despite their similarity in rank, Jon had never met the man, although he had heard a few whispers about how ambitious he was. It hadn't taken Jon long to realise that Intrepid was not a happy ship. From the moment he walked on board and saw the looks on the faces of the gangway staff, to the way the ship's officers behaved when he was invited into the wardroom for a drink, he had felt the undercurrent of resentment. However, Intrepid wasn't his, she belonged to this man and the navy didn't allow Jon to interfere, not overtly anyway.

'Good morning Tony. How is the old girl today?' Jon asked as he looked around the flight deck. They were both standing near the stern overlooking the docking bay. The rear of the ship could be

Conspiracy

flooded to allow landing craft to be launched directly from the stern and for this mission they would definitely be needed.

'We're all good today Sir,' Tony responded brightly. 'We've just had a signal from the Task Group Commander. He wants to do some more landing exercises with HMS Ocean and we are going to participate but only with the Sea Kings.'

Jon looked at the machines parked at the front of the large flight deck. With no hangar to protect them, they were normally kept up against the superstructure to keep much of the weather off them as possible not that there was much to worry about in the Gulf. Apart from the heat of course, it was still early in the morning but Jon could feel it building up. Intrepid didn't have any air conditioning and he knew that conditions below decks would only get worse as the day wore on. It had been one of the reasons that the ship initially wasn't considered for Gulf operations but operational need had overridden comfort in the end.

Parked on the flight deck were two green Mark 4 Sea Kings and two black painted Augusta 109 helicopters. The Sea Kings belonged to the navy but the 109s were part of a small squadron that supported the SAS. In fact, the original two aircraft had been 'liberated' from the Argentinians at the end of the Falklands War. Then they were virtually brand new and had luckily been rescued from the depredations of the surrendering Argentinian soldiers and the trophy hunting victorious British soldiers. With the acquisition of these two machines, several more were also acquired and had been supporting the Special Forces ever since. In two day's time they would be augmented by four MH6B 'Cayuse' machines from the US Special Forces. The small size of these helicopters belied the amount of firepower they could mount. All were fitted with a 7.62 millimetre minigun, two carried twin pods for four TOW anti-tank missiles and two were fitted with fourteen 70 mm Hydra rockets. Jon was looking forward to seeing them and having a go flying one. He had already managed a trip in one of the 109s. However, no matter how much firepower his little fleet of helicopters could muster, they were only there for back up. Sitting in the vehicle deck below their feet were ten US made Humvees. They had been offered by the Americans and his army staff, particularly Paul, had wholeheartedly agreed. The only other option was the dreaded army Landrovers which had already proved disastrously vulnerable in other theatres. Once ashore, manoeuvrability and the ability to cross rough terrain at speed would be the overarching priority and the Humvee was light years ahead of the Landrover even if they were fairly light skinned themselves. The final part of the inventory was five trucks loaded with special Nuclear, Biological and Chemical protection and detection equipment. All the troops and aircrew would have their own personal protective suits and respirators, this was the specialist stuff that would allow some of the experts to get close up and personal to potential sites. There were also two trucks crammed with communication gear and equipment to set up a capable command system once they were ashore.

Jon turned to Intrepid's Captain. 'Fine Tony, I'll leave all that to you but don't forget we have an 'O Group' meeting at eleven in my cabin. I just want to get our ducks in a row before the Americans arrive.'

So saying, he made his way back into the superstructure and to his cabin. There were several hours to go before he and his team met formally and he decided to go through some of the paperwork they had prepared for him, especially regarding the situation they were likely to find on the ground once ashore.

He hadn't got far when there was a knock on the door and Paul Roberts accompanied by a young Lieutenant Commander asked to see him.

'You're always welcome Paul, no need to ask,' Jon said as he put down the sheaf of paper he had been studying. 'And James, come in as well.'

James Pyke was the latest member of Jon's team. A young Warfare Officer, he had just been appointed as the team operations officer, responsible for managing the plethora of signals and operation orders they were having to comply with. He was a slim fair haired man and clearly very bright. What really annoyed Jon about him though was that he never seemed to be affected by the heat. He was always immaculately turned out, even in simple tropical shirt and shorts he looked like an advert from a men's magazine. However, there was no doubting his efficiency or skill, especially when it came to managing the enormous amounts of information they were inundated with.

'What's up chaps?' Jon asked. 'We're not due to meet until eleven.'

Conspiracy

Paul looked at James before speaking. 'This is a bit tricky Jon. It's nothing directly to do with our operation, it's about the ship or to be accurate about her Captain.'

Jon groaned inwardly but wasn't surprised. Stuck in his ivory tower with his own personal accommodation, it was hard to really get the measure of what was going on. However, Paul and James were members of the wardroom and would be far more immersed in all aspects of the ship's world. 'Alright, I've got an idea of what you're about to say but I'll only listen if you think whatever it is could affect our task in any way. Otherwise, there are other ways of dealing with it.'

'That's understood,' Paul said. 'And I wouldn't have brought it up unless those were my concerns as well. I'll ask James to speak first. As a senior officer in the wardroom, I'm treated rather differently and James has the inside track.'

Jon turned to James. 'Spit it out James. I know this is very sensitive but you have my word that anything we discuss here will go no further.'

James paused for a second gathering his thoughts. 'Sir, it started the day I embarked. As you know, I joined earlier than you when the ship was in Cyprus. When I went into the wardroom that evening, the Mechanical Engineer Officer who is a Commander was the only person in the bar. I went up and introduced myself. His opening words were 'Hello I'm Terry, the MEO don't call me Sir as there are only two ranks in this ship, Sub Lieutenant and Captain.' At first, I thought he was just being polite in an odd sort of way but then other officers came in and it was quite clear that the Captain was the main focus of conversation. At that point, the Captain's steward put his head around the door and announced that he would be coming down for a drink in five minutes. I was staggered when all the ship's officers finished their drinks and left. I was the only person there when he arrived. It was extremely awkward.'

'Does the wardroom have a standing invitation to the Captain?' Jon asked.

'I wondered about that Sir and had a quiet word later with the First Lieutenant and the answer is no. When in harbour, he just invites himself in whenever he feels like it. Apparently, it drives the Commander mad.'

Conspiracy

'I'm not surprised,' Jon said. 'The Captain is not a member of the mess and I've never heard of that happening unless he has had a prior invite. But there must be more to this than an awkward social situation.'

'That was just the start Sir. I had to be very circumspect as you can imagine. As a visiting staff officer, the ship's officers were not going to invite me into their private debates but it soon became clear that as the Captain is about the sole topic of conversation, I would become aware of the issues. It wasn't long before I was taken into their confidence. In fact, one of the reasons I'm here is that they want you to be aware of what is going on.'

'Shit James, this is starting to get mutinous.' Jon said worriedly.

'Tell me about it Sir,' James responded. 'Actually, there are two camps in the wardroom. I would say that about eighty percent are worried in some ways but several officers are staunch supporters. It has led to several heated arguments believe me.'

Paul nodded. 'At one point after dinner the other night I had to excuse myself. It was quite embarrassing.'

'Alright, I get that the atmosphere is somewhat poisonous but you haven't said why it's come to this James,' Jon said.

'It goes back to when the ship was warned off to sail here Sir,' James explained. 'Most of the ship's company thought they would be on draft elsewhere within months. Instead, they got a pierhead jump to the Gulf in an un air-conditioned ship. There are enough sailors on board who've done that before to know what it would mean and that was just the start. The Captain cleared lower deck and everyone thought he would give them a pep talk. Instead, he simply warned everyone that we were going into a hostile operational area and that, and I quote, 'some of you won't be coming home' and then walked off. It's almost become a wardroom joke and the sailors have picked up on it as well. The Commander tried to organise a Sods Opera on the way out and all the mess decks refused to participate. I've never heard of that happening in any ship before. There have been all sorts of silly little protests in the mess decks. The Commander is tearing his hair out and getting no support from the Captain at all. What's worse is that the Captain seems to focus on trivia and not the big picture. When I attended the first ship's operation brief, the MEO gave him a signal to release regarding the state of the boilers. He spent ten minutes arguing with the MEO about the title of the signal and didn't even consider the content. I couldn't believe it and when it was clear to everyone that he was actually wrong he still wouldn't have it. In the end I slipped away. And Sir, that was the really big issue, the one that makes me think this could affect our work.'

'What, that the Captain gets lost in the detail?' Jon asked. 'Come on there must be more to it than that.'

'Oh no, sorry Sir, the boilers. When we were flashing up to leave Cyprus the MEO had to stop the process as there was a problem with the water in them. It was contaminated.'

'Yes I was told that at home,' Jon said. 'I heard the engineers did a really good job sorting it out.'

'That was because it was what the Captain reported in his signals. He would hardly want the truth to be broadcast. Yes, the MEO's team did a fantastic job but it shouldn't have been necessary in the first place. It was sabotage pure and simple. Salt water was allowed to contaminate the boiler supply. There was absolutely no other way it could have happened. When the MEO reported it there was an almighty row between them. The Captain blamed the MEO and threatened to sack him. MEO apparently responded by saying that if that happened he would have no recourse but to tell the truth, including the fact that the Captain was lying in his signals to the UK. They've barely spoken since. Sir, this ship is literally on the edge of mutiny. The whole ME department are working under sufferance and they haven't caught the person who caused the problem in the first place. What's worse, is that he must be part of that team as no one else on board would have the technical knowledge to know how to do it. The Bridge and Ops room crews are not much better. No matter what they do, their decisions are nearly always countermanded whether they are right or not. It's only the Padre and Supply Officer who fully support the Captain and frankly that's probably because he won't have anything to do with them in the first place.'

Paul nodded in agreement. 'Jon, I don't know warships but I do know military people and this ship is fucked. Sorry to be so coarse but it's the best word I know to describe the situation. What's worse, we'll be relying on her very soon to take us into harm's way.'

Chapter 21

'Damn,' Rupert spat out. 'Give me the old Cold War days. I would have dragged the bastard in and kicked seven bells out of him until he told us what we wanted to know.'

Jenny looked at him with an amused smile. 'Would you really? I thought there were rules even in those days.'

Rupert grinned ruefully and then smiled. 'Alright smartass but you know what I mean.'

'It would make life much easier though,' Jenny replied. 'Do you want me to sum up what I've dug up so far?'

'Yes please.'

'Sir Giles Merriot. Advisor to the Secretary of State for Defence and also long time chum. They both attended Eaton and then went on to Oxford. He read economics and when he left, went straight into daddy's merchant bank. After a few years, he was head hunted and went to work for one of the big internationals. When daddy died, he inherited the lot, including the title and went back to the family business where he's been ever since. The bank is very originally called Merriot and Sons although that might have to change as he only has four daughters. The oldest is in her thirties and married, the others range down to seventeen but all seem to have inherited a gift for spending daddy's money. Mind you, Melissa his wife, seems pretty good at doing that as well. He doesn't seem to mind as on the surface they are loaded. However, I got our financial team to do a little digging. They have a large estate in Hampshire which is worth a fortune but also mortgaged to the hilt. The assessment is that his finances are viable, just. However, he won't be able to continue to allow his little darlings to try and bankrupt him for much longer.'

'And the bank? I've not come across them, what do they specialise in?' Rupert queried.

'Ah, this is where it gets even more interesting. As you clearly know, most of these Merchant Banks support small but rich sectors of industry. You probably won't be surprised to know that Merriot and Sons loan to the Oil and Gas industry almost exclusively. They do very well out of it. It's what keeps the family's head above water. Recently though, they seem to have been supporting American companies more than any others. There's nothing illegal about that but it's a little odd as US oil exploration is rather moribund at the moment. There would be much better investment opportunities elsewhere, in Russia for example.'

'Unless you knew something that others didn't of course,' Rupert replied.

'Exactly but it's hardly evidence of wrong doing. Of course, if those American companies were suddenly to gain access to Middle Eastern oil fields it would change everything.'

'And everyone would be applauding his business acumen,' Rupert replied wryly. 'So he has close contacts with Americans?'

'At all levels of commerce but it would also be natural to expect that he knows many in the administration.'

'Private life?'

'Ah, even more interesting. The rumour is that he and his wife now hate each other and rarely speak. She spends most of her time in the country and he hardly ever leaves London except to travel abroad. One has to wonder whether she has some sort of hold over him because I'm surprised they haven't formally separated. Neither are religious or anything like that. Maybe it's just that the divorce settlement would be too onerous. However, the financial guys downstairs don't think so. Getting rid of her even with a large bill would almost certainly ease the drain on his finances quite quickly.'

'Hmm, we should look into that. Leave it with me but frankly I don't think we'll have time to make anything of it. Apparently, they're planning to go in in a few week's time with or without another UN resolution. Anything else?'

'Yup, the juicy bit. Our Lord of the Realm seems to have quite an appetite for the ladies. He owns a flat in St John's Wood. It's actually only one street away from your place. It's currently occupied by a stunning young lady from Eastern Europe who seems to have plenty of spending money and no obvious source of income. If he's not staying there, he uses the Savoy and has a standing arrangement with a certain agency to supply ladies of negotiable virtue to his room. He has similar arrangements in New York, Berlin and elsewhere. He makes no secret of it and has a reputation amongst his peers as a bit of a lothario but has managed to keep it out of the press quite successfully.'

'Alright and what about his relationship with our beloved Defence Secretary?'

'Good question. When the Minister got his job after the last election, he nominated him as one of his advisors. He's never made it clear exactly what he expects of a merchant banker on his team but they speak regularly. They also socialise a great deal. It's not unusual, a lot of ministers use old school tie connections in this way.'

'Any sign of our man's social life spilling over into the ministers?'

'If you mean do they go out clubbing and shagging together, the answer is no. The Minister really is as devoted to his wife as the press make out. We're pretty sure he's never cheated on her in thirty years of marriage.'

Rupert sat back in thought. 'If we're going to get anything out of him in the short term, I'm buggered if I can see how. We must get the financial guys digging deeper but from what you say even his predilection for the ladies will be a busted flush. It seems his wife won't care. I reckon I'm pretty sure in assuming she knows all about it.'

Jenny gave him a strange look. 'Rupert, surely you could let me have a go at him.'

'What? No. Absolutely not. You've only just completed your induction training and have no field experience at all. This isn't bloody James Bond you know. You're not some sort of sexy spy from the films. It doesn't work like that.'

'Oh come on Rupert, I joined MI6 for the challenge. My looks are one of my assets I've always understood that. Why shouldn't I use them?'

'Because we don't do that. I would never ask you to prostitute yourself, so don't go there.'

'Who said anything about prostituting myself? Look, I've been thinking about this while I was doing the research. Merriot is in London all week at his office and his girl has apparently gone back home for a few weeks so he's staying at the Savoy. We could easily get the escort agency to put me on their books for when he calls.'

'Jenny. No.' Rupert stated firmly.

'Hear me out Rupert, please.' she replied. 'Look, when I was doing my induction courses we visited Porton Down. You know, the

Chemical Weapons lab in Wiltshire. There is a small team working for us down there. They showed us some of their latest ideas. One was a variation on Rohypnol, the date rape drug. They've tweaked it so not only does it act as an incapacitating agent but also has an element of a truth drug spliced in. The victim wakes up with no memory of what's happened.'

'No Jenny, not going to happen. Apart from anything else, requisitioning some of the stuff would be impossible. You have no idea how many hoops you have to jump through to acquire that sort of thing, let alone get authorisation to use it and from what you say it's not even proven to work. On top of that, you're not cleared for field operations.'

'Oh come on Rupert,' she said in exasperation. 'None of the work we've been doing for the last few weeks is officially sanctioned, one could even argue it goes directly against our own government's policy. Anyway, I had a word with one of the chaps down in Wiltshire who seems to like me for some reason and he sent me this.' She reached down into her handbag and brought a small pill container and flourished it with a triumphant smile. 'You know, I could always just hang around the Savoy Grill every night and try to pick him up myself. No law against that is there?'

Two nights later, Jenny was sitting in her new flat near Docklands when the phone rang. 'Miranda, you've got a call. The Savoy in an hour, room 721, name of Merriot.'

'Fine,' she replied. 'I'll be there.' Miranda was her stage name and the call was from the escort agency. Suddenly, she had butterflies. It was one thing to look at the situation clinically from an office, quite another to realise she was actually going to go through with it. For a second, she wondered whether this was one of the exciting things about actually being a prostitute, not knowing who you were going to meet and how it would turn out. She quickly dressed with the sexy underwear she had purchased just for this purpose and covered it with a sober dress and coat. Once it had been explained that they were helping national security the Agency had been very helpful in telling her how to behave, what to wear and do. No punter wanted a woman who clearly looked like a tart knocking at their hotel door. She just prayed that the drug worked, otherwise there would be no choice but to do whatever the man wanted. She felt guilty when the thought alternatively horrified and excited her.

Outside, a cab was waiting. It was actually one of their own and had been sitting with its roof light off until she appeared. There was no need to say where she needed to go. Within what seemed like minutes, it was pulling into the circular drive in front of the Savoy and she got out having pretended to pay the driver. He obviously couldn't stay but she knew there was help on hand should she need it. Quite how she would call for it she couldn't say. With another shiver of fear or was it excitement, she realised just how alone she was now.

Sir Giles Merriot was charm itself. When she knocked on his door he opened it himself. He was dressed in a hotel dressing gown and towered over her. She had studied his profile and knew he was fifty six years old, kept fit and was actually quite good looking in a rugged sort of way. What she wasn't prepared for was his presence. He had an almost magnetic charm that was quite overpowering. He took her coat like an old fashioned gentleman and ushered her in. 'Please use your phone,' was all he said as his eyes roved over her body.

Trying to ignore him for the moment, she took her mobile out of her bag and called the number Rupert had given her. Merriot thought she was calling her agency to say all was well. That was the message she said out loud. However, it didn't go to the agency but to the person in a room a few doors down.

'Now my dear, I've booked you to stay until midnight,' Merriot said. 'Oh and please call me Giles, you are Miranda?'

'Yes that's me Giles,' she said with what she hoped was a tempting grin. 'What would you like to do?'

'First things first my dear. Have you eaten yet? Because I have a meal ready in the dining room.'

Jenny realised that she was in a large suite. She hadn't really taken in her surroundings until then. Off to one side was a room with a table laid and a silver bucket held what was clearly a large bottle of Champagne.

'One thing I do like before we go any further.' Giles said with a grin. 'When I entertain ladies in my room, I do rather insist that they only wear their underwear so if you wouldn't mind removing that dress. You are very attractive and I would love to see what you are like underneath.'

Panic almost overcame her at his words. Partly because she was being asked to strip virtually naked. The underwear she had chosen left almost nothing to the imagination but also because she suddenly realised she would not have access to her little bottle of pills. Suddenly, she remembered something else the agency had told her.

'Of course, Giles,' she replied trying to echo his grin. 'But do you mind if I use the bathroom to get ready please?'

'Not at all, as long as you don't mind me watching you strip first,' was the reply.

Realising she had no option and also quite how out of her depth she really was, she slowly slipped the dress off her shoulder and down her waist. That was all there was to it and although she was still at least partially clothed, she suddenly felt completely naked and vulnerable. This was nothing like she had imagined it.

'I'll just be in the bathroom a minute,' she said with false gaiety and without waiting for an answer grabbed her bag before realising she had absolutely no idea where the bathroom actually was.

Giles obviously realised her problem. 'Over there my dear, the door on the right and through the bedroom.' He gave her bottom a pat and squeeze as she walked past him.

As soon as she was locked in the opulent bathroom she started to shake. 'Pull yourself together you silly tart,' she muttered to herself. 'This was all your idea so bloody well get on with it.' Opening her bag, she retrieved the pills. Only one was needed but where the hell could she put it? There was very little choice and in the end she decided on two. One she put in her skimpy bra, the other in the top of her stockings. She just prayed she could retrieve one before things got out of hand.

Dinner was surreal. Giles talked about all sorts of trivial things. He didn't quiz her about herself at all but spoke about himself at length. All the time, he was examining her body. She felt his gaze on her the whole time. She also realised what sort of arrogant egotist he really was. Although he was unfailingly polite, she got the impression that he looked on her as simply a toy to play with. Later in the meal, the conversation turned to sex and he started to tell her in great detail all the things he intended to do to her. Telling her in such graphic detail was obviously a big turn on for him. She managed to keep a smile on her face even though it was doing the exact opposite for her. Luckily, the Champagne cooler was as close to her as it was to him. She wanted to time it so she didn't have to drag his massive body anywhere. He would need to wake up in bed and if he collapsed at the table she didn't think she would have the strength to move him that far.

The meal finished and he suddenly declared that it was time to go to bed. It was clear he could no longer hold himself back. Praying she could get it right, she grabbed the Champagne bottle that was still half full and two glasses, saying they would need refreshment at some point. He grinned and grabbed her backside and steered her into the bedroom. While he was fumbling with her panties she managed to retrieve a pill and drop it into one of the glasses. As they reached the bed she poured two glasses and handed him one.

'Cheers Giles,' she said gaily and knocked her glass back in one. 'Come on drink up it's time to fuck.'

The look on his face was primeval as he also finished the drink, threw the glass on the carpet and pulled her down onto the bed on top of him. He then fumbled with the cord of his dressing gown and pulled it free. Underneath he was naked and clearly ready for action. The scientist had told her that another feature of the drug was that it was fast acting but hadn't actually said what that meant. She realised she had no idea how long it would take. It could be seconds or several minutes in which case she was going to have to continue in her role. His hands reached behind her back and instead of fumbling with the catch of her bra, he simply ripped it apart and threw it on the floor. His hands started to caress her nipples with surprising gentleness. He then put his lips and teeth to one and nipped it hard. She jumped in surprise and his hands slid down to her backside and started to slip her panties down.

'Oh Christ,' she thought. 'When does it stop?' But then she felt his hands slow down. They had been kneading and separating her buttocks and suddenly stopped. She looked into his eyes which were starting to glaze over. 'Oh thank God,' she muttered to herself as she pulled back. Within a minute, he was lying limply on his back breathing slowly. His erection had disappeared but his eyes still vaguely tracked her as she moved. She would love to have brought in a trained interrogator at this point but it was highly likely he would remember at least some of what happened next. If she could make him think it was all part of some erotic dream it was highly likely he would put it all down to too much booze. Her bra was destroyed anyway and staying topless would no doubt keep an image in his mind. She straddled his now inert body and started asking questions.

Chapter 22

Colonel Jacob Sharp climbed out of his little black helicopter and looked around the Intrepid's flight deck. It was starting to get seriously crowded now that his four machines had arrived. Wiping the sweat from his forehead he saw Jon waiting at the forward end in his white shorts and shirt, looking cool and contained as usual. Once the last aircraft's rotors had stopped, Jon stepped forward and shook Jacob's hand.

'Glad to see you back Jacob. It seems like ages since we were planning things back at Wilton. Have you brought all you promised?'

'Yes Sir, all machines as specified and the troops will transfer over from the Okinawa this afternoon.' Jacob was referring to the large American assault carrier sitting over the horizon to the east.

Jon was already in the picture. 'Yes, we've arranged for the Sea Kings to go and get them. Our Special Forces guys came out from UK in the ship so I'll get them to host your chaps and show them the ropes.'

'Looks like we're about set then Sir,' Jacob replied.

Jon looked at the Colonel. They already knew each other well from the planning meetings at Wilton before they came out here. Jacob was not what he expected of an American Special Forces officer. He was slim and wiry but seemed to have an almost professorial air about him. From his records, Jon knew he was very highly qualified academically and very highly regarded as a soldier having seen active service in several theatres, especially in recent years. It was just that with his short hair and round glasses he looked more like a school teacher than a professional soldier. However, Jon also knew that Special Forces officers were often deceptive in their appearance. Jon felt he was lucky to have him and his men on the team. The only thing that was slightly worrying was that he had been warned that Jacob was a very devout Evangelical Christian. So far, there had been no indication that this would be a problem but he just hoped he wouldn't start preaching at some point. Jon had some very strong views on the subject himself and he would hate to fall out with one of his staff over the issue.

Conspiracy

'What I suggest Jacob is that I get James Pyke to show you to your accommodation and give you a tour of the facilities. Join me for lunch and then we can watch the Sea Kings go and get your chaps.' Jon said.

'That's fine, maybe James could also show me my men's accommodation. I'd like to see what it's like.'

'Of course, but you'll have to apologise to them about the lack of air conditioning. Hopefully, we won't be stuck out here much longer. On that point have you heard anything from your side about timings?'

Jacob turned to look back at the aircraft as he spoke. 'Officially, I expect you know as much as I. However, the word on the streets is the middle of next week.'

'Hmm, we've heard that as well. One thing's for sure, we can't stay off the coast here indefinitely. But we won't be in the first wave anyway. I'm pushing for three days afterwards as we discussed but have yet to get final approval.'

Jacob nodded. 'It really does depend on what sort of a fight they put up. Have you heard the new buzz words the White House leaked to the press?'

Jon laughed. 'You mean 'Shock and Awe?' Yes I've heard it. I have to say only you lot would come up with something like that. If it was us Brits it would be more like 'Really Awful Frightfulness' which I guess doesn't have quite the same ring to it.'

Jacob laughed back. 'Oh I don't know Sir, whatever we call it, it's going to ruin their day, believe me.'

'As long as we're actually doing the right thing Jacob,' Jon said deliberately to try and sound out the man.

'Oh come on Sir, surely you don't have doubts? Saddam is the worst type of despot. He has to go,' Jacob stated firmly, with total conviction in his voice.

'Can't disagree with that Jacob.' Jon replied. 'But I thought we were going in to find these WMDs. After all that's our exact role with this unit. Certainly my government has firmly stated that regime change is not the reason.'

Jacob looked embarrassed for a moment. 'Our two governments seem to be playing this slightly differently Sir. Our President has repeatedly made it clear that getting Saddam out is a primary aim. Your Prime Minister has focused on the WMDs almost totally.

Conspiracy

However, I'm quite sure we will find them. Personally, I think we have a God given mission to sort out the region for the benefit of everyone.'

There it was. Jon realised that Jacob was actually only repeating the words of the US President almost verbatim but clearly believed them totally. However, nothing worried Jon more than when anyone called on God or religion to justify their actions.

He decided that now was not the time to enter that debate. 'Well anyway Jacob, whatever our personal views we have a job to do and personally I would like nothing better than to be successful. Let's just focus on the mission. Ah, here comes James. I'll leave it to him to show you around.'

As the two men went into the superstructure Jon was lost in thought. His doubts about this whole situation would not go away. Everyone was so sure the WMDs were there even though the UN Inspectors were still saying they had found nothing. Then there was his appointment to head up what was really an army outfit. He knew he wasn't really qualified to command it and so his position was really more of a public relations exercise. Presumably, when things were discovered, having his name involved would be seen as adding credibility. What worried him more though was that he was pretty sure there was something more to the whole situation, something he was missing. All that said, it also put him in the centre of things which meant he might at least have a chance to influence the situation.

Later that afternoon, Jon took Jacob to 'FLYCO' the flying control position that overlooked the flight deck at the rear of the superstructure. As the two men approached, they could hear raised voices from within the position. There was clearly some sort of angry exchange going on inside. Jon turned to his deputy. 'I think it might be politic if we hang back, don't you?'

Jacob nodded assent. However, they were now near enough that they could hear what was being said.

'You're a bloody useless man. When I ask for an ETA all you have to do is give me an accurate time. How difficult can it be?'

The reply was in a much quieter voice and couldn't be made out but Jon knew it was 'Dinger' Bell the ship's Flying Control Officer.

Conspiracy

The other voice was clearly the Captain. 'Buck up your ideas or you will be off this ship tomorrow.' The door was flung open and a red faced Captain Wright appeared. He seemed startled to see the two men facing him but then his expression rapidly changed to an ingratiating smile. 'Ah Commodore, Colonel, I was just checking on when the Sea Kings with your people are due back. Shouldn't be long now, if you will excuse me.' And he brushed past them before either could respond.

Jon looked at Jacob and shrugged his shoulders. 'Not our problem,' he said firmly. Jacob nodded.

They went into FLYCO. A balding and quite old Lieutenant Commander was sitting at the console which controlled the radios and flight deck loop system. He looked around startled for a second. Jon was pretty sure he thought it was his Captain coming back. The look on his face when he recognised that it wasn't would have been comical had it not been so serious.

'Afternoon Dinger,' Jon said, forestalling any comment he might make. 'Can I introduce you to Colonel Sharp who's my second in command and the chap who knows all about soldiery things?'

The Colonel held out his hand. 'Dinger?' he asked.

'Yes Sir, some poor unfortunates in the RN get nicknames whether they like it or not. Anyone called Bell is inevitably 'Dinger', then there's 'Chalky' White and loads more. It's a cross I have to bear. The Commodore knows all about it. Mind you he used to call me 'Sir' not many years back.'

Jon laughed and explained. 'Dinger was my Sea Daddy when I joined Dartmouth. That's a senior chap who gets given the task of looking after new joiners. Mind you in this case 'look after' is probably stretching the truth a little. He seemed hell bent on getting me into trouble half the time.'

Dinger snorted a laugh. 'Pot this is kettle over. I seem to remember the other half of the time you were leading me astray. Good times though Sir.'

Jon agreed. 'Just remind me to avoid any runs ashore with you Dinger, my liver and reputation wouldn't stand it. But back to more serious matters. Any sign of my Queens of the Air loaded with US Grunts?'

'There's been a delay Sir as I was explaining to the Captain,' Dinger said in a deadpan tone.

Conspiracy

Just then the intercom came to life. 'FLYCO, this is the Ops room. We have the Sea Kings on HF. They are forty miles away, ETA in twenty five minutes.'

Dinger responded. 'Roger Ops room please ensure the Captain is informed.' He turned and looked at Jon and an unspoken message was passed. Jon nodded back.

It wasn't long before the two aircraft were in sight. They changed radio frequencies when visual with the ship and Dinger gave the clearance to land, once he had checked the relative wind was in limits and gained permission from the bridge. Just as the first Sea King was approaching Jon noticed that the waked that had been streaming directly behind the ship was starting to curve. 'Dinger, the ship's altering. Tell him to overshoot.' Jon called urgently.

He was wasting his breath as Dinger was doing just that. Dinger then picked up another microphone as the ship began to heel into the turn. 'Bridge this is FLYCO we were just about to land on the first Sea King, you gave me a green light so why the fuck are you altering course?'

The Captain's angry voice came over the intercom. 'This is the Captain, you do not speak to the bridge like that Lieutenant Commander Bell. I decide when to alter course, not you. We will steady up when I'm good and ready. Once the aircraft are on board you are to report to me in my cabin.'

Jon reached over and motioned to Dinger to pass him the microphone. 'Captain Wright, this is the Commodore. Belay that last order, when the Sea Kings are safely on board you will report to my cabin. Is that clear?'

Chapter 23

Leaving Israel had been straightforward as had crossing Jordan. The Tarbil border post into Iraq was far from impressive. A series of long dilapidated sheds with virtually no one in sight. The two tankers had parked up the previous night in the large car park in front of the crossing. The next morning they started up and made their way to the border. As they pulled in next to one of the large customs sheds waiting for customs officers to appear, RJ climbed out of the cab of his truck and made his way to the one in front and called Pieter down.

'Is it usually this quiet? We seem to be the only people here.' he asked as he looked around.

Pieter looked at the scene as well. 'This is unusual, there's normally plenty of staff, most of them military and most wanting a little hand out. I suspect the military have other things on their minds at the moment.'

As he spoke, an Iraqi customs official finally put in an appearance. Pieter went over to chat and handed over their papers which were barely glanced at, probably because of the small fold of American dollars that was included with them. The vehicles weren't even looked at and then they were motioned on their way.

As he climbed back into the cab of his truck and motioned to Ahmed the driver to start up, another thought crossed his mind. All the work they had done to disguise the cargo had probably been a complete waste of time. It was this crossing that had always been considered the problem and they hadn't even bothered to inspect the tankers. He realised it wasn't a bad decision though, there were still hundreds of miles to travel.

As soon as they got underway it was also clear that there would be no military escort. He wasn't surprised, the lack of any soldiers at the border was a clear indication of what was going on in other parts of the country. However, this part of Iraq could be quite lawless especially on the long desert stretch which had no habitation of any sort for hundreds of kilometres. He just hoped that any bandits or rebel Kurdish bands were also concentrating their efforts elsewhere. It was only as they approached the Euphrates River that bisected the country, that they would see signs of civilisation again. The tanker's maximum speed was seventy kilometres an hour and at that rate they would need at least 12 hours on the road to reach their destination. In fact it would take at least double that. It was already close to midday, they had planned for an over night stop at the intersection with Route 21 which led south off the main Route 1 to Baghdad. This would be the road where they would head off, ostensibly to a farming area to the south west of the capital. In actuality to the separate facility already waiting for them. Pieter had wanted to drive through the night but RJ knew the state of the roads as they approached their destination and was adamant that they needed to arrive in daylight. The thought of wrecking the tanker with the special cargo didn't bear thinking about.

The monotony of the trip soon got to RJ and he started to nod off. He had agreed to do three hour stints with Ahmed, even though he didn't have any sort of Iraqi driving licence let alone one for HGVs. It was not as if anyone would be checking and despite no licence he had plenty of experience driving this sort of vehicle. This main route was actually quite well maintained as it was the main artery between Baghdad and Jordan and they were making good time.

It was getting dark and RJ was doing the driving when the truck ahead indicated to turn off and they pulled over for the night stop. The two tankers had built in bunks in the rear of their cabs and it was going to get cold over night but both RJ and Pieter had agreed to share a tent rather than suffer the stuffiness of a cab. The next day would be far more difficult. Most of the roads were still good but the last part would be difficult and the two men went to bed early. They would be up with the dawn.

RJ was woken from an unremembered dream by the sound of gunfire. He didn't hesitate and nor did Pieter who was milliseconds behind him as they flew out of the tent. The night was dark, there was no moon but the two tankers were silhouetted by the lights of two large old fashioned looking cars. There was some sort of altercation going on around the cabs of both tankers. There must have been at least ten men and it was immediately clear what they wanted.

'They can't see us Pieter,' RJ whispered. 'We're in the dark to them.' Both men had armed themselves but only with a nine millimetre pistol each. It was not going to be anything like enough fire power to stop what was happening but it would offer some protection. 'We need to get away from this tent and into cover. Over there.' He pointed to some rocks a few yards away.

The two men scrambled behind the rocks. 'The tent must look pretty much like a rock, it's the right colour. Hopefully, we won't be spotted. So what the fuck do we do now?' Pieter asked grimly.

RJ was about to answer when two shots rang out. 'I reckon that's the drivers gone. The silly arses must think the tankers have fuel in them. They'll be fucking sorry when they try to run one of those shitty old cars on fertiliser.'

Pieter laughed grimly. 'If they find the real cargo they'll be really sorry and so will half of Iraq.'

The two men watched helplessly as the hijackers mounted the cabs of the tankers and started them up. It was clear that they would be driven away and the chances of ever seeing them again were slim.

'With me Pieter,' RJ commanded. 'They may be happy with just one. The rear one is the one we want. We need to disable it and we've only got one chance.'

Still cloaked by the dark background, the two men half ran, half crouched towards the rear tanker. The remaining hijackers had now got back into their cars and were getting ready to leave. Pieter was the faster runner and was well in the lead when he saw his chance and before RJ could say anything, he leapt for the mudguard covering the rear wheels. Just above it was a ladder used to gain access to the top of the tank. He managed to grab the bottom rung, swiftly climbed to the top and ran forward. RJ had a pretty good idea what he was about to do and also ran towards the cab just as the whole rig started to move off. The driver was clearly in a hurry and also not very skilled. Even so, it was very quickly moving faster than he could run. Cursing under his breath, he realised he wouldn't be able to help.

Pieter flung himself down at the front of the tank as the whole thing lurched into motion. Reaching down with his hands, he managed to grab one of the coiled air hose brake lines that ran from the trailer section to the cab. Reaching around with his other hand he grabbed the small knife he always carried and started to saw frantically at the pipe. Although reinforced with wire, it was mainly made of hard plastic and with the strength of desperation, he managed to cut into it. It didn't need to be severed completely, a large leak would do. He then flailed his free hand around looking for the second one. By now the tanker was about to pull out onto the road. He didn't allow that to distract him and soon located the pipe and managed to cut into it as well. He briefly wondered how long it would take the driver to realise that the trailer he was towing, that weighed over forty tons, now had no brakes, before running back to the ladder. There probably wasn't time to climb down before it was moving too fast. As a trained parachutist, he weighed his chances and launched himself into the air. Contact with the ground blasted all the air out of his lungs but he managed a successful rolling landing. RJ ran up and helped him to his feet.

'He won't get far now,' Pieter managed to gasp out. 'I got both brake lines.'

The two men stood as the silence of the desert reclaimed the night. The only sign that there had been any activity were the tyre marks in the sand to one side of the road and the two pathetic bodies of the drivers who lay where they had been shot. The two men went over to them, dragged them clear and hid them out of sight. It was the best they could do. They then went and dismantled the tent. Pieter bundled it into a bag and they set off down the road.

'We saw some traffic yesterday so hopefully we will be able to stop someone.' Pieter observed.

RJ was about to reply when he heard something. 'I don't think we'll need a lift,' he said and broke into a steady jog. The faint distant sound was that of a vehicle impacting something else. He prayed it was their tanker and he prayed it was still intact, otherwise they could be running directly towards a cloud of poison gas.

The sun was just beginning to paint the horizon pink when they saw the wreck. The tanker was jacknifed across the road blocking it in both directions. Rammed underneath the front was the partly crushed wreck of what must have been one of the hijacker's cars. Slowing down and drawing their weapons the two men split to come up from both sides. There didn't seem to be any activity but it never failed to be careful. In fact, by the time they reached the wreck it was clear that both it and the crushed car had been abandoned. The tanker cab was empty and there was a considerable amount of blood in the crushed rear of the car.

'What do you reckon Pieter? The tanker must have got too close to the car ahead and braked hard. With only brakes on the front axle he was never going to stop in a straight line.'

'Agreed but we've got another problem. I can fix those air lines quite easily but look here.' Pieter pointed to a large puddle of green water spreading across the road from underneath the truck. 'The radiators fucked that's why they left it I reckon.'

RJ nodded. 'Ok but can you start it up and run it enough to pull clear of the car and park up on the road side?'

'We can only try,' Pieter responded. 'The engine should run for a few minutes before overheating.'

He jumped into the cab. Luckily the keys were still in it although he knew where there were spares. The engine fired first time and he didn't hesitate to slam it into reverse. Although the cab was almost at right angles to the trailer it still managed to lurch the whole rig back several feet. It was enough to separate the cab from the wreck. He shut it down and joined RJ at the wrecked car. With considerable effort, the two men were able to push it clear and off to one side of the road. Pieter could then drive the rig forward. The drop from the road to the desert sand was only a few inches so he was able to do a full one eighty turn and get them facing back the way they had come. By the time he stopped, the temperature gauge was on max and steam was starting to pour out from the engine compartment.

Pieter jumped out, pulled the bent covers aside and looked into the engine compartment. 'Good news, I think the radiator is actually alright. It's been shifted on its mountings and the bottom hose has pulled off. I reckon I can fix it in a few minutes at least well enough for us to be on our way.'

'Thank God for that,' RJ replied. He suddenly heard a chirping noise from inside the cab and recognised it straight away. It was his Iridium satellite phone. The Kurds must have missed it in the excitement of the attack. He was never meant to make a call on it unless it was a dire emergency and no one would ever call him but it had one key facility, it could receive short text messages. He quickly grabbed it and looked at the small LCD screen. The message was very short.

He turned to Pieter. 'We're running out of time. It all kicks off tonight. Right, we've got the water to wash off the top paint so we can also use some of that to top up the radiator. I guess it's time to join the Iraqi army old friend.'

Chapter 24

'Sharon? Who the hell is Sharon?' Rupert asked in frustration.

Jenny shared the feeling. 'I've no idea but look, let me go back and tell the whole story alright? I put my phone onto voice recorder as you told me but I think its best if I take you through my recollections first.'

Rupert sat back in his office chair. 'Sorry Jenny, I wasn't getting at you. It's just that this whole story is getting weirder by the minute.'

'If it's any consolation I feel just the same,' Jenny replied. 'Anyway, when he was clearly under the influence I followed your script as much as I could. I asked the foundation questions about his name, family and key points in his career. He was a bit hard to follow but coherent enough. So, then I went on to ask him about his relationship with the Minister and it was clear that they really are just friends. His prime role seems to be advising on financial and procurement issues. Although he did say that he also advised in other areas but wasn't specific.'

'That's not surprising and makes sense,' Rupert said. 'Go on.'

'It started to get interesting when I asked if he had any contacts with the US military. He said no but had several contacts with the Embassy in London. I then quizzed him about whether he knew about Jon Hunt's original mission. He confirmed that the Minister had told him about it and had gone on to warn someone from the US Embassy.'

'Did he say why?'

'He was a little vague on that one but if you listen to the recording it seems he thinks that he will be making money out of the forthcoming war and didn't want anyone jeopardising it. His actual words were, if I remember correctly, 'sort out Middle East, needs doing, won't harm my bank, had to warn Yanks.'

'And did you find out why he was the man who proposed giving Jon Hunt the command of this reconnaissance group?'

'He said the Americans asked him to propose his name to the Minister but I couldn't find out why. Probably because he didn't know himself.'

'Hmm, Ok. So did you ask whether he knew of any future plans?'

'That's where it starts to get really weird. Firstly, he started to ramble on about God's plan. When I tried to pin him down on what he meant. All he would say was that Sharon was God's plan and that it would all be justified. When I asked him what he meant about Sharon, he started giggling and said something like Our Jay was living Sharon, which makes no sense at all. Frankly by that time he was getting pretty incoherent. I think the combination of booze and the drug was getting to him. He fell asleep after that.'

'Right, so to summarise.' Rupert said steepling his fingers. 'He was definitely the leak and our guess that he is looking to make money out of the war was correct. After that it gets stranger. The question is what do we do now? If in fact, we can actually do anything.'

'Can't we warn the Minister that his friend is leaking classified information to America? Surely we can do that at least.' Jenny asked with feeling.

'Think about it Jenny,' Rupert said. 'We illegally interrogate the Minister's best chum and tell him that the result is that said chum is passing general information on to our closest ally. We'd not only be sacked but could end up in prison. I'm afraid that knowing what he's done in the past is now virtually useless. It's what's going to happen next is the important thing. You did a damned fine job but I'm sorry it wasn't good enough.'

Jenny chewed at her bottom lip. 'And all we know, or think we know, if we believe that old Israeli, is that some sort of plan is in place to ensure that WMDs are found to justify the whole thing. We don't really know whether there is intelligence that the UN don't have and they are hidden somewhere or even less likely that they are going to placed somewhere to be found at a convenient time.'

'And our friend, Jon Hunt has been put right in the firing line. Bollocks, we've got to do something but I'm buggered if I can see what,' Rupert said in frustration.

His attention was distracted by a noise filtering in from outside. A crowd of people were marching towards Westminster Bridge. The bridge itself was already packed. Most of the people were holding placards of some sort.

'You know, the BBC are reporting that three hundred thousand people are on that anti-war march but a mate of mine in the Met says it's more than a million. It's nice to see the government's poodle peddling yet one more lie.'

Jenny looked out towards Westminster. 'I don't suppose even ten million protestors will be able to stop the war happening now.'

'No, no one can Jenny, not even us,' Rupert replied sadly. 'And I fear that there's not a great deal we're going to be able to do once it starts either.'

It started that evening. Rupert was at home with Gina his wife trying to put his frustrations aside. The large glass of red wine was helping but the BBC was not.

'This modern technology is a double edged sword,' he said to Gina.

'Oh why?' she asked.

'Well, now we have coverage of war even in real time and from the enemy's positions.' As he said it, the television picture of Baghdad flared up as yet another missile hit a building. 'It shows us the horror of the whole process. People are dying in those buildings you know. But it also desensitises us to the whole thing. It reduces it to some sort of video game.'

Gina looked back at the television. 'It's not desensitising me. I think it's terrible. As far as I'm concerned there is absolutely no justification for this. Frankly, at this moment I'm ashamed to be British.'

'You're not the only one. There were over a million on the streets this afternoon who would agree with you. The UN have not sanctioned this even though our lawyers have managed to cobble together a feeble justification. I wonder what history will make of the whole thing. I just pray it's not the start of something even worse.'

Several miles away, Jenny was watching the same pictures but she had the sound turned down as she was once again listening to the recording she had made in the hotel room. The television reporting only made her feel frustrated and angry but even so she couldn't stop watching. Maybe it was because her attention was half focused on the TV screen but she suddenly thought she had heard something different. She rewound the recording back a few minutes and listened again.

'Oh fuck,' she muttered under her breath as she stood up and went to her laptop on a nearby table. As she waited for it to boot up, she listened again. The more she heard it the more she was convinced she was right. Once the laptop was on line, she did a quick search which only confirmed her fears.

She grabbed the phone and dialled Rupert's private number. When he answered, she cut him off before he could speak. 'I need to come over Rupert, right now. I'm on my way.' And she put the phone down. Grabbing the laptop and her phone, she quickly locked up and went downstairs. It didn't take long to get a cab and within fifteen minutes she was knocking on Rupert's door.

He immediately let her in. 'What on earth is all the excitement about Jenny?' he asked as he shut the door behind them. 'Come into the living room. Gina is here but she still has all her security clearances.'

'Yes but is she aware of all the off grid things we've been doing?' Jenny asked.

'Of course, we have no secrets.' Rupert replied as he ushered her into the room. 'Gina this is Jenny who works for me. I told you about her. Seems she has something to tell us?' he asked as he turned to Jenny.

Jenny took out her phone and replayed the relevant clip. 'I was listening to this while watching the TV and suddenly it became clear. I've confirmed it by checking on the internet.'

'Whoa, slow down Jenny. What have you confirmed?'

She gathered herself together. 'Sorry, let me backtrack. By the end of my little conversation with Giles he was starting to tire and slur his words.'

'Yes we've been through all that,' Rupert replied. 'But it doesn't help.'

'Oh but it does. Listen again.' Jenny replayed the audio clip. Seeing the blank looks on their faces she continued. 'We thought he was just rambling but if what I think is right then we have a real problem. He's not saying 'Sharon' he saying 'Sarin'. It's a chemical weapon, a nerve agent and I'm guessing that someone with the initials RJ was delivering Sarin.'

Rupert looked at the two women. 'Oh bloody hell. Why didn't I see that? And what's worse is that I think I know exactly who RJ is.'

Chapter 25

'Come in Tony,' Jon said as the Captain of Intrepid put his head around the door of Jon's cabin. 'Take a seat.'

'You said you wanted to talk to me Sir?' Tony said stiffly as he remained standing.

Jon didn't get up. 'Come and sit down. This is an informal chat. Don't look so worried.'

Tony sat down opposite Jon but perched on the edge of the chair with a pained look on his face. Jon realised he was going to have to take the bull by the horns.

'Tony, I've only been on board a few days but I have to say that the atmosphere here is worrying me.'

'Sir? Surely the ship is my business?' It was clear Tony wasn't going to be intimidated.

'You must know I understand that Tony but and this is important, if your business starts to adversely affect mine then I will have to step in. Do I make myself clear?'

'I'm sorry Sir but you'll have to be more specific.'

Jon was starting to lose his temper and forced himself to remain calm. 'Alright, this afternoon after you had chewed out the Flying Control Officer, which myself and Colonel Sharp clearly overheard by the way, you went back to the bridge and altered course just as we were about to recover two of my aircraft with my troops on board. Then, when Lieutenant Commander Bell quite correctly queried the bridge as to what the hell was going on, you rip his head off for a second time. Care to explain?'

'Sir, he swore at me. That was completely beyond the pale.'

Jon laughed mirthlessly. 'And you actions of jeopardising my aircraft were perfectly alright then?'

'No Sir, of course not,' Tony blustered. 'But I had my reasons for altering course. The Officer of the Watch should have told FLYCO.'

'But if you were on the bridge and had charge of the ship then you should have told him surely?' Jon asked mildly. It was quite clear to him that the Tony had made a school boy error. The question was, was he big enough to admit it. Jon suspected not and the next answer proved him right.

'I'll be honest with you Sir. The quality of my officers leaves much to be desired. I seem to have to be continually on top of them. It's been like that ever since we left the UK.'

'Tony you must know that I've just left command of the Formidable, a ship even bigger than this one. I know what it's like. You have to trust your people. You can't do it all yourself. It's surprising how much they respond to that sort of approach.' Jon said softly.

Tony's eyes narrowed. 'Maybe for you but we all know you're the golden boy. Fast track everywhere, best ships, best jobs, a chest full of medals and always appearing in the media. You were even promoted to Commodore before your time. Some of us have to work for what we've got.'

Tony's words caught Jon completely by surprise. Not only were they deeply upsetting, he knew they weren't even remotely true. Yes, he'd had some spectacular successes but that was as much due to circumstance as anything else. He had also had his share of failures but saying so to this man was clearly not going to have any effect. He knew that losing his temper would be counter-productive. In the short term, there was little he was going to be able to do. He would be taking his team ashore very soon and then Intrepid would only be operating in a low threat support role. He didn't like the idea but he would have to say something when he returned to the UK after this was all over. The thought actually made him feel sad.

'Tony, there's nothing more to say. You've made your position quite clear. I hope you understand mine as well. There will be no room for error from now on. Do I make myself clear?'

Tony nodded. 'If I may leave now Sir. I have a ship to run.'

Before Jon could reply, there was a knock on the door. Jon's Ops officer put his head around it and before anyone could answer, came into the cabin with a sheet of paper in his hand.

'Flash signal Sir,' James said urgently and handed Jon the paper.

Jon quickly scanned it and his heart rate accelerated. He then passed it to Tony.

'Well here's your chance Captain. Operation Enduring Freedom has been approved. First strike is tonight. You'd better get this ship in position. I want to be ready to disembark in three days time.'

Conspiracy

With the ship still in the vicinity of Bahrain, it would take several days of slow passage to arrive at her final destination whatever that turned out to be. The primary plan called for the ship and escorts to make for Kuwait Bay and disembark to the north of Kuwait city in order to avoid as much of the local population as possible. Once ashore, they would join up with other coalition forces at Um Qasr and establish a Forward Operating Base. As soon as they were established, there were a number of sites of interest that the helicopters would initially scout out and then if necessary the troops would go in, either using the Humvees or the Sea Kings depending on range and the terrain. Jon knew as a plan it was rather vague but he also knew full well how things could change. They would almost certainly be operating beyond the battle lines at least for the first few weeks. It was better to have a simple flexible plan than a rigid complex one. Unfortunately, it also meant that they were well back from the initial action.

For that reason, that evening, he was sitting in his cabin with Paul, Jacob and James, alternately watching CNN and the BBC. Jon found the whole emerging picture disquieting in the extreme. However, he was also distracted by watching his companion's reaction to the live events they were seeing. Paul looked as upset as he expected, James just looked fascinated but it was Jacob he was most interested to observe. He was sitting on the edge of his chair absolutely entranced. Every time there was a visible explosion from the city he gave a small cheer, it was almost as if he was at a sports match. On one occasion Jon distinctly heard him mutter 'praise the Lord.' Jon suddenly realised just how far apart he and his deputy actually were.

Suddenly, all thoughts of what they were watching were savagely interrupted. There was a massive rending crash and the sound of tearing steel. All three men were thrown violently onto the deck. A second later, there was a roaring, screaming noise. Jon knew exactly what it was. It was the safety valves on the ship's two boilers which had opened. He also had a bloody good idea about what had just happened. He just prayed that the damage wasn't too severe.

He scrambled to his feet. 'Paul, Jacob, go aft and see how much damage there is to our equipment and the aircraft. James get to the Ops room, I'm going to the bridge.'

Conspiracy

He didn't wait for an answer as he sprinted out of his cabin and ran to the ladders that would take him up the three decks to the bridge. He arrived out of breath but hardly noticed as he first looked out of the bridge windows. There, directly in front of them, was the superstructure of a large bulk cargo ship. Intrepid's bow was firmly embedded in the side of her. He quickly turned his attention to what was happening inside the bridge. Captain Wright was standing in front of a young officer. He was red in the face and shouting something. Jon couldn't hear what it was over the sound of the boiler safety valves which were still blowing. Suddenly, the noise stopped. The engineers had clearly got them under control. His relief was tempered by what he could now hear the Captain was saying. It was quite clear that the young Lieutenant was the Officer of the Watch and that the Captain was berating him.

The young officer was standing his ground. 'Sir, you had the ship. You told me to go to the chart table.'

Jon had already made his mind up. The remark was the final straw. However, he didn't go to the two officers. He turned to the Bosun's Mate who was standing open mouthed looking at the altercation. 'You,' he said firmly. 'Pipe the ship to Emergency stations. Now.'

The young sailor came out of his trance. 'Yes Sir.' He grabbed a microphone and hit the emergency alarm button. Jon knew that key ship's staff would have already worked out what was going on and had probably closed up anyway but many people on the ship would be confused and wouldn't know what to do. At first glance, the damage didn't look fatal but you never knew at this stage of an accident.

'Captain Wright, what the hell is going on here?' Jon called as he strode over to the two officers.

'Sir, we've had a collision.' The Captain blustered. 'This officer put us in a dangerous position and I didn't have time to correct the situation.'

The Lieutenant was clearly bursting to talk but was also reluctant to say something contrary to his Captain. In the end, his anger overcame his natural deference. 'Sir, that's not true. I called you when she was still three miles away as per your standing orders. You took over the ship when she was still a long way off.'

'That's enough,' Jon almost shouted. 'It took me several minutes to get up here. Captain Wright, is all that you've done since the collision is argue with your Officer of the Watch? Dammit, I had to tell the Bosun's Mate to go to Emergency Stations. What the hell are you playing at?'

The Captain looked confused. 'Sorry Sir, yes, you're right. I should have acted faster.'

'Captain, did you have the ship when the collision occurred?'

'Err yes Sir but we were passing clear behind her. She must have slowed down at the last moment.'

'What? You weren't watching her bearing? What the fuck were you doing?' Jon was past anger now. By his admission this was totally the fault of the Captain and he had clearly been trying to blame the young officer. This couldn't continue.

Jon turned once again to the young sailor. 'Bosun's Mate, pipe for the Commander to come to the bridge please.' He then turned to the two officers. 'What's your name Lieutenant?'

'Brown Sir.'

'Right Brown, as Officer of the Watch what should you be doing now?'

'Getting out the bridge cards and going through the emergency procedures Sir.' Was the prompt reply.

'Good answer. So get on with it.'

'Aye, aye Sir.' Brown looked relieved as he ran to the compass Pelorus where the cards were kept. Within seconds he had taken charge and was issuing the relevant orders.

'That's what you should have done Captain.' Jon said with contempt in his voice. 'Not trying to blame everyone but yourself.'

Just then, the Commander, the ship's second in command arrived. He was panting from the exertion of running up from so many decks below. 'Just come up from HQ One Sir. The forward collision bulkhead is intact and we don't seem to be taking on water.'

'Good,' Jon replied. 'Commander Peters, I am the ranking officer on this ship. Actually, I'm not sure whether I really have the authority to do this but as we are now on active service I don't feel I have any choice in the matter.' He turned to the Captain. 'Captain Wright, you are relieved of your command. I am instructing your Executive Officer to take over in command. You are to go to your cabin and remain there until this emergency is sorted out. Is that clear?'

Chapter 26

'Bloody Kurds,' RJ thought to himself. The attack on the trucks was screwing up his deadlines. With the war already underway he had little time in hand. They were going to lose at least twenty four hours now. He did have their contingency plan but he had no intention of using it unless things got seriously worse and there was absolutely no other option.

Pieter was as good as his word and soon reconnected the radiator hose and filled the system. He was then able to drive out of sight of the road. They got out a couple of buckets and filled them from the extra water tank and with two soft brooms started work on the paintwork.

'Bloody hell Pieter, this stuff comes off easily,' RJ said as his first few brushstrokes immediately started removing the blue paint. 'Its bloody lucky it didn't rain on your other trips.'

'Nah, we had the real paint on then,' Pieter replied. 'We only resprayed them as Iraqi army vehicles a couple of weeks ago. Then we put the temporary stuff back over the top. Anyway, it never fucking rains around here.'

'Fair point,' RJ agreed.

Once the tanker was a drab green, they drilled out the rivets holding the Israeli vehicles identification plates and riveted the Iraqi ones back in place. Finally happy that the vehicle would pass muster as an Iraqi army tanker, they changed their clothes and made sure they would pass for soldiers. Their last action was to retrieve two AK 47s from the hidden weapon store under the cab.

Their turn off from the main highway was only a few kilometres away and they were soon making good progress once again. However, RJ knew better than to relax. If something could go wrong it probably would. He would only relax once the tanker was under cover at the site and then only partially because they were going to have to unload its deadly cargo.

He wasn't too surprised when he noticed the engine temperature gauge starting to creep up yet again. 'Looks like you didn't completely fix the radiator Pieter,' he said in a worried tone.

'Yeah, I've been watching it too. We'll have to stop soon and let it cool down. It may just be an air lock in the system.' Pieter replied.

Minutes later, they were forced to stop by the side of the road to allow the engine to cool. There was no sign of any leaks but Pieter didn't dare take the radiator cap off until the whole mass of metal had cooled sufficiently. It was over an hour until it was safe.

The longer they waited the more RJ fretted over the lost time. 'If we go on like this it'll take another three days to get there.'

'Can't do anything more, we've lost water,' Pieter replied. 'There must be a pinhole somewhere. Are there any towns with a garage coming up?'

'Yes, there's Al Kasrah in about twenty klicks. We should be able to make that but will a garage be of any help? This is a big rig.' RJ asked.

'Could be and if nothing else we can always break an egg into the water. It can work, the idea is the egg yolk circulates and blocks the hole. But let's try the garage first. If nothing else we should be able to top up our water tank.'

An hour later, the once again overheating truck pulled up outside a rather dilapidated garage. There was one petrol pump and number of wrecked cars parked around the rear and no sign of anyone.

The two men jumped out and went into the building. A man came to meet them wiping his hands on a greasy rag. Inside the garage, there was an old Toyota Land Cruiser that he had clearly been working on.

'Can I help?' he asked warily, seeing the uniforms.

Pieter explained that their tanker had been damaged during an attack by Kurdish rebels and they needed to get the radiator fixed.

Without saying anything more, the mechanic went outside and Pieter showed him the problem. Like mechanics the world over, he then pursed his lips and started to explain just how difficult and probably expensive it would be to repair.

Pieter took the lead as he was the Sergeant and cut him short. 'We need to be on our way as soon as possible. We can pay in dollars so just get on with it.'

At the mention of dollars, the man's attitude changed. 'Fine, we need to pressure test the radiator and find the hole. When the engine is hot the water escapes as steam and you can't see it. Let me get it out and find the leak. I can solder or braze it up once I know where it is.'

'How long will this take?' Pieter asked.

'An hour to remove the radiator, another couple of hours to find the leak and fix it and another hour to put it back in. If all goes well that is,' the mechanic replied.

RJ looked at his watch. It was well after midday now. Any thought of getting to their destination today was gone. Even if the mechanic's estimate was accurate, they would still not get away until dusk at the earliest. Despite the mounting urgency, he was still loath to drive the last part of the journey in the dark.

Pieter looked at RJ and shrugged, then turned to the mechanic. 'Let's hope it does go well then, there will be a bonus in it for you if you do it quickly. Also, we can help if needed.'

The three men toiled to get the recalcitrant radiator out of the truck and then they took it into the garage.

The mechanic put a high pressure hose on it. 'There's the hole,' he said but he didn't really have to point it out as the small jet of water was quite obvious. He looked closely at the damage. 'I can probably fix it but I won't guarantee how long it will hold. It's in a very awkward place to get at. You would be far better letting me order a new one from Baghdad. I could probably get one for tomorrow afternoon.'

'Really? You know what's happening there at this moment? No one is going to worry about vehicle spare parts at the moment and anyway we need to get away as soon as possible. It's a risk we'll have to take.' Pieter asked.

'Tell me about it. I'm very glad I'm not in the capital. Ok then, I'll do my best. It's going to be late by the time we're finished. Are you going to head off straight away?'

Pieter turned to RJ who shook his head imperceptibly. 'No, we'll probably sleep in the cab tonight and set off at dawn.'

There was nothing more the two men could do at that point so they asked the mechanic if there was somewhere they could get a meal. He directed them back into the town and they set off. The place was very quiet. It was as if all the inhabitants were hiding, waiting for the inevitable to happen. They did manage to find one small café that served them a basic meal and then went back to the garage.

When they returned, the mechanic was shaking his head. 'Sorry but that radiator is scrap. I tried my best but there's no way that leak can be repaired. Every time I put a torch near it the hole just got bigger.'

The two men looked at each other and walked away so the mechanic couldn't overhear them

'Fuck,' RJ said vehemently. 'The idea was a dirty dash to the site in a day and now we're two days behind schedule and stuck here with a broken truck any ideas?'

Pieter only said one word. 'Contingency?'

RJ considered it for a second. 'No, not yet but it's becoming more of an option. The papers I procured for the trip are absolutely genuine. What would real soldiers do in this situation?'

'Call for help I guess.' Pieter replied. 'But is that a risk we can take?'

'For the moment we have no choice.'

Chapter 27

'This is Ronnie Jansen or RJ to his friends, not that I'm sure he actually has any.' Rupert said as he studied the picture being projected onto the screen in the small conference room.

'Doesn't look like much,' Jenny observed. 'He certainly doesn't look like a mercenary.'

'And what are they supposed to look like?' Rupert asked. 'No, this is one clever son of a bitch. If you ever wanted to start up a real 'A Team' like that TV programme, this guy would be on it. He's even done work for us in the past. Don't underestimate him Jenny.'

'So, what do we know about his recent movements?' she asked as she looked down from the picture on the screen to the file on her lap that contained all the information that MI6 had about the man. It was painfully thin.

'Bugger all. The last time we had direct contact was two years ago. He dropped off the radar after that. It's one of his skills. Of course, we weren't that bothered because as far as we know he's never been a threat. To us that is.'

'Hmm,' Jenny said as she continued to flick through the file. 'So he's ex South African Special Forces and jumped ship when apartheid finished. Did he think they would be out to get him? Was he involved in any of the repressive stuff? There's nothing here.'

'We just don't know but probably. These guys were all involved one way or another. But actually, my guess is that he just didn't want to be part of the new system. He wasn't the only one. He likes money that's for sure but I suspect it's also the excitement. Many mercenaries are like that. Very few of them die in bed. I met him once you know.'

'Oh, what was he like?'

'Quite a nice guy on the surface. But despite that, I got the impression that he wasn't someone to trifle with. Many SF guys are like that. Nice as pie until you cross them, then watch out.'

'So after ninety three, he seems to surface occasionally and then disappears only to reappear somewhere completely different.'

'That's about it. If he's involved in something in Iraq, I have no idea how we're going to find out.'

Just then the door opened and two more men came in. 'Jenny this is Pete and Joe, they work in different divisions to ours. They may be able to help and they know and agree with what we are doing.'

Jenny stood and shook the men's hands. Rupert was amused by their predictable reaction but didn't let it distract him. 'Ok, now we're all here. Pete here was RJ's handler when he did a small job for us. And before either of you two ask, you really don't need to know the details. Joe is one of our experts on chemical weapons amongst other things.'

Rupert then went on to tell the two newcomers the events of the previous days. When he got to the part about how Jenny had obtained the information he could see the cogs whirring in both men's brains but ploughed on. He then played them the recording that Jenny had made. The two men listened to the last part several times.

Joe spoke first. 'I agree with your assessment. That sounds like he's saying Sarin to me. If what you're saying is that it's going to be taken into Iraq, presumably to be discovered during the invasion, then that fits in quite well.'

'Oh, why's that?' Rupert asked.

'Sarin is quite easy to make and Saddam has used it before so presumably, he has had some sort of production facility in the past. Also, we happen to know that Israel keeps some stocks of it even though their public line is that they have never had chemical weapons. If this mercenary chap is up to what you suspect then starting from Israel makes total sense. Especially, as you have a clear American connection.' Joe explained.

Rupert turned to Pete. 'So do we have anything on what he did or where he went after our little job?'

'I've been looking into that this morning after you asked, 'Pete replied. I'm sorry but the answer is no. But there's one thing that might help. This guy tends to do a job and rest up for a while. If we assume that he did something like that after he left us then whatever he's up to and whoever he's working for is his next task. Not only that but he must have taken on the job much faster than normal. I expect the pay check was pretty substantial to get him to do so. It might be easier to trace him especially if we assume he's working for the Americans in some way.'

'I'm not sure that really gets us anywhere I'm afraid,' Rupert said. 'We need to know what his plans are and we've very little time. If we could just get some detail then maybe we could get a warning to our people on the ground. How deadly is Sarin Joe?'

'It's a liquid nerve agent. Although stored as a liquid, when released it easily turns into a gas. Inhale even a small quantity and you're dead in ten minutes or less. Even if you get a non-lethal dose, you'll probably have irreversible neurological damage. Saddam used it in his war with Iraq and on his own people, the Kurds in Halabja where he murdered over five thousand. You can see why it's exactly the right thing to try and hang him with. Finding it will justify just about anything the Yanks do once they are in control.'

'Oh God, this just gets worse and worse,' Rupert said wearily.

Jenny who had already looked up Sarin the previous night had been following another chain of thought. 'Rupert, Pete, if you wanted to recruit this RJ chap, how would you go about it?'

'Why do you ask Jenny?' Rupert asked.

'Bear with me, it's not like you have his telephone number is it?'

'Word of mouth normally.' Pete replied. 'In our case, we maintain a data base of contacts of all sorts. We put the word out that we wanted to meet and he contacted us. It takes time but as I said before, he doesn't normally do rush jobs anyway.'

'Do we know if he's ever worked for the US before this?' Jenny asked.

'Pretty sure he hasn't but what's that got to do with anything?' Pete asked.

'What if someone here in MI6 provided an introduction after he finished working for us? It would be logical would it not, especially as Pete says it all must have happened so fast?'

'Don't look at me,' Pete said. 'I was just his handler.'

'So how many people actually knew we were employing him?' Jenny asked.

Rupert spoke. 'Myself as head of department and Pete obviously. The Director authorised the mission. Then there was his task manager, Ronald Jones who Pete worked for and someone from finance to pay the bills although he probably didn't know much detail. That's it.'

'Then we need to talk to those people don't we?' Jenny asked.

'Bloody hell Jenny are you after my job?' Rupert asked with a grin.

Chapter 28

Life on board HMS Intrepid was frantic. The first priority for the ship's company was damage control. As soon as Jon was sure that the Commander had things in hand, he had headed aft to see what the situation was on the flight deck and vehicle deck immediately below. He tracked down Paul talking to one of the American soldiers by the command truck.

'We seem to have survived Sir,' Paul reported. 'No damage down here and all the aircraft were well secured as well.'

'Casualties?' Jon queried.

'One broken arm and a few bruises it seems,' Paul replied. 'What about the ship?'

'Bloody great chunk taken off the bow but we're in no danger of sinking if that's what you're asking,' Jon replied.

'Never liked bloody ships,' Paul responded. 'The sooner we're ashore the better.'

Jon could only agree and went on to tell Paul about what he had been forced to do on the bridge.

'Bloody Hell Jon, can you actually do that?' Paul asked.

'Bit late, I've already done it but if you have everything on our side of the fence under control I think I'd better go and get some signals sent to sort this whole mess out. Grab Jacob when you can and get me a detailed report on our status.'

So saying, Jon went back to his cabin and started writing. He was interrupted by a knock on the door. It was the Commander.

'Come on in,' Jon said when he saw who it was. 'It's Mark, isn't it?'

'That's me Sir,' he gave a weary smile as he took the seat that Jon had pointed to.

'So, how's the ship?'

'We've managed to back away now Sir and we're watertight. The merchantman says he's not too badly hurt and doesn't need assistance. He's heading off to Kuwait city. I'd like to stand down from Emergency Stations.'

'Not my call Mark. You're in command now,' Jon replied and he saw the look of relief on the Commander's face as he said the words.

'Yes Sir, err, how do we play this?'

'I'm just signalling the CTF, SNOME and Fleet about it now. I'm not going to ask for approval I'll be stating my intentions. Now, what are the chances we can get the ship to our disembarkation point as planned?'

The Commander considered the question for a few seconds. 'MEO says we have full propulsion and should still be good for about fifteen knots so I see no reason why we can't get you off as planned but I think we'll need a dock as soon after that as possible.'

'Good, you know this could be to my advantage. I was worried we might be held up waiting for the go ahead to disembark. It seems fate has made it imperative that we get off as soon as we can.'

'And the Captain Sir? What should we do about him?'

'Good question. I think maybe the Doctor should pay a visit and then we should fly him off back to SNOME's headquarters as soon as possible. I'll leave it to you to arrange but please feel free to use one of my aircraft as you see fit.'

They talked for a few more minutes and then the Commander left and Jon got down to finishing his signal. By breakfast, things were settled as much as they could be. Jon called Paul and Jacob in to discuss things over eggs and bacon.

'Ok guys, SITREP,' Jon said when they were seated. 'I've had acknowledgement of my actions in relieving the ship of her Captain. There will have to be an enquiry into the whole affair but because we're in a real operational environment it will all have to wait until this is over. A new Captain will be coming out soonest to take over. I'm not sure the Commander will be too happy, I got the feeling that he hoped to be confirmed in the position even if only for the short term but obviously our lords and masters think differently. However, it's good news for us as the new man is Brian Pearce.' Jon turned to Jacob. 'He's an old colleague and he was on my team for the last bit of work we did in the UK so Paul knows him well. He's a damned good choice. Now, the really good news. It's been agreed that we get ashore straight away. So plan on disembarking as planned in two days time.'

Jon was surprised to see a frown cross Jacob's face. 'Have you got a problem with that Colonel?' Jon asked.

'Oh no, sorry Sir not at all. It's just that I thought the idea was to wait out at sea until we knew we were needed.'

'Well, that's out of the window now,' Jon said. 'It means we may spend more time in the field but frankly that suits me. We'll be far more reactive if we're set up ashore.'

Just over forty eight hours later and Jon was standing between the two front seats of one of his Sea Kings looking between the two pilots as it made its approach to the airfield at Safwan. Until recently it had been one of the last Iraqi Air Force bases but was now abandoned. Fighting was continuing just to the north but the area had been declared safe and Jon had been authorised to set up his Command Post there. The vehicles had already been offloaded onto the beach at Kuwait Bay and made their way to the border at Um Qasr before turning north to Safwan. Jon had stayed on the ship to let the soldiers get on with their business setting up ashore and also because Brian had arrived that morning and Jon wanted to fill him in on what had been going on.

'I couldn't believe it when I was told about this Pierhead Jump Jon,' Brian said as soon as they were alone.

'Yes, sorry about dragging you away. But something had to be done. It may seem odd but Captain Wright crashing into that merchantman was just the excuse I needed. The man had just about run the ship into the ground by the time I arrived. I'm afraid it won't be an easy task to sort her out. Mind you, the Commander has his head screwed on the right way round. I'm pretty sure you can trust him. How was it all taken back at home?'

'Not sure really as I was given virtually no notice to pack my bags. However, several people did say that they weren't surprised. Wright had a bit of a reputation it appears. The only thing is, he will be back at home telling his side of the story while you're stuck out here for and indeterminate time.'

'I couldn't give a toss Brian as I'm sure you know,' Jon replied. 'I've got a job to do.'

Brian laughed. 'Now why did I think you'd say that? Mind you, this could be one of my shortest commands ever. Judging by what I've seen of the damage already I wouldn't be at all surprised if we never even make it back to Blighty. She was due for the scrapheap anyway.'

'Just keep her going for the time it takes for me to get the job done Brian. I can't think of anyone else I would rather have to cover my arse.'

'Nothing new there then,' Brian said with a laugh. 'Mind you I wonder what your job really is.'

'You and me both.'

So now he was independent. The helicopter slowed for the approach and Jon could already see that the tents were up and a neat line of helicopters were parked down one of the disused runways. 'That's the first thing that needs changing,' he thought to himself. It might look pretty but made a really inviting target for anyone with bad intent. He wondered whether it was the Colonel's idea, he wouldn't be surprised.

The Sea King landed and as soon as the rotors wound down, Jon opened the small personnel door and lowered the steps. Jacob and Paul were there to greet him.

Jon took a breath of desert air. He hadn't realised just how hot it was ashore. The ship had been far from cool but this was like walking into a furnace. He could feel the sweat start immediately.

'Afternoon Sir,' Jacob said. 'Welcome, we're just about set up. Communications are up and running and we'll have the accommodation sorted out by night fall.'

'Excellent and which is the tent with air conditioning?' Jon asked as he started walking towards them.

'Sorry Sir,' Paul said. 'But at least we can get out of this sun,'

Jacob steered Jon towards a large tent that had been erected against the back of the main command truck which contained the radio equipment. It wasn't any cooler inside but as Paul had said, being out of the burning sun was a slight improvement.

'What's the plan for the day?' Jon asked the two men.

Jacob answered. 'We need to review the latest Intel and update initial priorities. We have the list that we produced back in the UK and the ship but we've just got the latest real time picture. I think you'll see that we have an excellent candidate already.'

Chapter 29

'So, what progress have we made?' Rupert asked as he poured Jenny a glass of red wine. They had taken to using his house as their ad hoc headquarters as they considered that nowhere even in the main building was totally secure now.

'Well, you say the Director is above board and from what I've heard of his attitude to the whole situation that makes sense.' Jenny replied.

'Yes, I've known him for far too long,' Rupert said. 'If he's in this then we might as well all just go home.'

'Oh, like we are now,' Gina said with a grin.

'Good point.' Rupert said laughing. 'Of course, we can't rule anyone out but I'd stake my reputation on him knowing nothing about this.'

'Well, I checked with finance,' Jenny said. 'The chap who did the money for that operation left MI6 a few weeks later. There's no way he could have been involved in recruiting this mercenary. He went abroad and is working in South America. Seems he met a girl from somewhere in Chile and followed her there.'

'So that leaves me, Pete and his manager Ronald Jones. Dare I suggest we rule me out of this?' Rupert asked with a wry grin.

'I think we can safely do that,' Gina said. 'So that leaves two.'

Jenny looked up from some notes she had on her lap. 'Pete is highly unlikely. He could be double bluffing of course, as he was called into the situation cold. However, in my opinion he's just too far down the organisation to have the clout. He's just a worker bee.'

'Agreed,' said Rupert. 'And that makes Mister Jones our prime suspect. I pulled his service record today. There are two things that might point the finger at him. Firstly, his wife is American not that she's ever had anything to do with their intelligence services that we know about. Secondly, she is very much an Evangelical Christian. He's never intimated to me that he has similar views and I've worked with him over the years but these things do tend to rub off.'

'Sorry Rupert but why should religion have anything to do with this?' Gina asked.

'Remember what the US President said a while ago. 'God had told me to do this' or words to that effect. Many Americans, particularly the fundamental Christians see this as a holy crusade. It's not just the Muslims who have Jihads you know.'

'Sound like the most promising candidate then,' Jenny said. 'I always thought he would be. The question then is what do we do about it?'

'Well, one thing you're not trying again is your latest interrogation skills young lady,' Rupert said. 'No, we need something to hang him with but I'm buggered if I can see what and let's face it we're running out of time fast.'

'I'm not actually sure we need to. Can I change the subject for a moment?' Jenny asked. 'I had a thought today and would like to run it past you.'

'Go on,' Rupert said. 'Any ideas will be gratefully received.'

'Alright, I wonder whether we've been looking at some of this the wrong way round,' she said. 'Look, we are pretty sure that someone has commissioned a mercenary team to ensure that some evidence of WMDs are found. Now, why would they do that?'

Her question was met with silence for a few seconds and then Rupert answered. 'As insurance to ensure that they can justify the whole bloody mess. Come on, we've been over that a hundred times before.'

'Yes we have. But surely it means that they already know that there aren't actually any of these bloody things in the country, otherwise why take the risk of planting them?' Jenny replied. 'After all that's what the UN Inspectors are finding out. Look, turn this around. Suppose you were planning this. Remember, it must have all started several years ago. One of the first things you would want to know was the status of Saddam's weapon stocks, otherwise you wouldn't know how to design your strategy. With me so far?'

'Hmm, I think I know where this is going,' Rupert said. 'But keep going.'

'You can only do so much from outside. There seem to be pretty good estimates on how much Saddam used in the Iran war. And presumably there are some figures of how many chemicals were imported into the country. But you could never be sure so they must have commissioned someone to go in and do a hands on investigation. Give that person enough money to grease the right palms and he would have been able to achieve a great deal. I don't think whoever is behind this is short of cash. And there's more. Suppose he discovered that the stocks were just about all used up. He would need to locate candidate sites for the subsequent planting of evidence.'

Rupert sat back with a reflective look on his face as he thought through the logic. 'Ronald Jones worked in the Middle Eastern section after he left my team. I don't know the details but he was out of the country somewhere. 'If we assume that whoever is behind this has top level government approval from both sides of the Atlantic, even if it's been kept under the radar, then presumably there is a report about it somewhere. A formal report.'

'I'm ahead of you,' Gina said. 'When I worked as your secretary, I regularly had to access very sensitive material. If such a report exists it won't be on any computer or hard drive. Paper copies would have been used and all of them destroyed except for one master and that would be in the secure archive.'

'That's assuming that our procedures were used in the first place,' Rupert said. 'But I suppose we should try to find out.'

'How do I get in there Gina?' Jenny asked with her eyes lighting up.

'You don't, not without very high level approval anyway,' Rupert said. 'And that approval will be for one specific document and you will be escorted the whole time. There are two staff down there and they only allow one person in at a time. And before you ask, I am senior enough to authorise you but as I'm not aware of any such report I can hardly arrange for you to see it.'

'I take it the staff are male?' Jenny asked.

Gina answered. 'Yes, they've been there for years.'

Jenny laughed. 'Rupert, you get me in and then I might just come over all blonde. Come on, it's worth a try.'

The next morning Jenny dressed carefully. Nothing outrageous, just a higher hemline than usual, a blouse more see through than usual and some carefully applied make up. Rupert lifted one eyebrow when he saw her come into his office but refrained from saying anything.

He handed her a written memorandum, a special swipe card and solid looking briefcase. 'The report I want you to sign out for me is

Conspiracy

this one.' He indicated the Memo. 'It's on operation 'Dark Sword' you don't need to know what it's about. Show the Memo to the archivist and use the card to access the Middle Eastern section. When you've got the report, you place it in the brief case and lock it. Only I can unlock it. The reverse procedure is used to return it. All clear?'

She nodded. 'Assuming I can actually get some time alone, do you have any ideas on where to look?'

'Reports of this sort are fairly rare. As far as I know, the Middle Eastern section probably has no more than a dozen or more and they should be in date order. If we say no earlier than ninety eight and certainly no later than two thousand then you should have a very limited choice. The report I've actually authorised you to get is from that period.'

'Right, I'll be off then.'

'Jenny, be careful please. If this goes wrong your career could be over.'

She looked back at Rupert. 'There are far more things at stake than my career but don't worry, I'll be very careful.'

Ten minutes later and she was several floors underground standing before a heavily armoured door. Next to it was a telephone receiver. As she lifted it she saw the red light on the camera above the door come on.

'Miss Brooker for document retrieval for Mister Thomas,' she said into the handset in her very blonde voice.

There was a buzzing sound and then the door opened. A middle aged man held it open for her and she walked past making sure to sway her hips just a little more than usual.

Once inside, she was greeted by another man of similar age. They both looked at her as though she had come from another planet. Pretending not to notice, she handed the Memo to the man who had let her in.

'This is what I've come for,' she said with a massive smile. 'I'm new here, my name is Jenny what are your names?'

She discovered that the older man was Rob and the slightly younger but much fatter man was Brian. She kept eye contact with both of them as much as possible.

Twenty minutes later, she was back in Rupert's office. 'Here you are. There's your report and I accidentally scooped up another one.

Conspiracy

There were only two in our time period and they were right next to each other. My escort was too busy staring at my bum as I stood on tip toe to get them.'

Rupert nodded and quickly opened the brief case. He ignored the one he had ordered and made no attempt to even read the other, except to confirm that it looked to be what they wanted. Reaching into his desk he pulled out one of the new digital cameras that were appearing everywhere and started photographing the five pages inside. In a matter of a few minutes he had finished and put both files back into the briefcase.

'Be careful, the guys down there have a master unlock code for all the briefcases so you might have to watch it to make sure they don't see you have two reports when you take them out,' he said.

'They won't see anything trust me,' Jenny said with a laugh. 'Meet at your place for lunch?'

The two of them met again at Rupert's house at midday. Gina took the camera straight away and ran the pictures off on their printer. 'You do realise we could go to prison for doing this?' She said.

'Bit late for that now dear,' Rupert said. 'Let's see what we've got.'

He read the first sheet in silence and handed it to Jenny who did the same in turn for Gina. When they had all digested the contents, Rupert spoke first. 'Well, our friend Jones was the author. That sort of ties in with our suspicions that he also recruited the mercenary. Operation Alchemy, seems an odd title though.'

'No, I get it,' Jenny replied. 'Alchemy is the original science of chemistry and originated in Arabia. I can see why it was chosen. But this is exactly what we were looking for. An appraisal of the state of Iraq's weapon stocks as of the year two thousand, conclusions that there almost certainly weren't any and a list of potential sites. How does the author phrase it 'where they would be likely to be discovered in future.'

'Yes Jenny and we can get that list out to Jon so as a minimum he will know where to look. There are only ten locations and we already know about most of them. I think I'll be having a few words with Mister Jones in the very near future but frankly I don't hold out much hope for any results. But there's much more to this. Did you look at the original distribution of the report? Do you realise who must be aware of the contents?'

'Oh, sorry, I only glanced at it. Hang on,' she grabbed the report and looked at the back page where there was a small list of names. 'Oh shit. Oh my God. What a shame we didn't have this only a matter of days ago. But that means the whole thing was a lie.'

'But we knew that,' Rupert said.

'Yes but now we can prove it,' Jenny said with determination.

Chapter 30

RJ ground his teeth in frustration. 'We're getting nowhere,' he muttered to himself. He had spent most of the evening on the telephone. Not one number that he called actually answered. When the mechanic called them over to look at the little television that he kept at the back of his office he understood why. As usual, the local TV companies were a waste of time, merely pumping out propaganda or a picture of Saddam Hussein with martial music in the background. However, the mechanic's set was tuned to a satellite receiver and they could get both Al Jazeera and CNN. The picture from those stations told a very different picture.

'Fuck me, he lost just about all his command and control in the first twenty four hours,' Pieter said with awe in his voice. 'No wonder there's no one on the telephone. The mother of all battles looks more like the mother of all massacres.'

'Is there any way we can get this bloody tanker another two hundred kilometres Pieter?' RJ asked.

'Not without a radiator, absolutely not.' Pieter said. 'And who knows just how long it will be before the whole country is overrun and surrenders? We may be quite far north at the moment but we both know how quickly things can develop. It's getting critical my friend.'

'What we need is another tractor unit. Something to replace the useless one.'

'And where would we get one of those?'

'How about from those sods who took the other one?' RJ replied with a grin. 'Once they find it hasn't fuel in it what do you think they will do?'

'Yes but where will that be? You can bet your bottom dollar that they will be taking part in this war. The Kurds have a lot of scores to settle. It's probably why they attacked us in the first place.'

'Well, my thinking is that those cars they were driving would need topping up so they probably didn't go that far before they realised it was of no use to them. Look, we borrow the mechanic's Land Cruiser and go back up to the main route. If we can't find the tanker or something else suitable we reach a decision point. From there we can turn west and head out of this mess or if there's time we can still finish our job.'

'And if we bug out, we can still initiate the contingency before we go.' Pieter said.

'What? And a kill a few thousand innocent Iraqis? No we don't do that with the tanker where it is. Sorry but I do have some conscience.' RJ suddenly had a thought. 'What we could do though is alert the right people about where it is and make sure it's discovered at the right time. It won't be as effective as the original idea but will probably keep us in some form of good odour with our bosses.'

'Sounds like a plan and anything is better than sitting here doing fuck all,' Pieter replied. 'Are you going to get hold of your man in Baghdad to turn on the systems at the site?'

'He should be at the site waiting for us now. I'll try and give him a call.'

However, he wasn't too surprised to find that the only landline to the site appeared to be down and being so far out in the desert there were no mobile phone masts. He would just have to hope that Yussef stuck to the script in their absence.

It was close to midnight before they were heading back up the road in the Land Cruiser. The mechanic had initially been reluctant to let them use it but RJ solved the problem by simply giving the man more money than it was remotely worth and also promising to return it.

It didn't take long to rejoin the main Route 1 and the traffic was heavy on the opposite side of the road.

'Rat's leaving the sinking ship.' Pieter observed at the constant stream of traffic heading west towards Jordan and Syria. 'We seem to be the only ones heading east.'

'Are you surprised?' RJ asked.

'No, not really. But I'm not sure this is going to work. They must have had an overland route away from here. Stick to Route 1 and you end up in Baghdad which is hardly where they came from.'

'I've thought of that. We should be able to spot the place where they crashed the tanker. There should still be a wrecked car on the side of the road. My guess is that their turn off won't be far from there and it will have to be a noticeable track for a large truck to be able to use it. Not only that, it will almost certainly be heading north.

Conspiracy

So we look to the left as we travel along. There won't be that many suitable places.'

Sure enough, a few minutes later they saw the remains of the partially crushed car. RJ slowed down. In the dark it would be much harder to spot a track turning off the main tarmac road but they didn't have the luxury of waiting until daylight.

Suddenly, Pieter spotted something. 'Look there, the main road surface is flush with the sand and if that's not vehicle tracks then I don't know what is.'

RJ braked hard and looked where Pieter was pointing. 'Agreed, we have to give it a try. We've got enough fuel to go about fifty miles before we have to turn back and we've plenty of water. Let's see what we can find.'

The track consisted of reasonably well packed sand and they made steady progress. Even so, the horizon was starting to get light before they had made even half their agreed distance. Pieter had taken over the driving but both men were having trouble keeping their eyes open. It had been a long day. Suddenly and with no warning, the whole vehicle shuddered and a deafening screaming roar filled the air. Over their heads two dark shapes with flames spitting out behind them shot past them and into the distance. Both men reacted instinctively. Pieter slammed on the brakes and jumped out one side while RJ did the same on his side. They both ran away from the car and flung themselves flat.

It was only a few seconds later that it was clear that the two jets were not using them as targets.

'All clear,' RJ shouted to his friend. They both stood and looked ahead where the two aircraft had disappeared. Without warning, there was a distant crump and the silhouette of the two jets appeared in the distance as they pulled up into a vertical climb and then headed off to the east.

'F16's,' Pieter announced. 'Must have been on a morning patrol and seen something. Shall we go and see what it was?'

'Might as well but I've got a bad feeling about this,' RJ replied.

With it now getting quite light it didn't take them much time at all to get to where the jets had made their attack. Pieter pulled up beside the wreck of some sort of large vehicle. It was completely burnt out and still smouldering. It was also very hard to make out what it had been. Much of it was spread out over quite a distance. They got out of the Land Cruiser and carefully made their way towards it.

'Why waste a bomb on something way out here?' Pieter asked. 'It was hardly a threat.'

'Who knows, maybe they were just bored. You know what the Yank military are like. Or maybe their Kurdish friends told them about it.'

'Oh fuck, you could be right.' Pieter responded as he walked over to what had clearly been a door. He pulled it up and turned it over. There were traces of blue paint over green and a company logo could just be made out. 'Well I guess there's no point in looking for the tractor unit or even the bloody radiator then.'

RJ laughed mirthlessly. 'Not one that we could use anyway. Right, its decision time my friend. We can't move our tanker, not in the next few days anyway and there's no point going to the site without it. So, we either go back to the garage and wait for the Americans to arrive which could be dangerous or we bug out now.'

Pieter nodded. 'Your call but how long do you think it will take the locals to decide to help themselves to the contents of the tanker and then find it's not what they think? Fuck knows what they will do then but if they damage it badly it could really screw things up. I don't think our employer would be too happy with that.'

'Agreed,' RJ said. 'The Americans will find the facility empty which will appear odd at first but then we make sure the man on the spot suggests that maybe they've tried to remove the evidence. The only escape route from the Americans would be on the road leading to Route 21 and through Al Kasrah. There they find the tanker which has clearly had an accident whilst trying to make off with the evidence. If we keep a good lookout then we can make ourselves scarce just before they arrive'

'You'd better get on the satellite phone then and pass that on. I just hope that whoever they've got in place is good at his job.'

'Not our problem mate.'

Chapter 31

'The men are all ready for you Sir,' Jacob Sharp reported formally with a salute. Jon saluted back, walked forward and climbed onto the old crate they had found for him so he could address everyone. This was the first time he had had the opportunity to talk to all the people of his command. The last element had arrived that afternoon when they had been joined by a small specialist team of scientists who would be doing the in depth analysis of anything that was found.

'Stand Easy,' Jon called. 'Come on break ranks and come closer I don't want to have to shout.'

The men all shuffled forward until they were clustered closely around the ad hoc podium.

'I'm sorry I haven't had the chance to meet you all yet and it may be that I won't actually get the chance because we are going to start operations tomorrow,' Jon said, as he looked down on the two hundred of so faces looking back up at him. 'Let me first say that although our job is not to fight the enemy I consider it to be the most important one of this war. If these weapons exist it is my absolute resolution that we find them. When I say my job, I really mean yours of course.'

A small ripple of laughter greeted the remark. 'Now, we have military from two nations here and normally we would spend some time fully learning each other's methods and procedures. We don't have time for that unfortunately. As I'm sure you already know, because of our numbers, we are going to operate as three separate Platoons. Two will be national units, the third will be a joint unit because we have enough people who have worked with each other to make that effective. Immediately after this, we will break up into those three groups for detailed briefings. We have a list of places we want to investigate. Some are probably abandoned, some almost certainly are not. In terms of aircraft support, the helicopters will be held as a central resource but each Platoon will get its own vehicles. Operations will be coordinated from here and we have a direct line into the main command. We do not want any blue on blue engagements. For the moment at least, nearly all of our search missions will be behind enemy lines. Gentlemen, this is going to be hot, dirty and possibly quite dangerous work. I won't waste time giving you a pep talk, you are all intelligent enough to understand the risks. You are also intelligent enough to know how important this. Carry on please.'

Jon was about to step down when an American Staff Sergeant called out. 'Before you go Sir, we have something for you.'

Intrigued, Jon stopped as the Sergeant handed him a small cloth badge. He could also see quite a few grinning faces surrounding the man. He looked carefully at the badge.

'Sir, we've only been assigned a unit number so far so we thought that an emblem would be fitting, with your permission we would like everyone to wear one.'

'How on earth did you get them made up Sergeant?' Jon asked. 'And who came up with this idea.'

'Ways and means Sir, we were at sea on a large ship for some time waiting. But actually the idea came from one of your marines who served with you some time back. He thought you might like the idea.'

Jon looked again. The badge was circular with a yellow background and a grinning, black skull and crossbones stitched on it. He knew that it was one of the international symbols for chemical weapons but it was what was stitched underneath that really caught his eye. 'Jons Hunters' was stitched below the symbol. He looked at the Sergeant and round at the grinning men. This sort of thing was always good for moral and helping generate team spirit. He knew he couldn't really object. 'Great idea Sergeant, although I'll have to talk to the author about the use of apostrophes some time.'

'He said you would say that Sir.' The Sergeant said with a laugh.

'Who is this Marine? He must be here.' Jon asked looking around.

Suddenly, a Royal Marine Corporal was thrust forward. Jon recognised him immediately. 'Corporal Jenkins, you were in my Marine detachment in Formidable.'

The young Marine was clearly surprised that not only did Jon recognise him but also remembered his name. 'Yes Sir, during a certain bust up in Africa. Is the badge alright?'

Conspiracy

Jon frowned for a moment. 'Well, there are certain combinations of my name that could have been far worse. No, I think it's just the sort of thing we need. Well done.'

Two hours later, Jon was sitting in the large command tent with a much smaller audience. Jacob Sharp had centre stage and was giving an overview of their first operation. Attending were the three Platoon commanders and their immediate staff. Once again Jon was feeling like a fish out of water. Commanding a warship put him in the centre of the action. Here he was just a supernumerary although he had made it clear that once a site was declared safe from enemy action, he had every intention of being present for the searches.

'Gentlemen, our first objective,' Colonel Sharp declared as a white screen at the rear of the tent illuminated with a large aerial photograph. It showed a lake and at the bottom a complex of buildings. 'This is the al Qadisiyah Research Centre, which as you can see is along the shore of the same named reservoir. It's not actually a lake. There is a large dam further north which will be subject to a concurrent attack. Intelligence suggests that the site may actually be a chemical weapons factory. There are clear signs of activity including infra-red satellite pictures of what seems to be a large air conditioning plant which has been running for some time. All three Platoons are going to be involved. We will use our own MH6Bs for fire suppression but we have the facility to call in air support if we need it. This will probably be A10s. I want B and C Platoons to be away from here by ten hundred tonight in the Humvees. A Platoon will fly later in the Sea Kings. The two 109s will go ahead and do a last minute reconnaissance. A Platoon will conduct the assault. B and C will provide cover and back up from the north and the south. Any questions so far?'

There were none and so the Colonel handed over to one of his operations staff and the next hour was spent going over everything from communications to medical evacuation plans. When it was over, Colonel Sharp stood again. Jon had a good idea what he was about to do as he had been warned that preaching and a final prayer was his trade mark. Jon had no intention of letting him do either.

'That's alright Colonel, I'll finish up,' he announced loudly.

With an angry frown, the Colonel re-took his seat.

'That's the briefing everyone,' he said looking hard at the seated audience. 'But as we all know, a plan is only as good as the first few moments of battle and I want you all to be in no doubt that this will be a fight. As you've been told there are no obvious military units in place but we know that it is occupied. We also know that other units have found the fighting hard. The Iraqis are not just running away. They may have lost much of their command and control but they still have guns and grenades. I don't want any casualties. Our mission is not to take ground or fight pitched battles. We need to find these weapons, is that clear?'

There were nods all around the tent. 'Right go and get yourselves ready and good luck.'

After the tent had emptied Colonel Sharp came up to Jon. 'I was going to lead us all in prayer at the end Sir. We missed the chance,' he said in an angry tone.

Jon decided that this was the time to draw a line in the sand on the issue. 'Colonel, you've made it quite clear by your actions and remarks that you are a devout Christian. Good for you. I am not. Moreover, I have no intention of entering any sort of religious debate with you. This is my command and I am more than happy to let people have their own beliefs. What I am not happy to do is let one faction try to impose their beliefs on others. Is that absolutely clear?'

The Colonel actually took a step back at the vehemence in Jon's voice but it was clear he wasn't just going to give up. 'Sir, we are both from Christian countries. It is our duty to look after the men physically and spiritually.'

'Oh for fuck's sake Colonel. No, it isn't.' Jon was having to work really hard to keep his rising temper in check. 'Do you know that we have at least ten practicing Muslims in this force as well as two Hindus and at least twenty declared atheists?' He could see from the man's expression that he didn't. 'I took the time to review everyone's personnel files once I was given this job. Maybe you should do so as well. That is an end to it.' Before the Colonel could speak Jon turned and walked out.

Colonel Sharp stood in the tent in rising fury. He knew that this was as much a religious crusade as a simple war. He had been warned about the British Commodore. Apparently, his wife had died several years earlier and his girlfriend had been killed by terrorists only months ago. You would have thought that would have turned any man towards God, not away. Up until now he had been impressed by the man's approach to the operation. He had even started to admire him, especially after the way he had acted so decisively when the Intrepid had collided with the merchantman. Doing what he might have to do had been starting to prick his conscience. But if Hunt had turned away from the Lord then maybe it would all be a little easier.

Chapter 32

'Come in Ronald,' Rupert said to the knock on the door. He knew who it was because his secretary had buzzed him that Jones was on the way up.

Ronald Jones came in. He had a swagger to his walk. Rupert had always admired how confident he seemed. It was in contrast to his appearance which made him look like a down at heel bank clerk. He had short red hair, now showing signs of grey and always wore tortoiseshell glasses which Rupert detested, probably because they always reminded him of a rather nasty teacher at school. Rupert was still in two minds about whether they should let sleeping dogs lie in this matter but the chance to discover something more could not be ignored.

'Grab a seat,' Rupert said and indicated one on the other side of the desk. 'How are things? I haven't seen much of you after we finished that last little operation.'

'Fine Rupert, as you know I got a promotion and moved to another section. Since then I've been stuck behind a desk even if I did get some time abroad. There comes a time when they don't like to let you out to play on the streets anymore.'

Rupert laughed in agreement. 'Tell me about it. Now, I've been wondering if you can help me out in a little matter.'

'Oh, what would that be?' Ronald asked, clearly not aware of the ton of bricks that was about to land on him.

'Where do I start? Firstly, when we finished with a certain mercenary, as you said, you moved departments. Care to tell me where you deployed to?'

'Yes, I spent some time at the Embassy in Iraq before coming home for good.' He replied. 'But I'm sure you knew that. It was no secret.'

'No it wasn't but can you tell me of your extracurricular activities while you were there?'

'Sorry Rupert, that is on a restricted codeword list and you're not on it.' Ronald was now looking puzzled.

'Ah but I am now and the word is Alchemy.' Rupert looked hard at Ronald as he said the word. He wasn't surprised to see him flinch slightly although he covered it up well.

'You'll have to tell me something more than that Rupert. Just knowing a codeword doesn't prove that I can divulge anything to you. You know that.'

'No, of course, you're right Ronald. And to be honest I don't have anything to show you. However, maybe you can tell me why I shouldn't have you arrested for treason?' This time Rupert's words definitely struck home.

'What the hell are you talking about Rupert?' Ronald asked in an agitated voice.

'Let's look at what this department was asked to do last year shall we?' Rupert replied. 'We spent months producing a dossier for the government detailing our assessment of Iraq's Chemical and Biological weapons programme. The conclusions of that report, that the government are now waging war over, were that there were significant Weapons of Mass Destruction in the country and not only that but they were ready for immediate use. Can you tell me how you can square that with a report that you compiled based on an extensive in-country study, which concluded that there were no weapons at all?'

Ronald almost squirmed in his seat. 'That's above my pay grade Rupert. I simply did a job and filed a report.'

'And didn't see fit to raise it when you knew what was going on only a year later? And before you say anything else, like that it was your boss's responsibility to do that. I've checked and he has no knowledge of operation Alchemy. You were meant to be in Iraq doing routine liaison work in the Embassy nothing more. So, who the fuck were you working for?'

'I can't tell you that Rupert,' Ronald was sounding more confident now. 'You say you've read the report then you know who it went to. You might want to consider that before accusing me of treason. I would also like to know how you got to know about it.'

Rupert knew he had a valid point but wasn't going to let go that easily. 'That, to use your own words is well above your pay grade. But I'm curious. In that case why did you file a report in the MI6 secure archive?'

Ronald looked embarrassed by the question. 'Because that's standard procedure. To get it to the recipients I needed to go through departmental channels and had no choice. Although only a few people were cleared to read it, the system knew it was there.'

'You couldn't have simply put a blank folder into the archive?'

'I did think of that but by then it was too late. Look, I've done nothing wrong. Just because you weren't in the loop is not my concern.'

'Which takes me back to why you said nothing while we were working on that dodgy dossier. So it still begs the question who exactly you were working for? It would seem to me that it was someone outside MI6 otherwise it would have come to light.' Rupert said staring hard into the man's eyes.

Ronald was clearly going to dig his toes in. 'Sorry, I can't tell you. Surely you must understand that?'

'Very well Ronald. Let me make myself very clear. I now have a copy of the report which is secure and off these premises. You are quite at liberty to report me for doing that but then I would have to make its contents public and what reaction do you think that would generate? Your career would be over for a start. Imagine if the press heard.' Rupert didn't finish the sentence, he didn't need to. 'I suggest I would probably be in the shit but it would be nothing compared to what would happen to you.'

'So what are you going to do now?' Ronald asked tensely.

'Nothing Ronald, the war is underway and nothing can stop that. Of course, if your report is correct then they're not going to find anything and there will be egg on a lot of people's faces.' As he said the words, Rupert studied the man's face very carefully. Was that a flash of smugness just for a second?

'In that case, this interview is over,' Ronald stood and walked out without another word.

As soon as the door closed Rupert grabbed his phone. 'Go,' was all he said.

Jenny had stationed herself by the main entrance but well off to one side. After receiving the call from Rupert she didn't have long to wait. Ronald Jones strode out of the building with a purposeful step. She slotted in behind him, taking care to maintain a discreet distance. Ronald turned left and headed off down the south bank towards Westminster Bridge. At one point he stopped and took out his mobile phone. He didn't speak into it, merely stabbed at the keyboard for a few seconds before carrying on. There was nowhere for her to stop and take cover so she stood on the side of the road looking at the traffic and was forced to carry on with crossing over, even if it was definitely not what she wanted to do. The road wasn't too wide and she was able to keep her quarry in sight. Sure enough, he turned across the bridge towards Westminster. The bridge was crowded with the usual gaggle of tourists and she had to fight for a few minutes to clear a chattering crowd of Japanese schoolgirls. Once clear, she spotted him crossing the road and turning right down the north bank towards Blackfriars. Luckily the pedestrian crossing lights stayed in her favour but then it meant she was getting too close. She forced herself to stop and look at the water taxi on the river below her. She pretended to study the timetable on the post at the top of the steps while keeping a look sideways for her quarry. With panic rising, she realised he was nowhere in sight. The Ministry of Defence Building loomed over the pavement completely blocking any route away from the road. Where the hell was he? In desperation, she ran along the pavement but within minutes she had lost him. She wondered if he had known she was there all the time. Whatever he had done, it made her realise that she was still an amateur at this sort of thing. In chagrin, she pulled out her phone to call Rupert and tell him what had happened.

Two hours later Rupert called her into his office. Seated there were Pete and Joe. She raised an eyebrow in query.

'Jenny grab a seat. I've an apology to make,' Rupert said, looking far from apologetic as he made the statement. 'Look, you've not done any field craft Jenny and if I had warned you, you might have hammed it up, sorry.'

The tumblers clicked into place. 'You used me as a stalking horse. And I take it these two carried on with the real surveillance?'

'Yup sorry but we had little time and not many people to work with.'

'So how did he vanish like that?' she asked in a slightly annoyed tone even though she recognised the validity of Rupert's tactic.

Pete spoke. 'Simple, he went into the back entrance of the MOD building. You probably don't know but our passes are valid for there as well.'

'And I loitered outside the main entrance the other side until he came out,' said Joe. 'After that we played leapfrog. He must have been so sure that he had lost his tail that we had no trouble keeping him in view.'

'So, don't keep me in suspense. Where did he go?' she asked.

'The Horse Guards Thistle Hotel just off Northumberland Avenue. They've got a pay phone kiosk in the lobby. He spent about ten minutes on the phone. Then he came back. He thinks there's no way of tracing the call.'

'I've been up to see the Director,' Rupert said. 'And given him the whole story. It was an interesting conversation on many levels but I managed to convince him that our ploy is the best one. However, it now means that Mister Jones will be under twenty four hour covert surveillance. That said, I would be extremely surprised if he tries anything else.'

'I suppose the big question is did Jones fall for it?' Jenny asked.

'I'm pretty sure he did,' Rupert replied. 'When I said to him that his report indicated that nothing will be found, he reacted just for a second. And more importantly I never mentioned the list of potential sites that he put in it. I'm almost certain that he thinks we disregarded that as peripheral information. So he tells his lords and masters that we know he wrote the report but have merely concluded that it is counter to the official line we put out a year later which is why I was so pissed off.'

'So' who did he speak to?' Jenny asked.

Pete answered. 'GCHQ are pretty good. They should be able to trace the destination if not the actual conversation, we're waiting to hear.'

As if on cue, the door opened and Rupert's secretary came in with a buff folder in her hands. She silently handed it to Rupert and left. He opened it and studied it for a while. 'Why am I not surprised? So full circle then, not sure where this leaves us.' he said and handed it to Jenny.

She looked at the typed report. One thing leapt out at her, the name at the bottom. Sir Giles Merriot.

Chapter 33

'Is this tele-conference line secure?' the first man asked.

'Yes, it's not safe to meet face to face at the moment as I'm sure you appreciate.' was the terse reply from the other man thousands of miles away. 'Now, what news?'

'Not that good. Our man in Six was rumbled. The idiot filed a copy of the original report in their archive. It's now come to light.'

Silence greeted the remark for a few seconds. 'What do they intend to do?'

'It would appear that they think it's too late to do anything. At least until the war is over and by then of course, it will be out of date as it will be proved to be wrong. It could be used for some political leverage but shouldn't be an issue for us.'

'Well, my news isn't much better. The South African couldn't get to the site with the tanker. They were involved in a fire fight with some Kurdish separatists and it was damaged so that it can't be driven.'

'Oh God, it wasn't breached was it?'

'No and I know exactly where it is. The South African will make sure it stays in place. Then our man should be able to make use of it. It will look like it was being driven out of the country, trying to escape the fighting.'

'What about him? Is he sticking to the plan?'

'Yes, you know what these fanatics are like. He's been told about the tanker but there's no need to let him know about the report. It should not affect what he has to do. We won't talk again until this is over unless it's a real emergency. Goodbye.'

The screen went blank.

Jon and Brian were relaxing in the Captain's cabin back on board the Intrepid. Jon looked as exhausted as he felt. 'It may be hot on board but's it's got nothing on what it's like ashore.' He said as he gratefully took a large cold lager from his friend and proceeded to down it in one.

'And having to wear that combat gear can't help,' Brian said as he opened another can and offered it to Jon.

'Might make me look like a soldier but I still feel totally inadequate. It was one thing to accept the role from an office in London, it's bloody different out here. Anyway, how's the ship?'

Brian grimaced at the question. 'Well, we're still afloat but I can't see us making the thousands of miles home unless we can spend some serious time in a dry dock. I just can't see Her Majesty paying for that and then scrapping her when we get back. This could be the shortest command of my career.'

'She's done bloody well in her time. Maybe it's time to honourably turn her into razor blades. So, changing the subject, when do we expect this call from our mutual friend at home?'

'In about half an hour. The communications office will give us a call when he's on the line. Sorry I had to drag you back all of a sudden but this was the only way to get a secure line back to the UK. You just don't have the equipment for that in your tents. Anyway, how was your first operation?'

Jon leant back in his chair and looked at the ceiling for a second. 'In some ways it went really well. There was more resistance than we expected on the ground but those little helicopters pack some serious firepower. Unfortunately, one took a round through his engine and in the subsequent landing he did quite a lot of damage to the airframe. We're looking at salvaging it now. I've got Paul on the case. In the end we called in a couple of A10s and they really sorted them out. We found out later that there was a regular army unit stationed there. I'm not sure what that says about our much vaunted intelligence. Still, with our SF guys on the ground and the rest securing the perimeter we had the place under control in about four hours. Of course, it was only then that I was allowed to go and have a look.'

'What? You'd like to have taken part? I thought you said you weren't a soldier.' Brian asked.

'Maybe but they are my men and I don't like sending people into harm's way when I'm miles away from what's going on.' Jon said with feeling.

'Spoken like a true naval officer,' Brian laughed. 'We do normally fight as one company, don't we. So what did you find?'

'Nothing, nada, zilch, absolutely bugger all. The place was as clean as a whistle. It was one of the places the UN Inspectors hadn't managed to get to and we had high hopes. Or maybe I should say my

Colonel had high hopes. Frankly, I hope we never find anything as you well know. That said, the technical boffins are still looking. You never know there might be something hidden but it's looking extremely unlikely.'

'So scratch one from the list. How many more to go?'

'Good question. We now have ten likely sites but intelligence keeps coming in. The boys are going to be very busy over the next few weeks. This first operation was always going to be the biggest, purely because of the size of the real estate. After this, we will be going in at Platoon level. At least that's the current plan. And on top of that, if the regular troops stumble across something unexpected we will be supplying the experts to go and assess it.'

'So you'll be ashore for some time then?' Brian asked.

'How long is a piece of string? The main attack seems to be progressing pretty well. Most people reckon Baghdad will fall in a matter of weeks. Then who knows, maybe the rest of the country will just throw in the towel. We'll just have to wait and see.'

Just then a young Lieutenant put his head around the door. 'London on the secure line Sirs, if you want to come down to the communications office.'

He led Jon and Brian down a couple of decks and into the large space full of radio equipment. Off to one side was a small private office. Inside was a desk and a large old fashioned looking Bakelite handset and a speaker system.

'I'll leave you to it Sir,' the Lieutenant said. 'Just use it like a regular telephone but it's fully encrypted for UK only traffic. If you put the handset in that cradle you can use it as a speaker phone.'

Jon nodded and Brian closed the door. Jon put the handset in the cradle. 'Rupert this is Jon, I've got Brian with me and we are secure, over.'

Rupert's voice immediately responded. 'Good morning Jon, I've got Jenny with me listening in. We've got quite a lot to talk to you about.'

'That's fine Rupert,' Jon replied. 'We're listening.'

'Ok, well since we last spoke quite a lot has happened. We've got Jenny to thank for much of it. You can have the full debrief on that some other time.'

Jon looked at Brian with a raised eyebrow. There had definitely been a humorous note to Rupert's voice.

'Firstly and most importantly we are pretty sure that a quantity of Sarin has been taken into the country. We're not exactly sure when but funnily enough we think we know who's doing it. It's a South African mercenary who we know quite well from previous experience. What I would say is that if you come across him tread very carefully. He's extremely dangerous. We don't know what method they are using but we're pretty sure the route is from Israel and Jordan. It will have to be a large vehicle or even several but that's about it.'

'Understood Rupert,' Jon said. 'But unless you can narrow that down then locating him will be an almost impossible task.'

'Yeah, we realise that but at least you now know that our suspicions were correct and hey, you never know, something might come up. For one thing, if it's in a large vehicle, the roads in Iraq are few and far between.'

'Good point, anything else?' Jon asked.

'Oh yes. We discovered that an operation was conducted a few years ago to see if Saddam really did have any WMDs and it concluded that he probably didn't. We think it was this report that forced these people, whoever they are, to decide to bus some in. I've managed to get a copy of the report and it's in very safe keeping. It's too late to use it now that the war has started, shame we didn't get it a few weeks back. Leaking that to the press would have caused chaos, it could even have stopped this war in its tracks. Anyway, it also lists a number of sites that might make good places to find chemical weapons. Do you have a pen to hand?'

Brian opened a desk drawer and pulled out a signal pad. He turned it over so he had a blank side to write on, pulled out a biro and nodded to Jon.

'My secretary, Brian Pearce is poised and ready Rupert,' Jon replied.

Rupert read out a list of place names and Brian carefully wrote them down. When he had finished, Rupert continued, 'now one point about that list Jon and Brian, is that we're pretty sure the people who are running this show think that we've disregarded it. It might give you an advantage.'

'Hang on Rupert,' Jon said. 'Let me just look carefully at these places, most of them seem familiar. We even took one of them out last night.'

Conspiracy

He perused the names for another minute. 'Right, all of these are on our shopping list already except for a couple. I've also got a few more from recent intelligence. However, one in particular has caught my eye. This place Jurf Sakhar was discounted early on. It was known as one of the sites where Sarin and other nasties were produced in the eighties. However, it was also a nuclear site and because of that the Israelis bombed it to hell and back. The UN Inspectors were there only nine months ago and gave it a clean bill of health and we took it off the list. Apparently, it was completely wrecked and derelict.'

'Hmm well, its high on this list so maybe it might be worth a little peek at some time. It could be interesting if anyone of your people bring it up.' Rupert said.

'Right, to sum up then. We are now pretty sure that we are being set up to discover something. Which let's face it is exactly what we suspected. However, the key thing now is that we are pretty sure that one of the sites on that list will be the one. What's worse is that it may well contain real quantities of a chemical agent and my problem is that I don't actually want to find anything. Or as a minimum cast doubt on the veracity of anything we do find. Well, at least I'm more prepared.'

'Just be careful Jon,' it was Jenny's voice now. 'This seems to go to the highest level and doing something overt could ruin your career.'

Jon snorted with laughter. 'That my dear girl, is the last thing on my mind at the moment. So is there anything else?'

Rupert replied. 'No, that's about it but Jenny is right. Whoever is orchestrating this has fingers in some very serious pies. We know that government ministers are almost certainly involved and that's on both sides of the Atlantic. For God's sake Jon, take care.'

'Don't I always?' Jon asked.

'No, not that I've ever noticed,' Rupert replied with a chuckle in his tone.

'Fair point, thanks for all your work. I've got to get back to a very sweaty tent now. Keep in touch with Brian if anything else comes up. Bye.' Jon replaced the receiver and closed the connection.

'So, what will you do if you do find anything?' Brian asked.

'Don't think I haven't asked myself that question a thousand times old friend. If there's nothing I can do, then so be it. But give me a chance to screw this up for whoever is behind it all and trust me I will.'

Chapter 34

More time in the desert conditions hadn't seemed to acclimatise Jon very much but at least he was learning to ignore them, which was maybe the same thing. He had taken to having his daily Operations Group meetings an hour after sunset when it was cooler. It was two weeks after his visit to the Intrepid and nearly all the suspect sites had been inspected and nothing at all had been found.

Jon had been in his administration tent and was walking in the cooling air to the operations area when he suddenly heard a strange sound. The old airfield they were based on had been hastily repaired and various other units came and went. A wide variety of aircraft had been using the runway lately but this sounded like no aircraft that Jon recognised. If anything it reminded him of Silverstone and the scream of racing engines. His eye was caught by something in the distance on one of the airfield's perimeter tracks. It suddenly came into focus. A car was being driven at high speed. It was dark green and he had no idea what it was except that it was clearly incredibly fast. Jon caught sight of Paul a few yards away, also looking at the car.

'What the hell is that Paul?' Jon called out.

'If I'm not mistaken, that's one of the new Bentleys, the Continental.' Paul replied. 'It's a supercar they've only just started selling. What the hell it's doing here I've no idea.'

'Well I hope air traffic have cleared whoever it is to use it on the airfield.' Jon replied. 'Can you get on the phone and find out what the hell is going on while we convene for the O Group please?'

'I'm on it,' Paul said with a grin.

Jon continued in deep thought and entered the operations tent. Tonight they were planning on sending C Platoon deep into enemy held territory to the north. The plan was to link up with a Kurdish force south of the city of Mosul who claimed to have some intelligence about stored weapons. The report had come in the previous day. Although sketchy in nature, Jon knew that after Saddam had authorised the use of Sarin on the Kurds in the city of Halabja and over five thousand had been killed, the Kurds had a very personal interest in finding the evidence. The big problem for this one was going to be logistics. The Sea Kings had the range to get there but they would need fuel to return. It was really too far for the smaller helicopters and ground transport. Hopefully, at this meeting, Jon's operations team would have sorted it all out. There were numerous fuelling stations being set up with the advancing allied army and the Kurds were adamant that they had facilities in their main site. Even so, the hope was that they could all top up before arriving at their destination. Without firm assurances over fuel Jon was loath to let the operation go ahead.

The meeting lasted for over an hour and by the end Jon was content that all the risks had been identified and mitigated as much as possible. To draw the briefing to a close he stood up before the assembled officers. 'So gentlemen, to sum up, we leave tomorrow afternoon and it will take about four hours for the Sea Kings to make the trip. All the intelligence points to the target site being abandoned as the satellite imagery shows. Let's just hope our Kurdish friends are as good as their word regarding fuel. As this is not a contested reconnaissance, I intend to come along in one of the Sea Kings, not the least because we are running out of targets to investigate. Any questions?'

There were none and so the tent quickly cleared. As Jon was just flicking through some of the intelligence signals as a final check, Paul came in.' Ah, there you are Jon. I'm afraid you are going to have to put your Base Commander's hat on for this one.'

'Oh what now? You know I shouldn't have accepted that role, it's been a complete pain in the arse.' Jon had been talked into the duty as his outfit was the only resident unit on the field and he was the senior officer.

'That car we saw. Firstly, air traffic are really pissed. The first they saw of it was about the same time we did. Secondly, it was looted from the palace down the road.' Paul explained.

'But I thought that palace had been worked over.' Jon said. 'It was used by one of his sons wasn't it?'

'Yes and we all thought the place was wrecked. I'll let the two culprits explain.' Paul said and went over to the tent flap. 'Right, you two in here.'

Two sheepish looking Royal Marines entered. Jon recognised them immediately. One was Corporal Jenkins who was responsible for the team badges that they were all now wearing and the other,

Marine Brown, was another of the British contingent. They stood smartly to attention in front of Jon.

'Stand easy,' Jon ordered and the two men relaxed slightly as they came off attention. 'Would you two idiots like to explain yourself?'

Jenkins spoke. 'Sorry Sir, we saw that the track was empty and we did look around carefully before we entered it.'

'Jenkins, I really don't give a toss about that. What I want to know is why you were looting. You all know I've given strict instructions about that.'

'Sorry Sir,' Jenkins responded. 'But we weren't really looting. We had a make and mend this afternoon and just went for a look around. We had been told the place had been trashed by the Yanks when they came through the other week. It was Brown here who saw it.'

'Saw what Brown?' Jon asked in some exasperation.

'There were some out buildings at the back Sir. They all looked like they had been shot up or broken into but one was more intact than the others. It had a large garage door, one of those electric type ones. It was completely jammed which is why I guess no one had tried to go in. I used to work for the company who made those doors before I joined up and I know how to open them manually, so I did.'

'Go on,' Jon encouraged. 'You obviously found that car.'

'Yes Sir, I'm a bit of a car fanatic and that machine is one of the most powerful in the world. Sorry Sir but I just had to give it a try. It had a full tank of petrol and the keys had been left in it.'

'And you didn't try and stop him Jenkins?' Jon asked, looking at the other man.

'Well Sir, I know you don't like looting and we were hardly going to be able to just take it and hide it so we thought we'd just give it a go to see what it was really like and then hand it in to you Sir. We'd heard that you and Colonel Roberts race a car so I thought maybe you could use it.'

Jon had to stifle a chuckle, although he realised the Corporal did have a point, looting a complete car was not really possible. He also recognised the tactic but it wasn't going to work. 'Oh and that wouldn't mean that I was looting as well?'

'Well no Sir, you're the boss.' Jenkins replied with a grin.

'Listen, you two, are you on tomorrows shout? You're both in C Platoon I believe.' Jon asked.

'Yes Sir,' Jenkins replied.

'And where is the car now?'

'We took it to the Motor Transport guys Sir. They said they would look after it.'

'Don't worry Sir,' Paul interjected. 'I've been down there and told everyone in no uncertain tones to leave it alone. They've covered it in a tarpaulin for now.'

'Thanks Paul, although I haven't a clue how we're going to deal with it in the long term.' Jon turned to the two marines. 'Right, you two, bugger off. We'll say no more about this. I accept that you weren't exactly looting but God help you if I catch you playing any more tricks like this. Understand?'

Two relieved looking marines left the tent and Jon turned to Paul. 'Thanks Paul. We'll have to see what to do about it. I guess it's worth a lot of money.'

'About a quarter of a million would be my guess,' Paul replied. 'But leave it with me. I'll talk to command and see what they recommend.'

'Thanks, well I'm off for some sleep. It's an early start for me tomorrow.'

It was fully dark when Jon walked over towards his accommodation. For him, this was the best time of day. The desert sun had gone but the air was still hot with the radiated heat from the sand and there was the musty smell of spices and more conventional military food in the air. It was eerily quiet although muted voices could just be heard from the various tents dotted around the camp. Someone had finally connected a generator to the airfield perimeter lights and the distant, yellow, orange glow of the sodium bulbs made the desert behind seem even darker and more mysterious.

'So you've decided to accompany the mission tomorrow Sir.' It was Jacob Sharp's voice coming from behind him. Jon had done everything to maintain a professional relationship with the man but it was quite clear they would never be friends. The Colonel still hadn't forgiven him for banning prayers at all gatherings.

'Yes Jacob, it's time I went in with my men. Command wasn't too happy but caved in when I insisted.'

Conspiracy

'I'll be staying here then Sir. Keep the fort safe for your return.'

There was something in the Colonel's tone that grated on Jon but he couldn't put his finger on it. 'I would expect nothing less Jacob.'

The Colonel paused for a second and then changed the subject. 'Don't you love this time of the evening Sir. It's perfect for admiring God's creation and all His handiwork.'

Jon was pretty sure the Colonel was testing him with that remark. It was one of many that he slipped into conversations. Normally, Jon would simply ignore it. Tonight he had had enough.

'Really Jacob, so God created all this?'

'Of course, Sir. The Bible tells us he did.'

'So, he created all of us and all we can see and experience?'

'Yes Sir. Yes he did and isn't it wonderful?' The evangelical tone in the Colonel's voice had risen a notch.

'And he loves us all?'

'Of course, Sir, we are his children.'

'So, if he created us and all around us and loves us so much. Why did he create cancer? And why did he design women so that the go through agony to give birth? And why does he allow children to be born deformed. Why did he create mosquitoes that kill millions a year and parasites that bore into people's eyes and send them blind?'

The Colonel must have misheard the tone of Jon's voice because he answered as though he was a preacher talking to his flock. 'It's all part of his plan Sir. All we have to do is love and worship Him and we will be redeemed.'

Jon's answered with anger and scorn. 'Oh just fuck off Colonel. You expect me to worship and love an entity that killed my wife, my unborn child and my girlfriend because it was part of some sort of sick and perverted plan? You expect me to bow down and thank someone who tortures small children. What do you lot say? Every child is born with original sin and will go to everlasting flames unless they worship this maniac. That's just the worst form of foul moral blackmail anyone could invent. I don't know if a higher entity exists and frankly, I couldn't give a toss except to say that if it does, then the only thing it deserves is my derision and my loathing.'

The Colonel took a step back at the vehemence in Jon's tone. His mouth opened but nothing came out. Before he could say anything, Jon offered a curt 'goodnight' and walked away.

Chapter 35

Jon was back in his element. He was sitting in the right hand seat of a Mark Four Sea King. The aircrew had insisted that he fly the machine and he didn't argue. It was like coming home. He even found that he could remember where all the necessary knobs and switches were, along with all the pre-flight checks. Sitting to his left was Mike Donnelly the detachment Flight Commander and the Captain of the aircraft. Despite Jon's rank it was Mike who was officially in charge of flying the machine. However, Jon's trip into the past was about to end as they were due to land at the US Marine camp ahead for fuel. After that, Jon had insisted that the proper crew take the front seats for the final leg up towards Mosul. The first leg had been over relatively safe terrain and in daylight. The final part of the transit would be conducted low level, at night, on Night Vision Goggles and with the possibility of hostiles on the ground. Jon definitely did not feel current enough to fly that sort of profile.

'I've got the site visual,' Jon reported. 'Pre-landing checks please.'

The two of them went through the ritual of checks before Jon started to slow the aircraft down. Out to port was the second Sea King. As leader of the formation, the other machine would follow Jon as he manoeuvred. Seated inside Jon's Sea King were sixteen members of C Platoon and four of the weapons specialists. Piled up in the rear was all their equipment as well as personal protection suits and respirators for everyone. The other helicopter was similarly encumbered.

Jon called a quick 'Finals' over the radio and slowed the machine down to fifty knots. The aircraft's aircrewman opened the larger cabin sliding door and looked back towards the tail. As Jon flared the big machine into a slow forward hover taxi, the crewman called the clearance of the tail wheel to the ground. There was no runway as such but a large area of the desert had been flattened and in the near distance Jon could see two waiting fuel bowsers. Off to one side was a large camp of tents and vehicles. He gently ran the aircraft onto the ground ensuring that the large billowing cloud of dust that was blasted up by the helicopter's downwash stayed behind them.

Minimising the amount of sand going into the engine's intakes was very important if they were to last any time at all. Within minutes they were shut down. The Americans didn't like refuelling with the rotors running for some reason although it was standard procedure in the RN.

Jon jumped out and let the aircraft's regular crew take over. As he walked off the stiffness from two hours strapped into the machine, he noticed an American officer striding towards him. The man proffered a quick salute.

'Commodore Hunt? I'm Major Jones Sir. I'm this unit's operations officer. I've got some bad news I'm afraid,' he said. 'We've just got some new information about your mission.'

'Oh, what's up Major? It's not been called off has it?' Jon asked.

'Well that's up to you Sir. It appears that promises of fuel at your destination were a little optimistic to say the least. One of my men managed to get a telephone link to the guys you're going to meet. He managed to pin them down. They do have some but it's nothing like enough. And from what I can gather there's no guarantee about its quality.'

'Why am I not surprised?' Jon laughed humourlessly. 'We do have contingencies for this. Let me talk to my guys and I'll let you know what we decide.'

Jon called all the aircrew and the Platoon Commander into a huddle in the shade of his aircraft and explained the situation. 'Guys, the Sea Kings have the endurance to get there but it could get tight. So do we go or do we abort? I know what I think but I'd like to hear your views.'

There were no arguments. Everyone wanted to go on. With the continual failure of their search missions everyone was getting fed up with no results so Jon made the call to go with the mission.

They had a few hours to wait until it was dark. Unsurprisingly the forecast was clear and there was a decent moon for the transit north. As soon as the sun was fully set, they started up. Both aircraft were at their maximum all up weight, possibly even a little over but Jon wanted to ensure they had all the fuel they could carry. Consequently, they ground taxied away from the fuelling point and conducted a running take off to minimise the torque and engine power needed to get airborne. Soon, Jon was standing between the two pilot's seats with his own set of goggles on. The landscape appeared eerily green but quite clear and the two pilots kept the thundering machine at fifty feet or less as they shot across the desert.

Jon knew that no matter how wound up you were, after a while, unless something went wrong, things settled into a routine. After half an hour, he folded down the little jump seat behind the two pilots and stretched his legs out. It was to his surprise when sometime later he felt a hand on his shoulder.

'Time to wake up Sir,' the aircrewman said with a grin. 'We're almost there.'

'Good God, did I nod off?' Jon asked ruefully.

'Just for an hour and half Sir,' the crewman smiled.

Jon stood and took up his position behind the pilots just as they were starting to slow down, still amazed he had managed to sleep in such a loud, vibrating environment and still slightly groggy from the effects. The second Sea King had been told to hold off while they did a recce over the site. In fact, all it seemed to consist of was a small walled compound with a house against one inner wall and a number of vehicles parked up outside. There was no radio contact but luckily no one seemed to be pointing white lights at them. A bright light could easily shut down the goggles which was a bad idea if you were manoeuvring to land. Satisfied that there was a safe landing ground for both aircraft, the flying pilot turned the helicopter into wind and landed about two hundred yards from the wall of the compound and well clear of the vehicles.

The instant they were down, their troops disembarked in their fighting order with weapons held at the ready. They ran around the aircraft and took up defensive positions. No one was going to take any silly risks at this stage.

The reception party kept well clear until the rotors of both aircraft had ground to a halt and the engines had wound down. Then several men approached. With the muzzles of thirty SA 80 rifles tracking them they had the sense to put their weapons down first and approach with hands held high. Jon motioned to the Platoon Commander to go and speak to them. After a few minute's conversation, he signalled his men to stand down and everyone relaxed.

Two hours later and Jon was looking at a huddle of ruined buildings. 'I suppose I can understand why the Kurds thought this might have once been a chemical weapons facility. That is if you don't know what the fuck a grain silo looks like.' He muttered under his breath. The Kurdish fighters had been incredibly happy to see them all. They had the look of men who had been fighting all their lives. What they lacked in military sophistication they clearly made up with an almost feral ferocity. Jon was glad he was on their side. Unfortunately, their technical skill was in inverse proportion to their enthusiasm. Keeping a neutral face he turned to the leader of the Kurds, a scruffy looking man with a scraggly beard, who clearly hadn't washed for some time. 'Mohammed, my experts have cleared the site. I'm sorry but this is nothing more than an agricultural complex. This close to the Euphrates it looks like a place where the outlying farms brought their produce to store. Nothing else I'm afraid.'

The man didn't seem put out at all and just grinned at Jon. 'Ok, so you go back now?' he asked. 'We can give you fuel, yes?'

'Err, no thanks we have enough to get back,' Jon replied. He had seen the fuel the man was referring to. It was a stack of jerry cans with what was probably some sort of aviation fuel but there was far too little and it looked quite dirty. Fine for keeping a car engine running but definitely not a gas turbine.

The man looked disappointed for a second but then smiled. 'We use in trucks then. You want to stay for a meal? We have plenty of goat.'

The last thing Jon wanted was a breakfast of goat and so politely told the man they needed to get back now that the site had been assessed. Before he could be offered more hospitality, he called his men together. Each helicopter retained an external guard and everyone else piled in ready to go.

Jon took his place between the two aircrew as they started their checks. The first engine was started and all was normal. The pilot in the left hand seat then pressed the engine start button for the number two engine. It lit up normally but then suddenly there was a loud bang and Jon could see the turbine temperature going off the clock. Before he could say anything, the pilot reacted and slammed the fuel cock off just as the Central Warning Panel lit up with several warnings at once.

'Fire in the starboard engine,' the pilot called and pulled the extinguisher handle while at the same time the other pilot slammed the fuel cock shut on the running engine. Jon grabbed the hand held extinguisher behind the pilot's seat and ran out of the forward door which was still open. He shot around to the starboard side of the helicopter but luckily couldn't see any obvious signs of fire. He arrived at the same time as the aircrewman.

'Give us the extinguisher Sir, I'll climb up and have a look.' So saying, he nimbly climbed the side of the machine and unlatched the cover of the starboard engine. After a few seconds, he called down. 'Nothing burning but that engine is completely bolloxed, must have been all the escaping hot gas that set off the fire warning. Half the compressor has come out the side of the casing. It must have eaten something.'

For some reason, the only thing Jon could think of was that it was almost certain he would now be eating goat for breakfast after all.

Chapter 36

Colonel Jacob Sharp was almost tearing his hair out in frustration. Ever since they had deployed ashore, he had been expecting the intelligence to point towards the site and nothing had happened. It had to be discovered by surveillance as any attempt to direct people's attention to it could rouse unwanted suspicions. It was clear to him by now that whoever was meant to have turned on the power hadn't made it. He knew that the man had lived in Baghdad so all he could assume was that he had been affected by the bombing or the fighting. Either way, it was clear that the plan was in jeopardy. He had considered getting back on his satellite phone but there was nothing he could ask for that would help and the risk of interception, although slight, was still there. No, he was the man on the spot with the best chance of doing something but what?

As he was still pondering the problem. Paul Roberts came into the operations tent. 'We've got a downbird up north Jacob. One of the Sea Kings has lost an engine. Luckily, it was during start up so there was no other damage. Jon is coming back in the other one with the chemical team and some of the troops. I'm organising a spare engine to be taken back up there as soon as the aircraft gets back along with a team of maintainers to change it.'

'When does the Commodore actually get back?' Jacob asked looking at the map. 'Is he going to wait until dark?'

'No, apparently the trip up was uneventful and they've got better intelligence now from the local militias so they're coming back in daylight. They should be here by midday.'

'Shit, that means that we have no heavy lift if we need it.' Jacob said.

'Good point but we're running out of places to search now anyway.' Paul responded.

'Maybe but we both know how many more targets we've been getting as our troops move up. They seem to see WMD's everywhere they go.'

'True but they're almost at Baghdad now aren't they? Hopefully, the whole country will give up then.'

Jacob gave a small laugh. 'They've just about given up now. The only problem is that there doesn't seem to be a government or military command left to throw in the towel. I can see all sorts of local skirmishes going on for months if we're not careful.'

'Well it was never going to be easy. I just hope your government has as good a plan for the peace as it had for this war.'

The remark stung. These goddam Brits were always so critical. 'Of course they have. This country will be at peace with itself within months you wait and see. And then we will begin the work of bringing God to them.'

Paul burst out laughing. 'Good on you Jacob, you never give up do you? I think you might find that the Iraqi's expend just as much effort trying to bring you to Allah. But hey, I wish you the best of luck. Anyway, I'm off to see the squadron and make sure they have everything in hand before the Sea King gets back.'

He left the tent and didn't see the murderous look on Jacob's face.

Two hours later, the remaining Sea King returned. Jon climbed wearily out and called Paul, Jacob and the rest of his staff into the command tent.

He briefed them on the events up north and then asked for any updates. Everything seemed quiet so he excused himself and went back to his accommodation to try and get some sleep. Apart from a few fitful hours in the aircraft he hadn't slept for over twenty four hours. Despite being exhausted, he found oblivion hard to achieve. Partly, it was the heat but his mind was still buzzing from the adrenaline of the trip and his concerns over what was going on. He was amazed they hadn't found anything yet. Were all their suspicions unfounded? Was Rupert's intelligence simply wrong? Unless something new came up, about the only place left was that one of Rupert's list. Jon had asked around about it and the consensus was still that it was highly unlikely to be worth investigating. Firstly, because the Israelis had bombed the place back to the stone age a few years back. Then the UN had recently cleared it and then because it was so close to Baghdad it was unlikely anyone would be stupid enough to be using it.

He was just nodding off when a head appeared around the tent door flap. 'Sorry to disturb you Sir.' It was James, the Ops officer. 'We've got a shout. I'm setting up a brief now in the Ops tent.'

Jon levered himself off his camp bed. 'Alright James, just give me a minute and I'll be over.' He got up and splashed some water on his face. He was bone tired but since when was that an excuse for anything? Once in the operations tent, he sat at the front and indicated to James to start the brief.

'Gentlemen, we've just had a report from an American Ranger unit that they've liberated an old military site about thirty miles south west of Baghdad. They've discovered a vast amount of ordnance. They've got bombs, short range missiles and the remains of a few old Scud ballistic missiles. They are pretty sure that at least some of the weapons were used to deliver chemical agents and that some may well still be armed with them. Obviously they are reluctant to tamper with anything and they are in a hurry to get on towards the capital. We've been tasked to take over from them as soon as we can. This could be what we've been looking for all this time.'

Jon wasn't convinced. It was well known that Saddam had used these weapons in the past. This could just be the remnants of those campaigns. There would need to be some sort of manufacturing facility as well for this to be worthwhile. However, he kept his council as everyone else in the room was looking excited.

'Have we been told to move everything and take up residence there or is this just an investigation James?' He asked.

'This is so hot off the press I don't think anyone's got that far Sir,' James replied. 'We've got a lot of infrastructure set up here now. It would take several days to move.'

Jacob was getting excited by the news but not completely for the same reasons. 'Sir, I think we should do an initial recce as fast as we can. We can use the 109s to get the monitoring guys in very quickly and use the MH6Bs to give them protection. I can then take the rest of us in the Humvees and take over the military role from the Rangers. The site is about two hundred miles away so we could be there before dark if we move quickly. Once we've completed the initial survey we can then decide whether it's worth moving the whole outfit.'

'Good thinking Jacob,' Jon replied. 'Let's do it. We should have both Sea Kings back in a day or two as well which will help if we have to move the whole Operating base.'

The talk went on for another hour covering communications, logistics and likely contingency plans. Jon sat back and let much of it wash over him. He was studying the Colonel. He hadn't seen the man so animated since they had arrived ashore. If the man knew something about this new development then maybe they had finally found what they were looking for. Jon decided to give him his head.

As the meeting wound up, Jon stood to sum up. 'Let's do this as soon as we can. I want the monitoring teams in as soon as possible and then A and B Platoons on the road as soon after that as we can manage. After we've done initial assessments we will make the decision on whether to move the whole operation there. Any questions?'

'Yes Sir,' Jacob asked. 'Will you be leading this one?'

Jon had already decided how he wanted to play this and he wanted to give the Colonel some rope. Maybe he would hang himself, maybe not. It would be an interesting test. 'No Jacob, I'm still knackered after the Mosul operation. I would like you to take charge. Let me know when you have some definite results and we'll take it from there.'

Just for a second, Jon was sure he detected a look of smug satisfaction on the man's face. Then it was replaced with his normal bland expression.

After everyone had filed out, Paul came over to Jon. 'We didn't cover it in detail Jon but with all the troops going we're going to have to use all the Humvees. It will limit us if anything else comes up while they are away.

'Yes, I guessed that but we should have both Sea Kings here within forty eight hours or less and we can always recall some of the Humvees and the smaller helicopters. By then the C Platoon guys who came back with us will have rested and we will have at least some capability. But let's face it, if this isn't it, then there aren't that many places left to look.'

'Agreed,' Paul said thoughtfully. 'But we still haven't looked at this site at Jurf Sakhar. I'm not convinced that an old armaments dump is the place to leave the evidence we expect to find.'

'I agree but I'm also beginning to wonder whether we've just been too paranoid. We've convinced ourselves that this is all some sort of secret conspiracy. What if it's not? The Americans are going to take over this country whatever we find. Maybe that list Rupert found was just that, a list of potential sites and nothing more?'

'No, you told me they had solid intelligence that a shipment of Sarin was being brought in and they knew who was responsible. They must have a destination in mind. Look, if this new place comes in as a busted flush, there's only one place left on Rupert's list. That has to be it.'

A wave of weariness washed over Jon. He knew that Paul was probably right but just at that moment all he could think about was sleep. This could all wait until later.

Chapter 37

Jacob Sharp felt exhilarated, free and if truth be told, more than a little nervous. The road ahead was good tarmac, well illuminated by the Humvee's headlights and the moon overhead. However, he knew that once he turned off the main route the road would deteriorate quite badly. Luckily, he was in one of the best vehicles in the world to cope with that. He had also checked carefully with the latest intelligence. The battlefront was well clear and the area he was heading towards was not one that had been heavily contested. Anyway, if he was stopped it wasn't as if he didn't have the right to be on the road. He had all the paperwork and could claim it was all part of his job, which in a way it was. No, his only concern was that someone from his unit queried where he had gone to but if he got his timing right he would be back at the ammunition dump well before dawn. If they asked why he hadn't called in on the radio he would just say he must have been out of range.

The ground party had arrived in good time at the site of the weapons dump that afternoon. By then the monitoring team had already made an initial assessment and declared the area safe although there were some indications that there might be the residue of some chemical weapons around. The air of excitement amongst his men had rapidly evaporated when they saw just how large the place was and realised how long it was going to take to go through it all. Add to that the chances of booby traps and the task started to look unpleasant and dangerous in the extreme. He wasn't surprised when the Ranger's Commanding Officer quickly handed over the duty and moved his men out. He passed the initial assessment report back to their main base saying that all they would be doing that evening was securing the perimeter and setting up for what looked like a long slog. Once it was dark, he told the Platoon Commander that he was taking a Humvee to drive around the whole perimeter area and would probably be gone some time. The man seemed quite happy and didn't question his motives at all.

Jacob looked down at the small GPS receiver on the passenger's seat as it gave out a small beep indicating that he had arrived at his first waypoint. Sure enough, just ahead was a turn off onto an unpaved road to the right of the main carriageway. He turned the Humvee on to it. Only seven miles to go and he would be able to get the plan back on track.

That seven miles was hard work. This was a back road into the facility and was clearly rarely used. In places, it was completely covered in wind-blown sand several feet deep. He didn't dare contemplate getting stuck. He had several heart stopping moments when the wheels started to lose grip and spin. However, the Humvee proved once again what a capable off road machine it was.

It took over half an hour before the ruined sky line of the bombed out facility could be seen. The Israelis had clearly done a good job all those years ago. At least the ground was reasonably hard packed now and he knew where he was going. There at the far right was one of the few remaining intact structures. It was a large garage like building and he pulled the Humvee up outside and jumped out. Reaching back into the cab, he retrieved a large torch. Hopefully, he should be able to sort this all out in just a few minutes.

He went inside and there, just as he had been told was the pile of rubbish he needed to move. It didn't take long to expose the small access hatch which he pulled open. Shining his torch inside, he could see the ladder and climbed down. On the wall was the main power box. He pulled it open and pushed down the main breaker. The glare of the lights hit him and he had to close his eyes for a second to acclimatise. He then looked back inside the breaker box. Next to the main switch was the most important one. It was labelled in Arabic. That was fine because he knew how the word was written in their Godless script. When he made the switch, he listened carefully and for a moment was worried that nothing had happened. Then he heard a very distant whine of fans and machinery starting up. He had checked the satellite overflight schedule before he left the main camp. The next was due mid-morning tomorrow. If they didn't see the thermal bloom of the exhaust from the air conditioning he would be extremely surprised. It would certainly be spotted within days.

He left the main breaker and all the lights on, climbed up and secured the hatch. There was no point now in putting all the rubbish back, after all, he wanted the place found, although he did make a token effort to kick some in place.

He stood for a few moments with his eyes shut to regain some night vision and then headed back to the Humvee. As he did so, he looked at his watch. It was half past nine. Two and half hours to get to his next stop and then three hours to return. Allowing for an hour at the other end, he should be safely back in camp by four or five at the latest. It looked like the plan was back on track.

'Jon wake up,' the words seemed to penetrate from a far distance. He tried to ignore them but they kept repeating and then he felt a hand on his shoulder. The dream had been fantastic but he felt it slipping away and suddenly he couldn't remember it.

'Come on Jon, you need to wake up,' it was Paul's voice, he recognised it. What the hell did he want? He forced his eyes open. There was a bright light and a dim figure behind it. He realised it must be Paul holding a torch. Still groggy from sleep, he felt for his watch on the little bedside table but couldn't find it.

'What time is it,' he asked as he sat himself up.

'Half past seven in the evening. Sorry but you did manage a couple of hours,' Paul replied.

'No wonder I feel so bloody groggy. Anyway what's up? I assume you didn't wake me for the fun of it.'

'We've got a situation over at the armament dump. Our guys got there in good time and reported in. I didn't wake you then because there was little to report. There's no overt chemical threat so our guys are settling in and will start a full analysis tomorrow morning but then I got a call.'

'So, what's the problem?'

'Colonel Jacob has gone AWOL.' Paul said.

'What on earth do you mean?' Jon asked. 'How can he do that?'

'He told the Platoon Commander that he was taking a Humvee out to look around the perimeter of the arms dump. Not unreasonable as it covers a large area. But then one of the sentries saw him heading up the main road away from the place at high speed. He's meant to have a radio with him but hasn't answered repeated calls. They were so worried that they called us.'

Jon shook his head trying to fully wake up and work out what the hell was going on. 'Where does that road lead to? Maybe he's got a girlfriend stashed away somewhere.'

'Hah, not likely. And the road leads to Baghdad eventually but here's the interesting bit. It's only a turn off of seven miles and you reach guess where? Jurf Sakhar that's where. Look Jon, there's nothing else of interest along that road before you reach the front line. I can't possibly see any other possibility.'

'So, what do you think he's doing? If he thinks the site is worth investigating all he has to do is say so.'

'Really?' Paul said. 'You know how he's been behaving the last few weeks and I don't mean the God bothering bit. Whenever we've discussed this particular site he's hardly said a word which is really unlike him and then when you mentioned it at the briefing this afternoon he suddenly perked up.'

Jon didn't say anything as he thought about Paul's words. 'Alright, maybe he didn't want to draw attention to it unnecessarily. But why go blasting off into the night there now?'

'That's exactly what I've been worrying about as well,' Paul replied. 'Look, we think there is something planted somewhere but we haven't found anything yet. Whoever is doing this wants it to look completely authentic. But these people aren't fools. Surely they would want some control, someone on the inside to keep things on track if necessary?'

'You're saying Jacob is a plant?' Jon asked thoughtfully.

'Why not, he's perfectly placed and as far as motivation goes, we know there is a strong evangelical strand to this whole thing. And then there is you.'

'Eh? What do you mean by that?' Jon asked.

'You were parachuted into this job quite late and even you were surprised. I know that the official line was that you were well suited for the role and a bit of a media star. Just the sort of person to reveal Saddam's dastardly plans. But many also know that you are actually against this whole idea. Your States trip hardly stayed under the radar. So, maybe they also want someone on the team to ensure you don't fuck it up for them.'

'So you're saying that Jacob is a member of this conspiracy and possibly an assassin?'

Paul looked hard at his friend. 'Yes, that's exactly what I'm saying.'

Jon stood up and walked over to the far side of the tent without a word. He turned with a strange look on his face. 'For the last few weeks or so I've been trying to fathom the man out. I think I agree with you. No, in fact I'm sure you're right. The only question is what if anything we do about it.'

'In my opinion we should go after the bugger. If we can get him on his own maybe we can get the truth out of him.' Paul said grimly.

'How? We've no aircraft here and even if we had a Humvee they are too slow. It would take at least an hour and half to get one of the 109s back and then another hour to get back up to the weapon dump and he would probably be back by then. How could we explain that? If we went directly to Jurf Sakhar, he would hear the helicopter coming and just sod off. The only way your idea would work was if we could get there while he's still around and quietly at that. If we miss him we could then get back here without him knowing.'

Paul grinned. 'Want to know how we can do exactly that?'

Chapter 38

'You know Paul it really is time we both grew up.' Jon said with a grin.

'You may be right but bloody hell, is this fun or what?' Paul replied without taking his eyes off the road ahead which was illuminated by the powerful headlights.

'Alright, we know the bloody thing can do two hundred. At least you've slowed down a bit now.' Jon looked at the speedometer which was reading a steady one hundred and forty miles an hour.

'Yeah but I bet that's over reading. The car's only meant to do one hundred and ninety five.' Paul said. 'You do realise that none of our helicopters are this quick, even cruising at this speed.'

'Yes but don't expect the roads to be this good all the way Paul,' Jon said. 'Once we get off any of the main routes it will be a different matter.'

'I know, which is why we need to make up as much time as we can now. But this thing has four wheel drive so should be fairly good even on the poor bits.' Paul replied. 'I would go faster but the fuel consumption goes through the roof.'

Paul's idea to take the Bentley that the marines had liberated had seemed a bit farfetched when he first suggested it but the more Paul had explained the idea, the more it made sense. The car was ridiculously fast and actually had quite a lot of room. They went down to the Motor Transport tent and pulled the tarpaulin off the machine.

'Actually, I've a confession to make,' Paul had explained. 'After you told the marines to take it down to the MT guys, I came and had a good look around as well. As I said, the company have only just launched it so this must have been bought by one of Saddam's family very quickly. It produces almost six hundred horsepower and has a really large fuel tank. When it's full, it's good for over three hundred and fifty miles. It's got massive wheels and four wheel drive so it will easily catch the Colonel's Humvee, even off road.'

Jon agreed it was worth a try, after all there was little to lose. They were well behind the battle lines now and could always be back before it was light. However, before they left, he insisted on several precautions. They loaded the car with a personal Bergen each containing full NBCD kit and Jon found a case of water bottles in the galley tent. He then had another idea and raided the survival equipment store used by the aircrew and grabbed two flying helmets fitted with Night Vision Goggles.

As soon as Paul saw them, he nodded. 'Good idea. We can use them when we get closer. I've also put two SA80's on the back seat with night sights and a couple of hundred rounds of ammunition. There's five jerry cans of fuel in the boot although the tank is just about full anyway and I've also liberated a radio. Can you think of anything else?'

'Maps? How are we going to navigate,' Jon asked.

'There's a couple in the door pocket but the car has a built in satnav. I've checked and it has maps of Iraq loaded into it.'

'Alright, I've told the duty officer that we are taking the car and that I'll explain why when we get back. He was really curious but I pulled rank and told him to trust me. It seemed to work.' Jon said. 'So let's go.'

They both climbed in and buckled up. Paul fired up the massive six litre engine. Suddenly, Jon remembered a time many years ago when he and Brian were in another dangerous situation.

'Paul, its two hundred miles to Jurf Sakhar, we don't smoke, we've a full tank of gas, its dark and we will be wearing goggles.' He turned to look at Paul to see if he got the joke.

Paul said nothing but slammed the throttle down. 'Hit it,' he said as the car shot out onto the airfield.

Jon took over the driving after an hour. It was hard work concentrating at high speed. However, it wasn't long after he got behind the wheel that the road started to get rougher and he was forced to slow down. On one occasion, they rounded a gentle bend to be confronted by a flock of goats who were lying in the road, presumably because it was now warmer than the surrounding sands. He was travelling far too fast to brake and so simply steered off the road. Luckily, the sand on the road side was fairly flat and he managed to keep control. After that, he had to slow down significantly. However, it was only a few minutes later that Paul announced that they were approaching a cross roads with the main highway and the track leading to Jurf Sakhar was there. Jon pulled off just before the crossroads and both men put on the two borrowed aircrew helmets. Jon restarted the car with the lights turned off. Luckily there didn't seem to be any stray lighting in the car to Affect the goggles and so they pulled away, cautiously this time.

As soon as they had crossed the main road they saw tracks. 'I'm pretty sure that those are Humvee tracks,' Paul said. 'And they look fairly fresh.'

Following the tracks was fairly easy and also allowed them to spot where the other vehicle had had problems. The other vehicle had flattened the sand sufficiently that they didn't bog down and so they made good time.

'Shit, I've just had a thought,' Jon said. 'We've only got one set of tracks and they must be going in so he must still be there.'

'Well, that's what we want isn't it?' Paul asked. 'And if he comes out while we are here, we'll see him long before he sees us so we'll be able to pull over and hide.'

'Hah, yes but then he'll see our tracks. No, if we meet him on the way, we stop him and have a serious chat about what the fucking hell he's playing at.'

They didn't meet any other vehicles before they entered the ruined facility.

'Bloody hell, this place is really trashed,' Jon observed. 'I can't see how anything survived. Can you Paul?'

'Nope but look, we still have wheel tracks to follow.'

They continued through the ruined buildings until the tracks stopped before a scruffy but largely intact structure rather like an old aircraft hangar. It was clear that their quarry had stopped here as footprints leading into the building were obvious. However, they could also see wheel tracks leading away in a totally different direction.

'Well, now we know why we didn't meet up,' Jon observed. 'But let's see if we can work out what he was doing here first.'

They climbed out and Jon immediately rummaged around in his Bergen looking for the standard green right angled torch that they were all issued with. They also grabbed a rifle each. The place looked deserted but you could never tell. There was a little side door which the footprints led to and it was unlocked. Inside the place was empty. There was what looked like a small office at one end but they could see it was empty. At the far end where the footprints led, there was a pile of old oil cans and other detritus. They approached cautiously and both men could make out the outline of some sort of door or hatch in the floor. Wasting no time Jon, went up and pulled it open. Bright lights shone in their faces, almost blinding in their intensity. Both men waited a second to allow their eyes to become accustomed.

'Cover me Paul,' Jon said as he started down the ladder. 'There doesn't seem to be anyone around but you never know.'

When Jon was in the corridor he could hear the whir of machinery in the distance. Paul climbed down and joined him. Ten minutes later and it was quite clear the place was deserted.

'There something really wrong here,' Jon said as he looked into what was clearly meant to be some sort of communal area.

'What, like no sign of anyone or even any food in here? Or what is quite clearly a laboratory but no sign of any chemicals or a storage area that's completely empty?' Paul asked.

'That and the fact that it's bloody hot but the air conditioning is on,' Jon replied. 'Sort of like someone has only just turned it on.'

'Maybe like a US Colonel you mean?'

'Exactly. This is a sham but can you imagine what would be made of it, if it was discovered. It's exactly the sort of thing we were meant to find. And more importantly, I know what the good Colonel was up to.' Jon said.

'I'm ahead of you. There must be an exhaust for the air conditioning somewhere and even if its somehow well camouflaged, just the heat difference between here and the outside will stand out like a dog's bollocks to a satellite.'

'Exactly, I'm willing to bet it was meant to be turned on by someone else but they didn't make it. Probably the same person who set this all up in the first place. So the Colonel took the first opportunity he had to correct the situation. But there's something else. Rupert was adamant that Sarin was being brought in. It's not here so where is it?'

'Good point. Well, he's clearly headed off somewhere else. I think we should find out don't you?' Paul suggested.

'Maybe but what the hell do we do about this place?' Jon asked looking around. 'It's not as if we can just blow it all up.'

'Hang on,' Paul said and went back to the entrance. He looked at the wall and saw the locked box next to the main power breakers.

Conspiracy

'Remember one of the briefings we had back at Wilton about how the regime liked to have all these sorts of facilities set up with a self destruct?'

'Vaguely but they wouldn't have done that here surely? This is all for show.'

'Yes but they would want it to be as authentic as possible so why not.' So saying, Paul smacked the butt of his rifle at the hinges of the locked box. It took several swings but eventually the hinges failed and they could see inside. It was a spaghetti of wires and terminals. In the middle was what was clearly a heavy duty circuit breaker designed to electrically switch the system on. Paul looked closely at the mess. Most of the wires exited the box in a conduit heading into the facility. He followed it along and when a smaller conduit broke away he followed that. It disappeared into the ceiling.

'Hang on a second,' he said and went into the canteen room emerging a few seconds later with a chair. Standing on it he pushed one of the polystyrene tiles away and shone his torch into the void. 'Well if that's not a demolition charge it's a bloody good replica,' he called.

Climbing back down, he looked at Jon. 'What say you we blow this pace to kingdom come?'

'Excellent but where the hell is the big red button, it would hardly be in here?'

'Good point,' Paul said. 'Let's follow the other wires.'

They went back to the junction box. Paul could clearly see two wires leading out of the other side and disappearing into the wall. 'Must be outside somewhere. I've got an idea.'

They climbed out back into the large building. Paul went over to the little office at the other end. 'There's nowhere else,' he said. 'All the other buildings are trashed and this would be sufficiently far away. Let's look around.'

It was Jon who found it attached to the underside of the metal desk. 'Here Paul, this must be it.' He pointed to the well hidden switch right at the back.

Paul peered down. 'That's got to be it. You're the senior officer, you should have the honour.'

Jon hesitated. 'Are we doing the right thing Paul? If this place is found, at least it will legitimise what's been going on with this wretched war. Do we have the right to do this?'

'And give them the excuse to keep going? We know the whole bloody thing's a sham. If you don't, I bloody well will. This has to stop.'

'You're right but I had to ask.' He lifted the guard and pressed the switch.

Nothing happened.

'Oh for fuck's sake,' Paul exclaimed. 'I'm an idiot. Maybe I should have checked the arming circuit breaker. Turn the switch off Jon and for goodness sake don't touch it. I won't be long.'

Before Jon could reply, Paul sprinted off back to the hatch and disappeared. When he was back down he looked even more carefully at the arming breaker which was indeed in the off position. He also checked the main electrical feed. It didn't take long for him to spot something wrong. 'You cunning bastard,' he muttered to himself. 'You wanted this to look the real thing but didn't want the risk of it actually working.' He took a small penknife out of his pocket and undid the screws holding the main firing wires into their terminals. He had spotted that the wire's insulation hadn't been removed. It only took seconds to strip them back to copper and refit them. Then with a muttered prayer that there were no short circuits in the arming wires, he flipped the toggle on the main breaker.

Nothing happened.

Breathing a massive sigh of relief, he climbed back out and rejoined Jon. 'Clever bastard whoever it was who rigged this up. Mind you, he didn't realise he was up against one of the finest engineers in the British army. If you would like to do the honours again Jon.'

Once again, Jon lifted the cover and flipped the switch. This time there was a massive shock that they could feel through the soles of their feet. The whole building shook and there was the clatter as several sheets of corrugated iron fell off the roof. The whole building filled with choking dust.

They waited several minutes for the worst of the dust to clear and went back to the rear of the building. They didn't get far. The whole rear wall had gone and the floor was now a crater. It was clear that nothing remained.

'Well, we'd better go and find our Colonel and have a serious word with him.' Jon stated firmly as they emerged back into the night.

Chapter 39

Jacob had to stop and study the map again. It wasn't exactly easy to get lost as there were so few roads but this damned strip of tarmac just seemed to go on for ever. There had been one turn off about twenty miles back but there was still no sign of Al Kasrah. He knew he had no choice but to carry on. On looking at his watch, he realised he actually had plenty of time in hand. Wearily, he let out the clutch and forced himself to concentrate.

The road crested a rise and a left turn. Then suddenly there were lights ahead in the distance. Now all he had to do was find the tanker and the South African and not get shot in the process. He hadn't really thought about it until now but he was well to the west of Baghdad and although he hadn't seen any military units he was probably beyond the lines, in a sort of no man's land. One thing he certainly couldn't do was just drive into the town and ask around. He wouldn't last seconds. He kept going until he was within a mile or so of the first lit building and looked for somewhere to hide the Humvee. In the end, he simply drove it off the road and parked it in the desert behind some low rocks. They broke up its outline but would be of no use in daylight. That didn't matter as he would be long gone by then. He knew the location of the tanker. It was on this side of the town and next to the main road so it shouldn't be a long walk. It shouldn't be hard to find. He threw his uniform jacket into the cab and took out the headscarf he had acquired, wrapping it around his head in Arabic style. Again, he knew it wouldn't pass muster in daylight. He also grabbed the AK47 he had acquired. That would pass muster anywhere in the Middle East he thought wryly to himself. An American rifle would have been a dead giveaway. He set off down the road.

Only twenty minutes later, he saw the silhouette of a dark building on the left. It had a courtyard out front and what looked like a fuel pump. Cautiously approaching the building, he looked carefully around for any vehicles. At first there was nothing in sight but as he went around the back, there it was. An Iraqi army fuel tanker. He went up to it carefully. He could see immediately that it had been in an accident. The front was bent and twisted but he was surprised to see it relatively intact. He managed to get close enough for a detailed look then he froze as something cold pressed into his head behind his left ear.

'One wrong move and your brains will decorate the truck.' The voice was rough and gravelly with a distinct South African accent but quiet. A powerful hand reached around and relieved him of the rifle.

'How did you know I wasn't a local? You're speaking English.' Jacob had a good idea who this was.

'Don't make me fucking laugh. Putting a rag on your head doesn't make you an Arab. Now who are you?'

'I'm your contact you idiot, who the hell do you think I am?'

'Prove it.'

A new voice joined in. 'It's alright Pieter I know who this is. Colonel Sharp I'm really glad to see you.'

Jacob felt the pistol leave his temple. He shook himself down and turned to see the hulking form of one man and the much slimmer form of another South African standing next to him. He held out his hand. 'Probably just as glad as I am to see you.' The two men shook hands and RJ introduced Pieter who silently handed the AK back to Jacob.

RJ led him back to the cab of the tanker and the three men climbed in.

'Sorry about the crush,' RJ said. 'Life's been getting pretty difficult recently. The locals all think we're deserters which actually isn't a bad thing as most of them don't like the military. The problem is that they are convinced that the tanker is full of fuel which they would rather like to get their hands on. I showed some of them what it really is the other day but most of them think I pulled some sort of trick. We're constantly having to keep watch. Now, why are you here?'

'To let you know that I had to go to the site and turn it on. Your man never made it but it should be discovered very soon now.'

'So, we can get out of here now? There's a Land Cruiser we can use any time.' Pieter said eagerly.

'Hold fast Pieter,' RJ said. 'If we leave the tanker here it will be looted in minutes. Someone is bound to discover the real contents, then God knows what will happen. But that said, one option Colonel is to use a contingency plan we have.'

'Go on.'

RJ reached under the dash and pulled out a reel of wire. At one end was a small handle with a red button. 'This unreels for five hundred yards so you can get safely clear. Turn on the tanker's ignition and make this switch on the dash.' He pointed to a small toggle switch by the steering column. 'Press the button and a small explosive charge will blow the rear of the tank off and blow the contents into the air.'

'And kill how many people?' Jacob asked.

'Well that depends on the wind speed and direction but it if we did it here, it would wipe out the town. It disperses quite quickly after that.'

'Thank you for showing me but we are not in such desperate straits yet.' Jacob said. He had no qualms about actually doing such a thing, these people meant nothing to him. It was just that the whole plan was to have credible evidence of a government sponsored programme and indiscriminately killing a town of people wouldn't make much sense.

'Colonel, how did you get here?' RJ asked.

'I've got a Humvee parked about a mile down the road.'

'Does it have the guts to tow this rig?' RJ asked.

'Probably but I can't stay long. I really came here to see whether the tanker was still intact and make sure it could be found. I have to be back at my base before first light.'

RJ looked at his watch. 'How long will it take you to get back? It's just past midnight now.'

'About four hours, so I will have to leave here by two at the latest.' Jacob replied. 'There's no way I could get you back to Jurf Sakhar.'

'No, I wasn't thinking of that but in two hours we could get well south and into open desert and also closer to where you need to go. I would feel happy then that there would be every chance that it won't get looted. Frankly, that's the only reason we've stayed here so long.'

Jacob nodded, it made sense although he also knew that the two men had probably stayed more to ensure that they got paid when this was all over rather than out of any sense of purpose. 'Alright, I'll go get the Humvee. You say you have a Land Cruiser, you'd better get that as well because you'll need a vehicle to depart in once we dump the tanker.'

Fifteen minutes later and Jacob had the Humvee attached to the front of the large tanker. RJ was at its wheel and Pieter was behind in the Toyota. With all the noise of the vehicle, Jacob was surprised that none of the locals had put in an appearance. RJ explained that after they had discouraged their attempts at looting with a few rounds from their rifles, no one dare approach them after dark.

Jacob let out the clutch of the Humvee very carefully. As he felt it bite, he felt a jerk as the tow rope took up the slack. For a second, he wasn't sure that this was actually going to work, then with the clutch still slipping a little, they started to move. With the tanker pointing the way they needed to go, it was easy to pull onto the road and move off. Up until then, Jacob had been driving with no lights. The moon, which was nearing the horizon, was giving just enough light to see. He knew it would set very soon so once they were clear of the town he turned on his headlights. The tanker had some battery power left but RJ would only use the lights to signal a problem. The Land Cruiser would follow without lights unless it became impossible.

Slowly, Jacob let the speed increase. He was very conscious that the tanker had no brakes. They had agreed that in the event he had to stop suddenly, the Humvee would go right and the tanker left. The real danger would be that the tanker would then take charge of its towing vehicle and spin it around. Because of this, they had attached the Land Cruiser to the rear of the tanker with another rope. The idea was that it could brake the rig to some degree. Jacob knew there were no real hills on the route they were going to use but even a small incline could lead to the tanker going out of control.

Despite his worries, he managed to get his speed up to a good forty miles an hour but wasn't prepared to go any faster. He calculated that they could cover a good eighty to hundred miles this way before he had to leave which would be perfect. Soon, despite the inherent danger of such a clumsy rig he started to relax.

Chapter 40

'What the hell is up this road Paul?' Jon asked as they accelerated back onto the tarmac. Once again they had been able to follow the Humvee tracks but once on the road they disappeared. However, it was quite clear which way their quarry had turned.

'Desert, desert and more bloody desert,' Paul replied, looking at the map he had grabbed out of the door pocket. 'This is Route 22 which goes all the way to Saudi Arabia. In about seventy miles there's turning to Route 21 which goes north past several small towns and meets Route 1 which is the way to get to Jordan. I have absolutely no idea why he's gone this way. Do you?'

'All I can think of is that he's gone looking for this shipment of Sarin because it sure as hell wasn't back at Jurf Sakhar. So I'm bloody glad we brought our NBCD gear. I suggest we keep driving on goggles. We haven't actually come across any traffic yet but no one will be surprised to see us driving without lights. They all do it around here. It's an Arab thing I first came across in Egypt. For some silly reason they think that by only using lights when there are other cars about they will save the lightbulbs.'

They kept the speed down in order to save fuel but all too soon they came across the intersection with the route north.

'Which way Paul?' Jon asked as they stopped the car to consider their options.

'Well, there are no towns or even villages between here and Saudi on this road. But didn't Rupert say that the stuff was probably coming in via Jordan? In which case it would almost certainly have to come down Route 21 and as there's no sign of anything so far my best guess is to turn right.'

'All good points, so let's go that way. Any towns en route?'

'Not until a place called Al Kasrah. There are a couple of others but the road bypasses them. If the good Colonel is intending to get back before its light that's about as far north as he can get before he's going to have to turn around. Those Humvees can barely manage seventy on a good day.'

'Ok, we'll go that way and if we don't encounter him by that town you mentioned, we'll have to accept we've lost him and head home.' Jon said as he turned the car onto the new road.

Twenty minutes later, it was clear they had made the right decision. They had seen a few cars and trucks during their trip and most were driving without lights as Jon had predicted so no one took the slightest notice of them. This time it was clear there was something on the road ahead with its lights on as the goggles saw it from miles away. They had plenty of time to react and pull off the road well clear. They left the car and grabbed the two rifles, taking sight down the road. The night sights on the rifles gave much more magnification than the helmet mounted goggles. Unfortunately, the light from the first vehicle headlights simply whited them out. It wasn't until the car was opposite that they could make out what it was that they were looking at.

'I reckon we've found the Sarin,' Jon observed.

'The front of that tanker looks really smashed up. I assume that's why it wasn't at Jurf Sakhar.' Paul said. 'But they'll never get there before it gets light so what the hell are they up to?'

'Getting it as close as they can but for what reason I'm not sure.' Jon replied. 'More importantly what the hell do we do now?'

'Well, we've got two rifles. We could shoot it up.' Paul suggested.

'Good idea, except we've no idea how many men are in those vehicles or how they are armed. Do you want to risk that?'

'Sorry, only thinking out loud,' Paul replied. 'But they're going to have to stop and fairly soon I reckon. Why don't we just follow and see what they get up to?'

The two men went back to the Bentley and put on their helmets again. It proved surprisingly easy to follow the little convoy ahead from quite a distance. The light from the Humvee could be seen from several miles away in the goggles. It wasn't long before they came to the junction with Route 22 and turned left. Ten miles later, in a barren spot, Jon suddenly realised they were catching up and fast.

'Looks like we're at the end game Paul. I'll get as close as we can then pull off Ok?' Jon drove as close as he dared and then pulled over. The two men climbed out and reached in for their rifles and at Jon's insistence their respirators as well. It only took minutes to reach the place where the vehicles were parked up. The Humvee's headlights were off now and they could use the rifle's sights to get a good view of what was going on.

'There's only three of them,' Paul whispered as they watched them unhitch the Humvee from the tanker and then go to the rear of it and untie the Land Cruiser.

Jon was suddenly reminded of a time many years ago in the arctic when he was in a similar situation, with an enemy in his sights. However, that time the man was clearly a murderer and he had no doubt that taking him out was absolutely the right thing to do. This was different. In this case, one of the men was actually his subordinate and the other two were unknown. Despite the fact that he was pretty sure he was watching a dreadful crime being perpetrated, this was not the same.

'Do not fire Paul,' he whispered. 'We need to wait and see what happens.'

It didn't take long. The two men in what looked like military uniform of some sort shook hands with Colonel Sharp and climbed into the Land Cruiser and within seconds were speeding away back up the way they had come.

Jon remembered Rupert's words about how dangerous at least one of them probably was and gave a sigh of relief that they were out of it. That only left one man. As soon as the Toyota was gone, the Colonel climbed into the cab of the tanker. Jon stood and walked towards it with his rifle held ready. Paul stood and followed. 'No shooting, unless we have to. I want to talk to this bastard before we turn him in.' Jon said grimly.

Paul nodded. 'I'll go round the back.'

Jon was almost at the driver's door of the large vehicle when it opened and Jacob Sharp climbed out backwards. Half way down, he turned and saw Jon standing there pointing an SA 80 straight at his heart. He froze, the look on his face would have been funny if the situation wasn't so deadly serious.

'What exactly are you up to Colonel Sharp?' Jon asked in a surprisingly mild tone.

For a few seconds, the Colonel seemed incapable of speaking. His mouth opened but nothing came out.

'I'll tell you shall I?' Jon said. 'You've been to Jurf Sakhar to turn on the power and then came up here looking for a delivery of a chemical warfare agent. You were setting me and my team up to find them so that you could justify this whole fucking war. A war, which in reality, is a sham because Iraq actually has had no Weapons of Mass Destruction for years. Am I correct you utter bastard?' Jon almost shouted the last words.

The Colonel seemed to come out of his daze and flung himself back into the cab of the tanker. The move caught Jon completely by surprise and for a second he hesitated. Before he could do anything, the Colonel reappeared with something in his hand.

'I've no idea how you found out about this Hunt or how the hell you got here. But there's nothing you can do. And before you try anything this is a firing switch.' Held it up so Jon could see it. 'All I have to do is press it and the Sarin in the main tank will be ejected into the air. We all die, plus most of the people in the village only ten miles that way.' He pointed down wind.

'So that's it, is it Jacob? You're that much of a fanatic that you would sacrifice your life and that of thousands of innocents just to make a political point. What would your fucking God make of that? What will you say to him when he judges you?'

'Shut up Hunt. We have to bring God to this region and the only way is by force. A righteous war that will bring peace and Jesus to millions.'

'Not going to work Jacob,' Jon said with a calmness he didn't feel. 'Did you know that the facility at Jurf Sakhar was rigged to self destruct?'

Jon was pleased to see a flash of doubt cross the Colonel's face.

'Well, we did just that. There's nothing there now but a bloody great crater.'

'You're bluffing Hunt. Yes, I know it was rigged to look like it was meant to do that but it was also disabled.'

'We found that out and fixed it Jacob. It's not there believe me.' Jon had caught a movement out of the corner of his eye off to the left. 'So if you detonate this tanker all you will do is kill innocent people. It won't make any sense to the investigator, which by the way is me. Oh and I've got my respirator with me by the way. I notice you don't have one. Shame that as you won't be around to contradict anything I say.'

'Oh really? It will look like a load of Sarin was being taken out of the country and the tanker ran into an accident. Do you honestly think what you say will count for anything once the press get hold of it?'

While they had been talking Jon had been slowly walking forward.

'Stop there Hunt. No closer. You may not believe in the Almighty but I do and I've made my peace with him.'

Jon could see the Colonel's finger raise over the button at exactly the same time that the side of his head exploded. It was only fractions of a second later that the report of the SA 80 was heard. Jon leapt forward and grabbed the firing button from the dead man's hand before it was pressed.

There was silence again although Jon's ears were ringing from the sound of the shot. 'Thank you Paul.' he called. 'That was bloody close. Too bloody close.'

'So, what the hell do we do now?' Paul asked looking around the scene. 'We've got a dead US Army Colonel and a tanker full of chemical nerve gas. What's worse is we need to get rid of it without anyone knowing what it is.'

Jon was looking at the large tank. 'How big do you think that is Paul?'

'Thousands of gallons I guess, why?'

'Because if this was smuggled in, it can't be full of Sarin. Imagine what a customs inspector would do if he inspected it? He'd be dead in seconds. No the stuff must be hidden inside it in something else.'

'Hmm, good point Jon. Hang on a second,' Paul went to the rear of the tanker and studied the warning symbols. 'We've assumed this is a fuel tanker but these symbols are for fertiliser. That makes a sort of sense. Why would you import petrol into a county that makes its own? They must have had it camouflaged in some way when they crossed the border and then repainted it somehow but they kept the hazard symbols. Only one way to prove it. I suggest we put our respirators on just in case.'

Having done so, he went to the rear where there was an outlet valve and cracked it partly open. A stream of brown liquid fell to the round. They waited for a few seconds.

Paul turned to Jon. His voice was muffled by the respirator but still clear enough to hear. 'If that was Sarin it would have evaporated by now,' he said as they both studied the muddy looking puddle.

Before Jon could stop him, Paul pulled the side of his respirator away from his face and took a small sniff. 'You can take it off Jon,' he said as he removed the black rubber mask.

Jon did the same and almost choked on the strong smell. 'Bloody hell, what is that stink Paul?'

'Ammonia, the tank has what it says on the tin. That's a liquid nitrogen fertiliser.'

An idea formed in Jon's mind. 'Is it flammable?'

'Oh yes, one of the hazard symbols makes that quite clear. Why?'

Jon explained. Paul thought for a moment. 'We'll have to be bloody quick. It's sure to be found once its daylight.'

'Come on then.' The two men scooped out a shallow depression next to the tanker and unceremoniously dumped the Colonel's body into it without saying a word.

'What the hell do we do with that?' Jon asked looking at the Colonel's Humvee.

'I'll drive it back. We can say we found it abandoned. We're meant to be out looking for the Colonel anyway.'

'Ok and then I'll get the hell out of here.' Jon said.

'We'd better fill up the Bentley from the tanks in the boot first,' Paul said. 'I get the feeling you're going to test the fuel consumption figures quite hard. It's not quite so far to the ammunition dump but it's still at least two hundred and fifty miles. How about you try for two hours?'

'Is that a challenge?' Jon asked with a grin.

As soon as they had refuelled, they set off in the two vehicles. Jon left the Humvee behind as soon as he trod on the accelerator.

In only a matter of minutes, he realised he had made a dreadful mistake. This was his second night with virtually no sleep. He was exhausted before they had started out that evening and he had been running on pure adrenaline ever since. Driving this monster of a car at speed needed solid concentration. In some ways, what was worse was the road was actually in good condition and pretty straight so winding it up to ridiculous speeds was easy. First, he tried turning on the air conditioning which worked for a while. The radio would only receive stations in Arabic although he did find one playing western music. After a while, he turned the radio off and started to sing out loud to himself. Again that helped for a while. At one point he found his eyes drooping so he slammed on the brakes and pulled over.

When he got outside, he jogged up and down the road for a few minutes before attempting twenty press ups. He managed ten.

That seemed to work and he sped off feeling better. The road unrolled in front of him in the car's headlights. It was so featureless it was almost impossible to tell how fast he was going unless he looked at the speedometer.

'Hello Helen,' he said to his wife. 'Nice to see you and Ruth.'

'Jon, this is fun,' Helen said. 'Do you usually drive so fast?'

'Yes, he's terrible like that,' Ruth chipped in.

'Do you two girls have to back seat drive all the time?' Jon asked in frustration. These two women were always having a go at him.

'We're not back seat driving,' both girls said at once.

'Wow that light's bright,' Helen said.

'And loud,' Ruth shouted.

Jon opened his eyes just in time to wrench the wheel to the left narrowly missing a lorry of some sort with headlights ablaze and the driver furiously leaning on his horn. The car started to slide. He knew he dare not suddenly lift off the throttle but no matter which way he steered he couldn't catch it. It was the classic 'tank slapper'. After several swerves, the car spun and there was nothing he could do. He remembered what Paul had said in these circumstances when racing. Slam both feet hard on the clutch and brakes and let go of the wheel. He didn't have a clutch so two out of three was all he could do. He just prayed that if the car left the tarmac it didn't dig in on the sand because he would be upside down in an instant. It seemed to go on for ages but was probably only a few seconds. It didn't dig in and when he came to a halt, he was amazed to see he was back pointing the right way and still on the road.

'Fuck me, that must have looked amazing from the outside,' he muttered in a shaky voice.

However, the scare had really woken him up this time and as soon as he had calmed down he set off with grim determination. In the end he actually made it in slightly less than Paul's target. Afterwards they calculated that he averaged close on a hundred and thirty five for the trip. When he was twenty miles away, he pulled over briefly and managed to make radio contact. He told them what he wanted so that when he arrived, the MH6B was ready, fully armed and rotors turning.

Jon skidded the car to a halt by the helicopter, jumped out and ran to the little machine. One of the crew handed him an American flying helmet which he put on. It was already plugged in.

'Good morning Sir,' the pilot said over the intercom. 'You have a little job for us I understand.'

'Absolutely. You're fully armed?'

'Yes Sir.'

'Good, then this is where I want to go.'

Dawn was just starting to lighten the horizon when they reached the stricken tanker. Jon got them to fly over the area carefully. It was deserted and there were no signs of any road traffic.

'This is what I want you to do,' Jon told the two crew.

The little machine let down into the hover a hundred yards upwind of the tanker. The 7.62 machine gun stuttered and holes started to appear along the bottom of the large tank. Soon, brown liquid was pouring out into the ground. The machine then transitioned into forward flight and turned until it was several miles away. It then turned back to run in towards the target. Suddenly, a streak of flame shot out and a TOW anti-tank missile slammed into the chassis. The whole rig disappeared in a tower of flames. A few seconds after the first explosion, there was a secondary gout of fire. It was blue in colour and only lasted a few seconds. There was no need to fire any more missiles. The helicopter kept circling upwind of the wreck until the fire had burnt out.

Jon knew that Sarin was volatile and flammable. None of it would have escaped and there would be absolutely no evidence left to show it had ever been there. The heat of the fire would also have completely cremated the remains of Colonel Jacob Sharp, Unites States Army.

'Thank you gentlemen. That was good shooting. We can go home now and I apologise in advance if I start to snore.'

Chapter 41

Two days later and they were still only a third of the way through the bomb dump. Jon had remained tight mouthed about the activities of that night. He admitted that they had gone to look for the Colonel but had never found him. His explanation about the tanker was that they had encountered it on the search and felt it was a health hazard and an excuse for him to let some of his men have some target practice. If anyone thought the explanation was rather thin, they kept their counsel.

The disappearance of Colonel Sharp was reported and a military investigation team had arrived and taken statements. Paul and Jon made sure they had their stories straight and explained they had found the abandoned Humvee on the side of the road but with no sign of the Colonel. When asked, Jon had said that Jacob had been acting slightly strangely in the previous weeks but he had no premonition that the man was suicidal or in any way disturbed. In the end, nothing could be found or proved and the team left.

Jon was getting ready for the evening Ops brief. Over the previous day they had moved the entire operation up from their old airfield site and the place was still a little disorganised but with the re-appearance of the two Sea Kings, the move had gone quite quickly. He was just getting up from his desk where he had been reading a digest of the day's findings when two men entered the tent.

'Commodore Jonathon Hunt?' one man asked. Both men were in civilian clothes, wearing dark suits which Jon found extremely odd.

'Yes and who wants to know?' he asked angrily. 'Who let you in here?'

'Sorry Sir you are required to come with us.'

'Am I hell. Who are you and what do you want?'

Jon realised the men were extremely well built. If it came to a struggle he would lose. He stood up, getting ready to shout for help when he felt a sting at his neck and the world turned black.

'Anyone seen the Commodore?' The Ops officer asked as the time for the evening brief arrived and went. It was very unlike the

Conspiracy

man to be late. In fact no one could remember it ever happening before.

Paul stood. 'I'll nip over to his tent, maybe he's overslept.'

The remark caused a ripple of laughter amongst the assembled staff.

When Paul got to Jon's tent it was deserted. He had a quick look around but nothing seemed out of place. As he came out again, he caught sight of a Marine. 'Jenkins, have you seen the Commodore anywhere?'

'Yes Sir,' the Corporal replied. 'He just got into a car with two men. They drove off that way towards the entrance.'

'Were they in uniform?'

'Err, hard to say Sir with it being dark but they looked like civvies to me.' Jenkins replied.

Paul's blood ran cold. He ran back to the Ops tent and grabbed the telephone and made the switch for the Command Post by the entrance. 'This is Colonel Roberts. Has anyone arrived or left by car in the last half an hour?' He listened for a short while and slammed the phone down and turned to the assembled officers. 'Commodore Hunt appears to have been arrested.'

Mayhem erupted. 'How do we know that?' Someone called.

'Because according to the soldier manning the gate, the two men in the car showed CIA identifications.'

'What the hell do we do?' James asked.

'Are the Sea Kings serviceable?' Paul asked.

'Yes Sir, both of them.'

'Right, scramble one and get me out to the Intrepid as soon as you can.'

The phone on Rupert Thomas's desk rang and he automatically picked it up and listened for a few seconds. When he realised who was on the other end, he forgot the routine report he had been reading and concentrated.

'You're sure, Brian? He asked.

'Yes,' the voice of Brian Pearce at the other end replied. 'About four hours ago. I've only just found out as they had to fly out to me. Is there anything you can do?'

'Jesus, I don't know. Look, leave it with me. There's certainly nothing you can do at your end. He's probably in the air by now.'

Conspiracy

'Do your best Rupert,' Brian replied and the line went dead.

Rupert ran to his office door and called to his secretary. 'Sarah, I need the extraordinary rendition flight time table and I need it yesterday.'

She could hear the urgency in his voice. 'Yes Rupert, I'll run down and sign it out. I should be back in in a few minutes.'

He went back to his desk and dialled Jenny's number telling her to get up to his office as fast as she could.

Jenny and his secretary came in simultaneously. 'Here you are Rupert,' Sarah said, handing him a pink folder with the blue cross denoting a classification of top secret.

'What on earth is going on?' Jenny asked.

Rupert spoke without looking up. 'Jon has been arrested by the CIA. I've no idea why and they have absolutely no right to do so but since when did that stop them doing anything they want. I would suspect it's something to do with his actions in Iraq but I've no idea what he's been up to recently. Against advice from some of us, the government have allowed the CIA to land aircraft here to refuel on the way to the US. They are called extraordinary rendition flights because they don't bloody well exist. Because we are friends with the bastards we have a copy of their movements which don't bloody well happen of course. Right, here, there's one due this afternoon from Iraq. It's landing at Northolt in an hour and then straight on to Washington. It has to be that one. Fancy a quick drive across London?'

It might have been too early for the rush hour but no one had told the traffic that. While Rupert tried to find out more on his mobile phone with no success, Jenny tried to fight her way up to the North Circular Road. By the time they could see the airfield at Northolt it was almost too late. As they pulled in to the Main Gate they could see a white private jet just starting to taxi away from the hardstanding by the control tower. It had no markings on it except for small black national registration letters near the tail.

'That's the one,' Rupert said. 'That was the registration on the timetable.'

The RAF Corporal who was looking at their passes seemed to be taking an inordinate amount of time. 'Is there anything wrong Corporal?' Rupert asked. 'We really are in a hurry.'

'No problem,' the Corporal replied. 'Your passes are fine but if you want to take your car in here you'll need a temporary car pass. If you just park over there in the temporary bay and go into the office, I'm sure they'll issue you one in no time.'

'Fine, we'll do that,' Jenny said through tight lips.

The Corporal seemed in no rush to lift the red and white striped barrier barring their path. However, as soon as it was clear Jenny floored the throttle and shot past a clearly very surprised young man with her tyres leaving black lines on the tarmac.

They shot around on to the perimeter track and could clearly see the jet making its turn to line up with the runway.

'No good Jenny,' Rupert sighed. 'It's too late.'

'Is it bollocks,' she answered and swerved the car on to the grass and then on to the main runway so that they were heading straight towards the aircraft which was now finally lined up.

'I've always wanted to see how effective these air bags are,' she said grimly. When they were only a few feet away she slammed on the brakes but even so the front of the car slammed into the aircraft's nose wheel at over forty miles an hour.

The air bags did indeed work and the car slammed to a halt at the same time that the nose wheel oleo collapsed. The nose of the aircraft dropped but luckily on to the back of the car. It was all silent for a second and the two dazed occupants shook themselves to clear the powder released by the multiple air bag explosions.

Jenny was first out. Not the least because Rupert's door was jammed. He followed out her side and they both had to crouch low to get clear of the aircraft's belly which was only just above their heads. As they emerged, they could hear the sound of the two jet engines spooling down.

Suddenly, the front passenger door of the aircraft slammed down only inches from the two of them and an extremely angry face peered down at them.

'Do you know what you've just done?' the man almost screamed at them. 'This is a diplomatic flight, with diplomatic immunity.'

'Actually, that's not quite true and you know it.' Rupert replied in a surprisingly restrained voice. 'This is a CIA operated, rendition flight and it definitely does not have diplomatic immunity. So please don't try to lie to me. All you have is permission to land here and take on fuel. What you definitely do not have is permission to break international law.'

The red faced man was joined by another. 'Who the hell are you? You seem to be well informed.'

'I am a Deputy Director of MI6. You might have heard of us? And I have strong suspicion that you are illegally detaining a British National on your aircraft. Care to comment?'

Before anyone could say anything else, there was a screech of tyres and two Land Rovers pulled up. Half a dozen Air Force personnel carrying rifles piled out and surrounded the aircraft. Behind them was a fire engine and two red Land Rovers.

A man dressed in a Sergeants uniform came up to them. 'What on earth is going on here? Is everyone alright?'

Rupert stepped forward. 'No one has been harmed Sergeant,' he offered his ID card. 'As you can see, I am a senior intelligence officer and this is my assistant.'

Jenny gave the Sergeant her very blondest smile and she could see his level of anger drop several notches in the process. She also offered her ID card. 'I'm sorry about the unconventional way we used to stop this aircraft taking off Sergeant,' she said. 'But the men on it are illegally kidnapping a British National. It was really important that we stop them.'

'That's not true,' an American voice called from the door. 'This is a mandated, government approved flight and we have immunity.'

'They tried that on us,' Jenny said sweetly. 'It's a lie. Anyway, if they are not in the process of an illegal kidnapping then surely they will have no objection to us looking inside.'

'Not necessary my dear,' the Sergeant said and then called up to the aircraft. 'I'm sorry Sir but you have just had an accident in an aircraft on a British runway and I have to act in accordance with English law. I require you to evacuate the aircraft immediately on the grounds of safety. Let's face it, you're not going anywhere soon are you?'

The man's head disappeared from view for a few seconds and then reappeared with a look of resignation on his face. 'Very well Sergeant, you win.'

The two pilots came out first looking quite intimidated by the number of armed men watching them, then the two CIA agents appeared with a third man between them. He was dressed in a baggy orange jump suit and blinking in the afternoon light as if he had been kept in the dark.

As soon as they reached the ground, Jenny ran up and hugged him. 'Welcome home Jon, sorry about the way we had to do it.'

Epilogue

'What's this?' The First Sea Lord queried as Jon passed him a white envelope.

'Surely you can guess Sir. It's my resignation,' Jon said firmly.

'No, sorry Jon, I'm not prepared to accept that and you know why. This office will almost certainly be yours sometime in the future. The Royal Navy needs people of your calibre.'

Jon laughed humourlessly. 'Maybe Sir but this person doesn't need the navy any more. I'm sorry Sir but I want out. This war we've just fought was a lie and hardly anyone in the military queried its validity even though most of us knew it was a sham and I include myself in that. We should have. I'm sorry but I don't want any part of this any more. I've done more than my fair share over the years.'

'Yes, you have. But I have to ask though. You've managed to avoid spending much time behind a desk for most of your career. Is it the prospect of not getting a command again and spending most of your time in Whitehall that's behind this?'

'I expect you think I'll say no to that Sir. But actually yes, that is one of the reasons as well. Despite all their promises, we know that the politicians are hell bent on saving as much money from our budget as they can and I don't think I can preside over a continually shrinking navy while still being asked to do the impossible. Sir, my mind is made up.' Jon looked the man in the eye.

The Admiral sighed. 'Fine, it's your right after all. I can't actually order you to retract it but if you change your mind don't be surprised if we take you back with open arms. Now, can I ask something else?'

'Sir?'

'Can you tell me what really happened in Iraq? It seems you and that REME Colonel did something or discovered something that pissed off the CIA enormously, even though they are now apparently denying anything even occurred.'

Jon, Paul and Rupert had agreed that they would not fully disclose all the details of what had happened but Jon felt that this man at least deserved some answers.

Conspiracy

'Sir, I'm not prepared to go into the detail but I will give you a digest. Firstly, there were no Weapons of Mass Destruction in Iraq and our government and the Americans knew that before the war started and I'm not referring to the UN weapon inspector's report. Secondly, there was an attempt to plant them. The American Colonel that went missing was instrumental in the attempt. Paul Roberts and I stopped him. Believe me, none will be found.'

The Admiral looked surprised at Jon's words. 'Surely that information should be made public? It sounds like a massive crime has been committed.'

'I agree about the crime Sir and had we discovered the truth before the war started, that would have been a different matter. But if we did make it public now it would only destabilise the situation even more. At least now that no WMD's will actually be found there will be no excuse to continue with the annexation of the Middle East.'

The Admiral started to say something but closed his mouth as the meaning of Jon's last words hit home.

'And what about you Jon? It seems you must have made some seriously dangerous enemies. Aren't you worried about your own safety?'

Jon laughed. 'Paul and I are probably the safest people in the world right now. It's been made known that full documentation has been placed in several secure locations. I know it sounds like a bad line from a film but if anything happens to us, it will be released.'

The Admiral looked hard at Jon. 'I really hope you're right in that assessment Jon. There are some really vindictive bastards out there.'

'I understand that Sir. I've made my bed and I'm prepared to lie in it.'

Later that day, Jon met up with Rupert and Jenny for lunch. Rupert had already explained to Jon what had been going on while he was away after they had left Northolt. 'Just had some more news Jon. A certain government advisor was found dead in his car this morning. He had done the old hose pipe up the exhaust and into the car trick.'

Jon was completely unsympathetic. 'I hope that's the first of many Rupert. However, knowing how these politicians work, I expect most of them will either deny everything or claim they were always right. It's a shame we can't make this whole story public. Anyway, I have some news for you as well.' He told them what he had done that morning. Both of them immediately proceeded to try to talk him out of it.

When it was clear that he had really made up his mind and that nothing they could say would make him change it, Rupert asked him. 'So, what are you going to do Jon? Have you actually made any plans?'

'Yes, you may all laugh but I'm looking at property on the Isles of Scilly. I visited there some years ago and always promised myself I would retire there. Look everyone, I'm tired. Its time my life changed direction. I want some quiet time to myself. I'm going to buy a boat and do some diving, drink too much scotch and think. Sorry if that doesn't sound like me. I'll still get some excitement, Paul wants me to continue sharing his car on the circuits. Basically, just for once, I want to be selfish. So that's it.'

It was clear there was no moving him and so they all wished him well. Privately Rupert reckoned he would last six months but maybe this was what his friend needed.

After the meal, Jenny stayed behind and cornered Jon before he could leave the restaurant. 'Can I come?' She asked in a small voice.

'To visit, yes of course, whenever you want,' he replied with a smile.

'No, not to visit. Permanently, with you.'

Jon sighed and looked at this stunning, gorgeous girl. Who in their right mind would say no? 'Jenny, you're lovely in so many ways. You're bright and great company and I know you're fabulous in bed.'

She blushed at the remark but Jon continued, smiling. 'But you're fifteen years younger than me. I know what would happen. At first, it would be wonderful but over time, you would feel stifled and to be brutally honest I still haven't got over the death of Helen. With Ruth, we were just friends, very close friends I admit but that's as far as that went. So, I'm sorry but no.'

He leant forward and gave her a hug and kiss on the cheek. As he inhaled the scent of her hair, his resolution wavered and he almost changed his mind. Forcing himself to maintain his expression, he looked her in the eyes. 'Goodbye Jenny.'

He turned and walked away.

Conspiracy

Author's Notes

Conspiracy theories abound these days. I'm sure the internet should take much of the blame as it allows sharing of information so readily. I generally don't believe in any of them despite the apparent solid evidence that 'appears' on the web. An example is whether men actually landed on the moon. Irrespective of the photos showing double shadows and all the rest, in my view there is absolutely no way that it could have been faked. There were just too many people involved for it to have been covered up.

However .... Have a look at the massive portfolio of evidence that supports the case for at least some of the events of 9/11 being faked or covered up. I suspect that much of it falls into the same category as the moon landings or Roswell in the fifties but some of it is very, very convincing. I use some of these events in the book. I will just throw three into the ring:

1. Most people don't realise that three buildings came down that day. The twin towers everyone knows about but there was also 'Building 7' which was adjacent but not hit by any aircraft. In the years before the attack it had been heavily modified and strengthened. Yet, having been on fire for a few hours, it collapsed vertically as though all the internal supports had been simultaneously sheared. Many demolition experts have testified that it couldn't happen unless deliberately demolished. A counter argument is that no windows exploded as they would have done if demolition charges had gone off. The answer to that is that Thermite could have been used which is a more modern procedure and does not cause an explosive blast. An analysis of the steel supports would have easily have determined the truth. For some reason they were all removed and smelted down within a week of the collapse.
2. What hit the Pentagon? The building probably has more external CCTV coverage than any other building in the world. So why has only one recording ever been released and that is taken from the side and barely shows anything at all? There was one television report made from outside just after the attack and the

Conspiracy

journalist is asking, where is all the debris? This report was never aired again. Official reports claim that the aircraft was flying so low that it hit five streetlight standards before impacting the side of the building. This was a massive airliner lying at 500 knots, piloted by a terrorist with only a few hours on light aircraft and he managed to fly it straight and level only feet from the ground? You would think that such a sight would have been seen by many witnesses, after all, he would have to line up from some way out. NO witness have come forward. There are photographs of the hole in the side of the building and it's just that, one circular hole. So where did the wings and engines go? What's really odd about this is that the authorities don't seem to want to produce any counter evidence to naysay the conspiracy theorists, like better CCTV or bits of aircraft. Maybe they can't?

3. And that leads on to my last point. There was a full enquiry into everything after the event so why did the FBI then admit that they had 'accidentally' shredded thousands of relevant documents before they could be called for?

I've no idea why these things did or did not actually happen but many experts are still querying the whole thing today. But there is another way of looking at the situation. Ask yourself where would the world be if 9/11 hadn't happened? There would have been no excuse to invade Afghanistan and therefore, probably no momentum to go for Iraq. Then ask yourself what would have happened if large quantities of WMDs had been found? These are unanswerable questions of course but they make a good plot for a novel.

Readers might just notice that I was very much against the second Gulf War! Like many, I've never been so ashamed of my country and all I can say is I'm glad I left the Royal Navy a few years earlier. Just before the war started, the Prime Minister went on the BBC's Question Time programme. I tried to find the clip on web but there's no sign of it (another conspiracy??). His words to the audience were (as closely as I can remember):

'We must remember that Saddam Hussein represents a direct threat to the security of the United Kingdom that could be enacted within forty five minutes.'

Conspiracy

This was a blatant lie and I knew it as soon as the words came out of his mouth. The big question was why no one in the audience didn't immediately question him (maybe the BBC edited it out, who knows?). How did I know it was a lie?

1. The only 'part' of the United Kingdom that was under any sort of threat was the sovereign base on Cyprus, which one of Saddam's missiles might just be able to reach. Why he would want to threaten that, Blair never bothered to explain.
2. At that exact moment, there was a massive Task Force poised and ready off the southern coast of Iraq. If he and/or Bush had ordered the attack at that time there is no way on the planet that such an efficient military force could have actually got things going in forty five minutes. So how on earth would Iraq have been able to react faster? I think what he was alluding to was that it takes forty five minutes or so to set up and fire a Scud missile but 'accidentally' omitted to mention that even in Iraq there was a command and control system that would have to order the firing.

Of course, one has to wonder why Blair was so keen to focus so hard on WMDs. In America, it had been stated policy for many years that they wanted to get rid of Saddam. They had also been making the case that Iraq was a state that sponsored terrorism (although the opposite was probably the case as the last thing Saddam wanted was Islamic fundamentalists threatening his regime). So Blair was out on a limb and putting all his bets on finding WMD. A cynic might suggest that if he focused on despotic rulers that should be deposed, people might start asking why, in that case, we weren't threatening Zimbabwe and that nice Mister Robert Mugabe or other dictators around the world for that matter.

The net result, of course, was that there were no WMD and Blair ended up looking like an idiot. However, one has to ask why he was so certain. Did he actually start believing his own lies? The UN Inspectors and even MI6 were not sure at all. I guess he's never going to tell us. But it was a good hook for my plot.

Estimates of the deaths caused by this unnecessary and illegal war range from 100,000 to 1.4 million. Even if it's the lower number I do wonder how our ex-Prime Minister can look at himself in the mirror in the morning. If any reader is interested in trying to get justice and even get paid in the process, have a look at 'http://www. arrestblair. org/'. I'll say no more.

Some years ago, my wife and I went diving in the Red Sea at Taba and stayed in a hotel next to the Israeli border. We went across one day and swam with dolphins. The hotel did have a Casino and on the last night I won enough to pay our bar bill, despite my darling wife pinching some of my chips and losing them when I wasn't looking. A short time after we left, Islamic terrorists drove a truck full of explosives into the main entrance and blew up half the hotel.

Motor racing – I raced cars for twenty five years and still do occasionally. I started after the navy sent me back to sit behind a desk. I guess some people just like a bloody good adrenaline rush. I do and so did Jon. The race at Silverstone is a bit of a composite of several of mine.

Part time Studies are quite common. In my case, I spent nine months on one with four others looking at Helicopter Support issues. Giving one to Jon albeit with a hidden agenda was quite feasible.

The Joint Helicopter Command actually came into being as I describe. I was part of the team that looked into it during the Strategic Defence Review. I also claim the credit of the army taking it over. I had just completed the study into Helicopter Support so had visited all air stations in the UK that operated helicopters. I also knew the savings that were being claimed for shutting the Naval Air Station at Portland. It was my suggestion during a MOD meeting, that at least one airfield could be shut. When asked if they would do such a thing the RAF said no, the army said yes and so got the job. They never did shut a base.

Raids on suspected WMD sites were conducted by various Special Forces units right from the start of the invasion of Iraq. Putting these under a centralised command would have been quite feasible.

Water soluble paint is often used. A British Lynx helicopter in the Gulf just before the second Gulf War was painted red by the ship's Flight and took Christmas cake around the fleet with Father Christmas dangling from the winch. It was grey again the next day. Commando Sea King 4's were often overpainted white for arctic operations.

Arabic drivers do often drive without lights to 'save wear on the bulbs'. If you are in an Egyptian bus going to your hotel at night it can be quite terrifying.

Anyone who has read this whole series of books might remember the prologue to the first one 'Sea Skimmer'. That section is about a journalist seeking out Jon to ask him about Exocets during the Falklands War. Jon, retired from the navy is living in a small house, on his own on the Isles of Scilly.

This may not mean that Jon and Brian won't sail again………….

Swan Song

Retirement does not suit Commodore Jon Hunt. He is enticed back into the navy to teach young pilots how to fly. However, the plans of a Saudi Prince, who is hell bent on destroying the relationship between his country and the West soon drag Jon back into action. Taking command of the 'Swan Song' a superyacht converted into a covert intelligence gathering ship, Jon is soon not only confronting the Russian navy but also ghosts from his past.

Conspiracy

Printed in Great Britain
by Amazon